# A PERFECT PLOY
Barbara Nicholson

## ALSO BY BARBARA NICHOLSON

*One Wrong Turn*
*Twenty-One Seconds*

This book is a work of fiction. All names, characters, and incidents used within this novel are products of the author's imagination. Although places and events may exist, they are used within this novel fictitiously. As a fictional novel, nothing within it should be construed as real. Any resemblance to persons, living or dead, actual events or locations is entirely coincidental.

PUBLISHED BY SOFTWARE Systems LLC
    Lewes, Delaware
FIRST EDITION
Book cover design by Getcovers.com

ISBN:
ISBN-978-1-7333542-4-0

To all those who care enough to become involved
and not allow evil to flourish.

# Chapter One

## Monday Morning

## Kauai, Hawaii

AMY PRYCE FELT THIS Hawaiian paradise was doing its job, beginning to erase the memory she came here to forget. The six-mile run she just finished also helped.

On the fourth floor of her time-share rental building, she passed beneath the closed windows of the end unit, the one originally assigned to her. It sat across from an outdoor elevator, where a suited man waited. She shook her head. *A business suit? In this heat?*

Yesterday, an interesting tour of the island, followed by a relaxing day at the beach, further helped her unwind. This morning Amy credited the already strong Kauai sun, slung high in the sky at this early hour, for both her upbeat attitude and the perspiration penetrating her clothes.

Reaching her current unit, ready for a refreshing shower, she slid the twirly band off her wrist and inserted the key. Pausing to cherish the moment before entering, she closed her eyes and drew in a deep breath of the fragrant scent wafting from the overflowing flower boxes atop the railings that faced each door. The elevator chimed. She opened her eyes.

She turned as a cop exited her original unit and took the few steps necessary to reach the elevator. The suited man had his hand across the door, allowing a couple with a stroller to exit. An unsettling thought struck her. *Is he here because of what we did?* The moisture snaking down her spine became a line of crawling ants.

Pushing away the thought of a shower, Amy withdrew the key and rushed toward the policeman as he stepped in. Amy called out, "Excuse me, officer, did the rental manager send you?"

He looked toward her but didn't answer. Instead, the suited man released his grip on the door, gave the policeman a quick nod, turned, and faced her. "I'm Detective Palakiko. Can I help you?"

*A detective? They sent a detective?*

Taking in his dark hair and tanned skin, she stiffened, steeling herself for the confrontation to come. Ready to defend her actions, she said, "You can't be for real. What we did isn't a crime."

"What *did* you do?" His piercing stare sent a chill through her despite the heat.

She wanted to explain. Intended to explain. Ran over to explain. But the fact it necessitated a detective stunned her, leaving her mute.

When she didn't speak, he asked, "Did you know the couple in the end unit, number 401?"

*Did? Past tense?* Without intending to, she took a step away from his imaginary blow. "Why? Did something happen?"

"There's been a death," he said, studying her.

"Who? Billy? Mabel?"

"Did you know them?"

Amy felt a sudden heaviness pressing on her, pinning her in place, as if the earth's gravitational pull was stronger here than in other parts of the world. "We just met," she said.

"When was that?" He stuffed his hand into his pocket, his expression serious.

"I arrived late Saturday afternoon. They assigned me 401 for the week. I was exhausted when I got here. I fell asleep. It felt like only minutes when I heard voices outside my windows."

"Voices? Were they angry? Threatening?" The detective fished out a small pad and pen.

"No. Just annoying, dragging me out of a deep sleep." Amy watched him turn to a blank page. "So, I got up to investigate."

"Then what happened?"

Her mind flew to Saturday. To those eerie voices.

"What do you see?" Amy heard an unfamiliar voice ask.

A deeper voice, sounding disappointed, said, "I can't see anything except the floor. The slats are angled downward."

Inside the time-share rental, Amy Pryce's tired brain jolted her awake. Someone was talking. *Are they speaking to me?* Confused for the moment, she struggled to peel open her eyes. *Where am I?* When she did manage to get her lids up, they opened to strange surroundings: a bland, white stucco ceiling and those unfamiliar voices.

Slowly, it came back to her. The eighteen-hour, twice-delayed, three-plane ordeal from DC.

The reflection in the mirror—from a picture above the bed of a surfer riding in on a wave—helped the fuzziness of sleep disappear. *Hawaii.* Her racing heart began to slow. She relaxed, exhaling a long breath, realizing the voices weren't in the room. They were outside.

"Now what are you doing? Get down." That voice now clearer, louder. "You're going to break your..."

Interrupting, the resolute but quieter one said, "This isn't right."

Amy maneuvered to the edge of the bed, yawned, and rotated her neck and arms in slow motion, stiff from the exhausting journey.

With finality, Amy heard, "It's supposed to be ours!"

"But it isn't. It will be fine. Can't we just go? It's not worth risking a fall."

Curious, Amy rose and ambled over to the windows, grasped the handle, and cranked, adjusting the slats of the jalousies to a wide open position.

As she did, they struck something.

Or someone.

Apparently sensing her distraction, the detective asked again, "And then what happened?"

Back in the present, Amy said, "I went outside and found an elderly woman standing there. She had a hard-backed suitcase lying on its side near her feet, and she was holding a purse." *And a tissue at her nose.* Watching him make notes, Amy thought it best to leave out the part about whacking Mabel with the slat. By way of apology, Amy had invited them in to check the injury and been relieved to find there was no serious damage done.

Amy took a deep breath before continuing. "Next to her was a tall man with a mane of pure white hair, standing very erect but looking forlorn. I asked them in. They told me their story. Billy proposed to Mabel here." A slight smile formed at Amy's recollection of the couple, causing her normally hidden dimples to appear, one on each cheek.

"Billy? Mabel? Are you referring to Mr. and Mrs. Plomasen?"

"Yes. His name is William, but everyone calls him Billy." She looked away from his unrelenting gaze. Amy moved a hand to her now cramping stomach as the reality that one of them had passed away started to sink in. "They're here to celebrate their tenth anniversary."

"Tenth?" The detective questioned.

Amy understood his doubt. The woman was eighty-nine and Billy ninety-five. He was very proud of his age, having mentioned it to Amy several times. "Yes." She nodded.

"When did you see them last?"

"Saturday night. That's when I met them. We talked. I found out they wanted the unit the office had given to me. They had requested that specific one, but their flight was delayed. I arrived here first. It didn't matter to me. But, for them, it had enormous significance." The detective jotted another note. "In addition to his proposing here, they wanted it because it's the closest one to the elevator. Which is not an issue for me, because I almost always take the stairs."

"What was their demeanor?"

Amy thought back, reflecting on the elated couple and how enamored she had been with them. "Blissful with each other." She paused for a few moments. "Except for when they told me they found out a few weeks ago he has cancer. No one could tell them how much longer they would be able to vacation here—or anywhere else—so they vowed to do it now. They cashed in some of their certificates of deposit early and chose to relive one of the happiest days of their lives—here. After hearing their story, I offered to switch."

The detective's raised eyebrow caught her attention. "What? They were charming. We switched. I moved to their unit, 405, and let them have mine. What's the big deal?" Her mother's stoic independence and her father's gentle kindness instilled in her a combination of strength and compassion. She called on either when necessary.

"Do you know how many CDs they cashed in? Was it everything they had?"

"No. I don't. I didn't ask."

"So the last time you saw them, you would say they were happy?"

Amy's mind spun. "Of course they were. I just told you so. They were looking forward to celebrating and reliving their engagement here. Why are you asking?" That question made her realize he still hadn't told her who died. A horrible thought hit her. "Both of them?"

He didn't answer. His expression did.

"How?" When he didn't respond, she said, "How could they both be dead?"

"Our investigation is just beginning."

His answer didn't tell her a thing, except maybe to confirm it did involve both of them. Recoiling, her back struck the railing. Her hand grabbed at it for support as her mouth went desert dry. "It can't be. It isn't fair. They were so happy. So full of joy." A wave of sadness washed over her for this couple she had just come to know.

Turning from him, her hands clenched the railing surrounding the center court as she fought to regain her composure. She took a long moment to focus on the towering palm in the open center, tracing its route from the ground below to the floors above.

After giving her some time, the detective asked, "What did you say your name is?"

With an effort, she answered him, her voice shaky.

"Here's my card." It required her to turn to retrieve it. It read, Detective Kimo Palakiko, Kauai Police Department. The bottom portion contained a printed address and a handwritten phone number. He let her study it a moment before asking, "Did you use the stove?"

Surprised, she said, "No. Not the stove. Nor the air conditioning. Nor the bath. Nor much of anything else. I was so drained when I got here, I dropped my luggage and headed straight for the bed." She also recalled skipping all other nightly rituals, including brushing and flossing, but didn't think he needed to hear that.

The detective flipped his notepad closed with an action that spoke of practice. "I think that's enough for now. I need to see some ID from you. And I'll need you to come in and get fingerprinted for elimination prints."

She nodded. "I just came back from a run. I don't have anything with me. It's in my room."

"No problem." He extended his hand for her to lead the way. She wanted to know more, but he was asking all the questions. And not sharing anything.

She began walking. The detective followed. After a few steps, she whirled around. Her abrupt stop caught Palakiko off guard. "Can we at least go check in the freezer? He proposed to her over chocolate chip ice cream. They were here to reenact their special moment. It would be a comfort to know they at least had that."

With urgency, he said, "I need to see some ID."

She started to ask another question, but he said, "Now."

All of a sudden, he was in a hurry.

# Chapter Two

## Monday Morning

## Kauai, Hawaii

*WHAT HAPPENED?* Amy's mind wouldn't stop asking that question. Sitting alone on a green and yellow flowered couch, a duplicate of the one a few doors down, she feared something awful had happened to the Plomasens. Although she couldn't imagine what. The detective left after taking down her information.

Amy felt empty. She longed to call home, but decided it would have to wait. A long-overdue shower to snap out of her lethargy was what she needed now. With sadness still clinging to her like a cloak, she rose and headed for the bath.

She turned on the faucet and stuck her hand in the water, waiting for it to warm. Watching the shower head spew out its spray, it occurred to her that death had surrounded her far too much for her twenty-seven years. Beginning with her brother Tommy's, when he was seven and she nine. Then, more recently, witnessing a gang member gut open a fellow member during an argument. Adjusting the shower head, the irony of this Hawaiian vacation hit her. One designed to help her recover from witnessing that brutal slaying now included more death.

Her arms sagged as she washed, tortured by the weight of what might have happened. She shut the water, shivering as she stretched for a towel. Draping it around her, a thought sprang to life. *I still have the second key to the unit. When we switched, I only handed them one. I can go and take a look.*

The thought reinvigorated her. She dressed, dragged her shoulder-length brown hair back, secured it with a scrunchie, and rummaged through her bag for the other key.

Outside 401, she hesitated for a second before letting herself in, unsure of what awaited. She used a hand to cover her nose from the unpleasant and stale smell that hit her when she entered. With caution, she treaded down the long hallway hiding the bedroom and bath on its other side.

Darkness surrounded her as she reached the openness of the sitting room and slider to the lanai. Thick curtains covered the length of the slider, except for an opening at the end which allowed a tiny sliver of the intense outside sun to trickle in.

The unit sat empty. And quiet. Too quiet. *Take slow breaths.* The silence gripped her as she forced herself to breathe. The air conditioner wasn't running, yet the place felt cold. She flicked on the light. With the place illuminated, it seemed far less foreboding.

With deeper, slower breaths, she took a few tentative steps through the sitting area. Knitting needles and a wide skein of blue yarn peeked out from inside a small tote bag alongside a chair. A paperback book and two magazines rested on the end table. The slider was locked.

Amy turned around and moved past the kitchen into the bedroom. She searched for any signs of a struggle, finding nothing unusual. The frosted jalousies were shut. Rumpled sheets covered the bed. Clothes hung neatly in the closet. Toiletries lined the bathroom counter along with a set of false teeth soaking in a liquid. For some unexpected reason, that sight tugged at her, causing her to choke up.

She made her way back to the kitchen, stopping at the stove. It, and the surrounding counter, were dotted with black powder. The black stains on the refrigerator handle reminded her why the Plomasens' came here. Amy pictured Mabel's face as she recited Billy's proposal to her verbatim. "We are so compatible, Mabel. It would be a shame for us not to spend the rest of our lives together. Don't you agree?"

Mabel said her, '*I most certainly do*' response flew out without hesitation. Surprising her, because her mouth agreed before her brain registered what her heart already knew.

Other sections of the kitchen contained remnants of black dust, but the amount of residue on and around the stove made her wonder. *Could this be the culprit? A gas leak? It could explain how they died.*

As Amy surveyed the mess around the stove, another possibility—an unspeakable one—-struck her. It made the detective's line of questioning make sense. *Is he thinking suicide?* Reflecting on the detective's interest in their finances and their state of mind, she began to wonder if they would do it. *No. Not them. Never.*

Dismissing that possibility, Amy reached over and opened the freezer door.

Inside, a half-gallon of chocolate-chip ice cream along with a plastic tray of ice cubes stared back at her. She pulled out the ice cream, setting it down on the counter. A sense of satisfaction exposed her dimples as she smiled, picturing the couple licking their spoons, enjoying their moment, reveling in their reenactment. Curious to see how much they had eaten, she placed her fingers under the lip of the carton, pulled up, and lifted.

The lid dropped from her hand. A chill colder than the icy concoction itself spread through her. She grabbed for the counter. In front of her lay an untouched container of ice cream. Its undisturbed swirl at the top still waiting to be broken.

*It can't have been suicide! Not without them celebrating first. That's what they were here for.*

A sudden fear made her return the container to the freezer and head for the exit. When she reached it, she closed the door with a slow, reverent motion. As if for the final time.

As if sealing their tomb.

# Chapter Three

## Monday Late Morning

## Kauai, Hawaii

THE MORNING'S EVENTS left Amy rattled. Feeling alone and confused, she wanted to discuss it with a loved one. She reached out to her dad but failed, having to leave a message for him. The time difference made it afternoon back in DC. That meant Amy's best friend and roommate, Bonnie Fitzpatrick, would be at work. Hoping she would be available to talk, Amy dialed her, grabbed an energy drink, and paced, waiting for her friend to answer.

Bonnie cooed when she did. "Don't keep me in suspense. Tell me all about Matt. What's he like?" Her friend's excitement blew away some of the heaviness pressing on her.

"Matt," she exhaled. "With the morning's chaos, I almost forgot about him. He never called. Consider that the first bad news of the morning."

Bonnie's excitement faded. "I'm sorry. I know you were hoping to hear from him." After a brief silence, Bonnie said, "What's the other bad news?"

"Are you sitting? Remember the couple I told you about? The ones I switched with. Well, brace yourself." It took a few seconds before Amy could say, "They're dead."

"Dead!" Amy pictured her friend bolting upright. "You're kidding, right? What happened?"

"I'm not sure." Amy walked as she talked. Her mindless path covered the bedroom, the kitchen, and full rotations around the coffee table in the sitting area. "I don't believe it myself. I went for a run this morning. When I got back, I noticed a cop come out of my original unit. He..."

"Amy, are you alright?"

"I'm fine. There was also a detective waiting for the elevator." Amy retrieved his card from her pocket. "His name is Kimo Palakiko. I told him about the switch."

Bonnie's voice lit up. "Oh. A detective?" Bonnie's enthusiasm for all things involving romance hadn't stopped since meeting her soulmate, Jeff, and finding happiness. Amy pictured Bonnie adding his name to a list of romantic prospects for her. "He sounds promising?"

"Can you stop! Will you please just be serious for a moment." Amy's words spilled out louder and much harsher than she intended. Hearing herself, she stopped moving, unclenched her fist, and loosened her grip on the phone. "I have no interest in this Palakiko guy. He is just so... Annoying."

"OK. If you say so."

"Sorry. I didn't mean to snap at you. I think the detective is thinking they committed suicide. If he's right, or if that's true, then maybe..." The phone was silent for a breath. "I can't shake the feeling that I should have picked up on it somehow. I should have realized something didn't seem right. Maybe I could have stopped them."

"Really? I recall you telling me how happy they were. 'Blissful,' I believe you said. You described an almost ninety-year-old woman as 'gushing like a teenager.' So how could you have known? I don't think anyone would have picked up on anything from the way you described them to me."

"Maybe not. But something is wrong. I know it." After a long silence, Amy resumed her pacing. "I don't think they did it. They wouldn't commit suicide."

"And why is that?"

"My gut."

"Your gut?" Amy could appreciate Bonnie's doubt. But the guilt wouldn't leave her. *If only I...* Amy didn't know how the sentence ended.

Amy heard Bonnie sigh. "You only met them once, and your knowledge is limited to what they told you. You don't know whether they would. Or they wouldn't." She paused for a moment. "Did you consider the possibility they did it so they could guarantee some afterlife connection? Live together.

Die together. Spend eternity together. Some people think in those terms. And if so, I would call that a happy thing, wouldn't you?"

Amy rotated her neck trying to free the knot in the back of it. "Bonnie, I went back into 401. Guess what I found. An untouched carton of ice cream. They never re-enacted the proposal they came here for. They wouldn't have committed suicide—not without celebrating first. It's the reason they were here."

Amy could hear Bonnie exhale in frustration. "What did the detective say?"

"He didn't say much. He did ask me if I used the stove. That tells me he suspects it."

"He said that?"

"Well, not in so many words..." She flopped down on the couch, leaned back into it, and stared at the ceiling. "Bonnie, I'm so confused, but I can't walk away from this. You are the only one who knows how guilty I feel about what happened to Tommy. And my promise to him to fix things in this world that I come across. To not walk away."

Witnessing what her brother's death did to her parents, she had promised herself early on that she would be the one to compensate for it. To succeed. To make them proud. To never add to their burden and grief.

And to uphold a vow she made to Tommy to guarantee he didn't die in vain.

Bonnie said, "Are you sure you're not looking for an excuse to get out of starting the job I worked so hard to line up for you when you get back?"

"No, Bonnie. It's not that."

"So what are you thinking of doing?"

"I don't know. Right now, I'm late for an appointment I scheduled before I arrived here with a local professor on Hawaiian history. I'll meet with him. Then... All I do know is I won't be able to live with myself if I just walk away from this."

Amy had been hoping for additional moral support from Bonnie. She knew Bonnie tried, but how could she ever *really* understand? She wasn't the one who convinced a younger brother to negotiate with his school bus partner into taking turns sitting by the window, so a stray bullet during a gang dispute would find its way through the glass and cut short his life.

# Chapter Four

## Early Saturday Morning

## Toronto, Canada

"LOOK THIS WAY," SHOUTED a local reporter from the crowd. Susan Fleming stood behind a vivid purple ribbon that stretched across the lawn of a newly renovated, ranch-style home. Even at this early hour with a morning chill in the air, the neighborhood bristled with activity. Over a hundred people waited, drawn to the event by the offer of a free breakfast.

Handing her a gigantic pair of scissors, Frank Gigliano said, "Want to do the honors?" He moved to stand beside her. Putting on a wide smile, Susan lifted the ribbon in one hand and held the shears high in the other. The local reporter maneuvered through the crowd, snapping pictures from different angles while she and Frank held their pose.

Susan and Frank worked for a charitable organization, The Stratford Living Legacy Foundation. It funded the remodel and installation of a modern, efficient kitchen in the home behind them in order to provide meals to the area's homeless. This half-a-million-dollar project, one of their smaller efforts, didn't necessitate two representatives. But late yesterday, Susan and Frank each received a text from the chair and final member of their three-person committee, Mike Shore, indicating there would be an emergency meeting afterward.

The young reporter gave them a thumbs up, indicating he had all the shots he needed. With one quick clip, Susan parted the ribbon to a smattering of applause.

As the crowd filed in for their culinary reward, local officials and church representatives plied Susan and Frank with handshakes and messages of thanks. A young fire recruit approached them. "We have a reserved table set up for you inside."

"Sorry, we can't stay," Frank said. "Another time."

"I can make you something to go," he offered with an enthusiastic grin.

"Thanks, but no. Duty calls," Frank said, reaching into a pocket and pulling out his car keys.

Susan turned back toward the last stragglers heading in and smiled at another satisfying accomplishment. "It does smell good, Frank."

But her mood darkened when they reached Frank's sedan. Susan admonished herself for agreeing to carpool with him. After Mike's urgent-sounding text about today's meeting, Frank had called, offering to pick her up. In a moment of weakness, she agreed. His careless driving confounded her—he always drove in such a hurry. As the Chief Financial Officer, it stood out in such stark contrast to the cautious and meticulous attention to detail Frank exhibited with his work.

She inhaled a deep breath for the ride ahead and got in.

With her seatbelt not yet fastened, Frank pulled away, asking, "Any thoughts on why we are meeting with Joey Stratford and his wife, Eunice?" Joey Stratford, the current president and CEO of Stratford Industries, worked for the company his grandfather started. With money his grandfather made from it, he also founded a charitable foundation—the one Susan, Frank, and Mike now worked for.

"All I know is Mike got a call from Eunice asking for it," Susan said. Then, concerned about his driving, she decided to limit her conversation, hoping he would concentrate. No luck. The city of Toronto, with its myriad of demolition and reconstruction projects, was flying by.

At a red light, she took in one of those sights: an old building, ninety percent demolished, save for a twenty-foot clock tower. Braced in place, it stood erect in the center. Around its base, construction workers carried, scurried, and jackhammered like hornets whose nest had been disturbed.

Frank gunned it when the light turned. "I don't think his wife will be there. The twins were only born a few weeks back. Prematurely. I imagine she's tied up with them. I believe they are still not home."

"I heard." Susan said, taking comfort in the fact their destination was close at hand.

"And the unexpected births coming so soon after the humiliating board fight Joey survived. I'm amazed he got the raise he asked for. And at how he managed to retain his title as president and CEO. I heard the staff isn't happy with him." Frank turned into the hotel's driveway. "There was a lot of talk going around that he is already overpaid and using his lineage as leverage."

Susan released a long-held breath as Frank parked near its entrance.

In the lobby, they met Mike Shore, who, in his late seventies, would be retiring soon. At least Susan hoped he would. As his replacement, she would be ready for her own retirement if he didn't make that move soon. Despite his request for casual, he appeared well-dressed, only without his familiar smile.

Susan asked, "Mike, care to tell us what's going on?"

"Eunice wouldn't say."

"Then why are we here?" The two companies founded by Joey's grandfather—theirs and Stratford Industries, the one Joey worked for—were purposely designed to act independently. The only interaction between them was a required yearly contribution from Stratford Industries' profits to the charity. Employees of either company were ineligible from benefiting in any manner from the foundation's generous outreach. "Did you remind her that they, or any of their employees, won't qualify for anything from us?"

"Susan, I am well aware of what the rules are. I'm not certain what this is about, but last night she sounded close to tears. I couldn't get anything out of her. She told me she and Joey were desperate to talk to the full committee. That they would explain when we were all together and that she would arrange everything for today. I tried to press her, but to no avail. We're only here as a courtesy because of who they are."

Susan hoped he was right because otherwise, Mike would be in an untenable spot. "Alright, Mike. It's just with the heavy workload we have, time is valuable."

As they approached the elevator, Mike suddenly asked with surprise, "It isn't anyone's birthday, is it?" Susan and Frank stared at him. He said, "When I arrived, I checked with the concierge. He told me the presidential suite is reserved for us." Susan's look of confusion matched Frank's. "If this isn't a surprise of some kind for one of us, I can't fathom why we need that large a room."

Susan's curiosity and suspicion were aroused. *Neither can I.*

# Chapter Five

## Late Saturday Morning

## Toronto, Canada

APPARENTLY ALERTED by a well-tipped concierge, Eunice Stratford stood waiting for them, holding one of the suite's double doors open for the Stratford Foundation's Evaluation Committee as they exited the elevator. They sidestepped past her to enter.

"Thank you all for coming," Eunice said as the door clicked closed. "I can't believe we have the use of this room. It is such a steal."

Susan gaped at her. *A steal?*

Mike leaned down and pecked Eunice on the cheek. "Of course. It's our pleasure to be here." Susan and Frank exchanged handshakes with her.

Eunice guided them through the desolate space, past an ornate lacquered table devoid of its normal huge vase of fresh flowers. She led them to a black-marbled wet bar at the far end of the room. There, a tray holding tall glasses of ice water with a wedge of lemon speared on each, waited like soldiers. "I'm afraid I can only offer you water. If anyone would like something..."

They all declined, cutting her short.

Mike asked, "Eunice, where's Joey?"

"He's not able to make today. He sends his regrets."

Mike said, "I see. Well, we're all here." Susan gave Mike a questioning stare which he ignored. He asked, "What did you need to talk to us about?"

"Let's sit first," Eunice said. She led them to a piano where chairs upholstered in fabric matching the drapes sat in disarray. They each selected a seat and repositioned them into a smaller group. Eunice chose hers last, a Queen Anne, asking Mike for help in placing it across from the three of them.

"First," Eunice said, her voice quavering, "I want to thank you for meeting with me."

Susan settled in, already irritated with the woman, wondering how long this would take, hoping she would get straight to the point. As soon as those few words left Eunice's mouth, she began to sob. *Oh no, not this.* Over the years, Susan had seen her share of tears from applicants who intentionally—or unintentionally—used it as a device to further their cause.

Dinosaur tears, too large to have come from those small slits, flowed openly down Eunice's cheeks. She made no attempt to remove them as Susan studied the petite woman with pixie-style, short, poker-straight hair, wondering if she even weighed a hundred pounds.

It struck her that Eunice epitomized the polar opposite of herself. Susan's lightened blond hair could be found at the furthest end of the spectrum from the jet black of Eunice's. Moreover, where Eunice's form looked tight and firm, hers displayed the consequences of too many meals, too often.

In contrast to the tears, Susan noted Eunice appeared relaxed. Curled up in the roomy armchair, reclining with her feet tucked under her—something Susan would never be able to accomplish. She guessed her height to be no more than five feet, recalling Mike bending down to deliver his welcome kiss despite her four-inch heels, which now lay off to the side of the chair.

Mike asked, "Do you want to take a moment?"

The tears just stopped. Too quick for Susan's taste, adding to her curiosity and increasing her suspicions about the woman.

After using the back of her hand to wipe her face, Eunice continued in quite a composed manner—her demeanor completely flipped. "I think you are all aware of our recent..." She hesitated, perhaps unsure of what to say next, cleared her throat, and in a stronger voice, said. "I'll get right to the point. Our twins were born premature—at a little less than five months. They are being cared for at The Devereux Clinic for Health. They have extremely qualified doctors and a specialized unit to treat them."

Never married, Susan tried to imagine how difficult this must be for the woman. Her feelings toward Eunice softened.

Eunice went on, "We found out yesterday that the older of the two boys has a malformed heart, a condition requiring surgery." Her reference to one of the children as *the older of the two* reminded Susan that Eunice refused to name them. She referred to them only as Baby A and Baby B, because naming them would be too painful if either of them did not survive.

Mike said, "I'm sure I speak for all of us when I say I'm very sorry." Frank uttered something as well, and a nod of Eunice's head told them she accepted their sympathies.

"At this point, he is too weak to be operated on. They are hoping if they can bring his weight up, they might attempt it in the next week or two. We've spent an unbelievable amount of our funds on them. This unique facility, the medical staff, the specialists..." Her voice trailed off. After a moment, she said, "Some experts must be flown in because the babies are too fragile to move."

Eunice stopped for a bit before exhaling a heavy sigh. "Frankly, at this point, we've exhausted our savings."

Susan sat stunned, knowing that Joey's salary, already in the millions, should be adequate to cover their medical costs. Although she imagined Mike and Frank found Eunice's statement as surprising as she did, she trusted Eunice could read nothing by their expressions. Normally, they did not make any comments or give opinions in public until after the three of them had discussed the issue. In private.

When none of them spoke, Eunice awkwardly continued, "Well, I guess that's why I've asked you here."

In the expansive space, the silence seemed to have its own echo.

Her fear about today's meeting was now a reality. Relief spread through her that she didn't have the job yet. If Mike were to entertain her request in any way, he would be breaking one of the cardinal rules of their very specific company dictate.

Leaving the rejection to him, Susan adjusted her gaze, shifting it from Eunice to the parquet floor.

Mike started, "Eunice, I'm pretty sure you are aware of...."

She cut him off. Her hands flailed. "Yes. I know about your stupid rules. I am aware there's one concerning any financial distributions to employees of our company or yours. But may I remind you these are the great-grandchildren of the man who gave you that money. And now, quite honestly, we need it to save the lives of those babies. I don't care what your idiotic rules say. We need your help."

A rush of heat slammed through Susan, her cheeks turning beet red in a flash, thankful no one would notice since her focus remained on the floor. She resented people who viewed their organization as nothing more than an open checkbook. It enraged her that this arrogant woman, knowing the rules, was wasting their time. While compassionate about their health issues, she also knew they should be able to cover the expenses involved.

Eunice stopped speaking, focusing instead on the tissue being wrung in her hands atop her lap. Susan and Frank waited for Mike to make the next move. After an awkward silence, he asked, "What exactly do you want our help with?"

Mike's question sent Susan's already overheating body near to a boiling point. *Mike, you can't. And you know it.* She could no longer hide the flush. She tried to catch Mike's eye, finding Frank's look of concern instead.

"In order to continue to provide the critical attention they need, Dr. Zoric says several things are needed, including money to compensate his staff."

"I see. What sum of money are you seeking?"

*Mike, why are you asking? You know we can't do this.*

Frank cleared his throat, hinting his disapproval, but Mike's focus remained on Eunice.

"Two million dollars." Then, with more force, Eunice added, "And we need it now."

*Is that a threat?* Susan's antennas sprouted. *Is it because she is the wife of a CEO that her words sounded like an order, her request like a demand, or is she just a distraught mother pleading for the welfare of her child?* Susan couldn't decide. Her pulse was jackhammering faster than the one she witnessed on the ride over.

Mike's voice brought Susan back to the issue at hand. "Thank you, Mrs. Stratford. You are probably not familiar with how this works, but we will delve into your request, discuss the matter, and reach out to you with our decision." With those final comments, they left an unhappy Eunice, alone, in the massive room she described as a steal.

At the elevator, they stood in silence. Susan's migraine made it unbearable to speak. She entered first, realizing the avant-garde meeting had at least distracted her from dreading the ride back.

Frank walked in last, letting out a long whistle as he hit the lobby button.

When the doors closed, Mike raised a hand. I know. I know. There's nothing to discuss. I'll call her on Monday and inform her how much we regret it, but our hands are tied."

*Thank goodness, Mike. For a moment, I thought you might actually acquiesce.*

# Chapter Six

## Monday Morning

## Toronto, Canada

IN THE CENTER OF HER cedar-lined closet, Susan Fleming stood fuming at Mike Shore's summons to the office. He wanted to discuss Eunice's request. Shorty, the white Angora with one ill-formed paw Susan rescued as a kitten, tiptoed in, eager to investigate. "Don't you start. I'm already annoyed. There is nothing to discuss. And Mike knows that."

Shorty circled her feet twice before sitting and staring up at her. Susan took in a long breath and bent to pet him. "I realize I'm taking a long time, but I can't decide what to wear. It's always business attire at the office. But Mike said, 'This is only a casual get together.' What does that mean?" As he nudged his head against her hand, a calm settled over her. The amount of pleasure she derived from this imperfect little creature always amazed her. He gave her a simple meow.

She stood, resumed scanning down a rack, and came to a drab gray pant set. At first, she questioned why she kept it, favoring darker colors that contrasted better with her highlighted hair. Then, she plucked it off the hanger.

*You are the perfect color for my mood.*

SUSAN ENTERED THE FOUNDATION'S posh conference room at this early hour to find the morning sun pouring in at full strength. It penetrated the ten-foot, floor-to-ceiling windows as if it owned the place. The wow factor of this palatial setting, with its unobstructed view of the CN Tower, no longer impressed her. She found Frank flipping through a pile of papers atop the dark cherry table in front of him. She said, "Looks like you've been busy."

"Yeah." He put down the steaming cup of coffee he held in his other hand. "I started delving into The Devereux Clinic for Wealth," deliberately misspeaking its name. "What they charge is unbelievable."

"Don't tell me. A ridiculous amount for an aspirin?" She dragged out one of the high-backed chairs across from Frank.

"They're way past ridiculous. I'm trying to determine what's so unique about those physicians. I printed out backgrounds on all of them. They carry impressive credentials, but I'm not so sure they are that exceptional to warrant these excessive rates."

Susan sat and rolled her chair to the table. "It's a private facility. What did you expect? I would assume they are expensive."

"Speaking of expensive, you should see how many zeros are attached to the suite Eunice booked for our, what, half-hour meeting?"

"You mean her *steal*, don't you?" Susan quipped.

"I told Mike next time we make the arrangements."

"Why? Are we paying for it?"

"Mike told me to cover the bill."

"I can appreciate her trying," Susan said, "but our hands are tied. I'm not expecting any more meetings with her."

"I hope not. In addition to the outlandish charge, they billed us for two days. I had to straighten that out with them. I told them it was only for one. By the way, what's your take on today's agenda?"

Before Susan could answer, Mike strode through the door, placed his briefcase on the floor, and took his usual seat at the head. Without preamble, in a strong and determined voice, he asked, "Well, are we ready to save the lives of our founder's great-grandchildren?"

Frank rolled back his chair aghast. "Are we ready, Mike? Are you serious? We have no information. No details. No clear understanding of what the money would be used for." His objections were flying out like fastballs. "Let's say we ignore the fact we shouldn't be discussing this," he paused, his hands in the air, *"we haven't discussed it."* Under normal circumstances, they each did their own research, with Frank's financial analysis and conclusions coming first. Followed by any concerns either Susan or Mike might have before they would discuss the request as a team.

Silence followed Frank's outburst.

After a short while, Frank added, "And it's only a possibility their lives will be saved. They can't give us a guarantee. Why are we ignoring the rules we've been governed by for all these years? Why the exception?"

Susan cut in before Mike could answer. "There is nothing to discuss. We can't." She paused for a moment to study Mike. *Is he going senile? Is he on some new medication?* "Mike, do you want to ignore a cardinal rule, one excluding us from considering any employees of Stratford? And, for the CEO no less."

"I agree with Susan," Frank said, his pen clicking open and closed in rhythmic fashion.

Mike hoisted his briefcase up, the pale of his hands in stark contrast to the dark of the table and the black of the case. In slow motion, like a turtle with nowhere to be, he took his time opening its lid, selected a sheet of paper, and held it up in midair as Susan and Frank exchanged looks. "Here is a case in what could be interpreted as a breaking of, as you say, a cardinal rule. Remember Roland O'Connor's wife. Her kidney transplant. Roland is an employee at Stratford."

Frank's pen stilled for the moment. "That's not the same," he argued. "We helped his wife *before* Roland got hired."

"Semantics, interpretations." Mike sounded annoyed. Frank's nervous clicks resumed. Mike leaned back, locked his fingers across his chest, and continued. "We all listened to Eunice. The woman is a mother, and she is obviously in pain. Her children need our help, and, as she reminded us, the money we distribute these days did come from their great-grandfather." He looked to each of them in turn. "Both of you are aware of how stringent I am on adhering to our legal responsibilities. I believe we need to make an exception this one time."

Frank put down his pen, grabbed his wrists, and stretched his hands high above his head. "Well, it seems like you've already decided. I understand your argument, but based on what I've found so far, it's a waste of money. It's not that I don't want to assist with the health of those kids. I do. But the clinic overcharges. Further, we have no idea what the two-million-dollar infusion would be used for." He dropped his arms, his palms slapping the table. "I'm sorry, but I would turn this one down in a flash."

Susan spoke up. "I realize this is a sensitive issue. A hard one. Hard decisions are a part of our job, Mike. You know that. But this foundation is designed to be an independent entity. We are supposed to operate autonomously. It is a basic tenet of the company. I can't tell you how concerned I am about this. I'm upset to hear you waver on what has been such an important issue to you in the past." She exhaled with purpose. "We would be setting a precedent here. I'm worried about going down that road."

Frank's squashed his empty coffee container and hurled the cup into the wastebasket in the corner of the room. "Three points."

Mike cleared his throat. "I've given the situation some consideration. I believe the rest of the board will go along with this exception. After bouncing it off one or two of them, I think they will support our decision."

*He checked with the others on the board before we even discussed it?* Susan's glance toward Frank told her he seemed just as surprised. The foundation consisted of seven board members, the three of them and four others. *Now I'm certain something is going on with him.*

Mike snapped his briefcase shut. "In the past, we've always arrived at unanimous decisions." He returned the briefcase to the floor with some force. "I would like your support on this, despite the fact you both may have some misgivings."

Frank leaned forward, resting his elbows on his research papers, covering his face with his hands. Susan turned her focus to a peaceful garden setting hanging on the wall behind Frank. In contrast to the serenity in that garden, the tension in the room could be measured on a Richter scale. For the most part, they did function as a cohesive team, agreeing in general. Susan didn't want to jeopardize that relationship.

Mike broke the uncomfortable silence. "I can see you are both having difficulty with this. But I genuinely believe if their great-grandfather lived today, he would agree to an exception in this case."

Frank brought down his hands. "In the past, we've denied dollars for critical, life-saving requests, some including children."

"Yes. I know we did." Mike said, solemn but unmoved.

Struggling with the issue, Susan warned, "Once we start ignoring rules, we won't be able to stop."

"I just told you the board will support us on this exception," Mike said.

She looked away to consider the matter. *If Mike, the by-the-book man, is willing to abandon his strict adherence to the rules, knowing his commitment to them, perhaps I need to reconsider. And, with the millions we give away each year, this* is *a nominal amount.*

Mike again shattered the quiet. "We've had our discussion. It's time to vote." He spoke in a superior tone, "Can I say we are all in agreement?"

Frank took a moment, then shrugged. "Fine. Not sure I like it. But I'm in."

*My logic tells me no, but maybe Mike is right. There are times when—no matter how rigid—rules need to be broken.* Susan relented. "Yes, me too," she said.

Mike's relief was palpable. "I'll inform Eunice the three million dollars is approved."

# Chapter Seven

## Monday Early Afternoon

## Kauai University Library

"I'M SO SORRY I'M LATE," Amy said to Professor Jim Longo. She recognized him by his six-foot-four height—information she obtained from the college website. He was adding a book to one of several stacks on the table in front of him when she entered the Kauai Community College library at the SW Wilcox II Learning Resource Center in Puhi.

He turned and extended his hand as she took in his slim build and fit-looking physique, finding him not unattractive for his fifty-plus years. "Longo or Jim, please," he offered.

She gave him a quick laugh. "I think I like the sound of Longo." Although here to relax for the week, Amy intended to delve into something of interest during her stay. Recalling a college girlfriend who traveled to Kauai during breaks, she asked for her advice. Her friend highly recommended her uncle, who taught Hawaiian history, referring to him as *a goldmine of knowledge.*

"Longo, it is. And no apology necessary for being late. You'll come to realize everything on Kauai is more relaxed. I guess you've been enjoying some of the luxuries our island offers."

"Well, not exactly. It's not the reason I'm late. But let's not go into that." Surveying the quantity of books occupying the table in front of them, Amy asked, "Are these all for me?"

"You did ask for research material," he said, sounding satisfied with his selections. He stared down over glasses perched at the edge of his nose. "I told you the library here is well stocked." His pride for Hawaii radiated, although his biography indicated he hailed from Colorado and has only lived here for the last twenty years or so.

He selected a book from the table. "This one covers the history, which begins with the canoes that brought the first settlers here." He handed her a thick book about the Polynesian islands.

Amy chuckled. "Wow. This is an awful lot to absorb." Her knack of approaching people often resulted in people being eager to share. Although this time she might have overdone it. "Be careful what you ask for, isn't that what they say?"

His slight grin accentuated his dark mustache, an oddity with the salt and pepper of his hair. Reaching for a colorful, glossy-covered publication entitled *The Gardens of Hawaii,* he flipped to a marked page and pointed to a stunning flower. "Is this the one you were inquiring about when we spoke?"

Amy glanced at the picture of a long-stemmed plant with green striped leaves. Its opened pod of bright orange, leaf-like petals spiked outward in various directions, forming the flower itself. The unusual one that caught her attention at random spots along her run. "Yes. They seem to grow wild. And they are breathtaking."

"It's called the Bird of Paradise because it resembles a bird in flight. Appropriately named, wouldn't you agree?"

"Without a doubt." Over the last five years, in a variety of situations, Amy had queried a large number of experts, delving into their particular area of knowledge. She always approached them with humility, with a sincere interest in the subject matter, expressing an eagerness to learn from them, and promising to be non-judgmental. This approach allowed her to ask some tough questions when necessary. Although she had already accumulated a vast store of information on a wide variety of topics, her intense curiosity still yearned for more. It also didn't hurt her inquisitiveness that when Amy smiled, a dimple appeared in each cheek giving her a cherubic look.

"Well, I imagine you'll want to begin," the professor said. "But first, let me give you a quick summary of what I have gathered and organized for you." He placed his palm on the pile in front of him. "These are all on the history of the island." Indicating an adjoining stack, he said, "Those are on the Hawaiian language."

With a sly expression, he asked, "Did you know our alphabet consists of only 13 letters? That there are only five vowels and seven consonants, a-e-i-o-u and h-k-l-m-n-p-w? Or that Hawaiian is the shortest alphabet in the world?" He seemed to enjoy giving her this little quiz. "We do have one additional character, the glottal stop called okina—it's a little character resembling a comma. All of our words end in a vowel. Nineteenth-century missionaries wrote it. And, along with English, Hawaiian is also recognized as an official language of the state."

"Now I'm convinced I've found the right source," she said, flashing him one of her dimpled best. "And I think I should be taking notes."

Stepping to the side, he continued. "Here we have books on agricultural products of the area, including the sea, and...," he moved to a final section, "a description of each of the eight islands and their unique characteristics."

His last comment brought to mind yesterday's helicopter tour. It churned up a pang of unhappiness since Matt, the pilot who promised to call, didn't. It also reignited her interest in Niihau. "Longo, you say I can find info on each of the islands. Including Niihau?"

"Ah, the forbidden island," he raised an eyebrow. So named because of a polio epidemic back in 1952 when it required a doctor's note to visit in order to halt the spread of the disease. I must say, that little rock has garnered quite a mystique for itself."

"I understand it's a private island."

"Yes, owned by the Robinson family."

"That's interesting."

"It's quite a long history. I can give you a brief synopsis if you are interested. But why do you ask?"

Hesitant to mention the fact that during the ride with Matt she challenged him to do something daring, she simply shrugged. "It surprises me that one of the Hawaiian Islands is private. That's all."

"Allow me to give you a further explanation of the situation over dinner if you're free tonight."

*Is he asking me on a date?* It caught her off guard. Her research described him as single, but in his early fifties, he was almost twice her age.

"My niece told me to take good care of you. There is a luau at the Kauai Island Hotel this evening. It is a very touristy presentation, but it would be a nice introduction to many of our traditions. And I find we all learn more with visual aids."

*Hawaiian hospitality?* Unsure of his intent, she asked, "Is it casual?" She employed the stalling tactic—albeit a truthful one—-to allow her a few seconds to decide. Packing in haste, her current attire consisted of casual tops and shorts, flip-flops, and running shoes.

"Everything here is."

Matt said he would call. She still hoped to connect with him, but...

# Chapter Eight

## Monday Late Afternoon

## Kauai University Library

AFTER PROFESSOR LONGO left, Amy settled in with a book from the island pile. She found an aerial view of the island of Niihau. The warmth of the sun and the quiet of her surroundings sent her back to yesterday morning.

And thoughts of Matt.

She found the heliport with ease. Stepping out of her rented jeep, she marveled at the imposing R44 helicopter. It sat on a square piece of concrete-covered ground a short distance away, its blades at a standstill. Even dormant, its imposing power sent a thrill of anticipation tingling through her.

To her side, a sheet of wood mounted on two-by-fours outlined the shape of the island. A dotted line snaked through it. She stepped closer, scanning the highlights: Waimea Canyon, the cliffs of the Na Pali Coast, Wailua Falls, and the Alakai Swamp with its rare birds and vegetation.

The voice from behind startled her. "You must be my eight o'clock."

Amy turned around. "Sorry. I didn't hear you."

"Because I'm wearing my sneaky shoes." An attractive thirty-something guy with military-short blond hair stood in front of her, pointing to his sneakers.

Flashing her dimples, she gave him a questioning look.

"I guess it's more effective with the young kids," he said with a shrug of muscled shoulders. "It goes along with the 'Are you ready for the ride of a lifetime?' question." He put out his hand. "I'm Matt." The strength in his grip surprised her.

"Amy."

"Well, I guess you're my only passenger for this one." He drew his phone out of his pocket, lowered his head toward it, and poked in entries as he spoke. "The dotted-line on the map shows you the typical route we follow, but we can spend more time in any one area you desire."

The warm breeze and the newness of the day put Amy in a flirtatious mood. "So, I guess that means... I can tell *you* where to go?"

He lifted his face to reveal a wrinkled nose, a creased forehead and an I-don't-think-so expression. "Not sure I like how that sounds." He winked. "But yes, for the next hour or so, I'm at your disposal." Matt led the way toward the waiting chopper. A few steps later, he came to an abrupt stop and turned. "Forgot to ask, on or off?"

"On or off?"

"The doors." Leaning in closer than necessary. "Do you like to live dangerously?"

Until he asked, it didn't occur to her that the chopper resembled her rented, open-aired jeep. The seats were visible on both because the doors were removed.

"Dumb question." With mischief in her voice, she said, "Dangerously."

"Follow me," he said with a grin of his own.

He bounded into the aircraft after helping her in, then walking around it. Once in his seat, he began flipping switches and adjusting levers as she settled in. The blades began whirring at frightening revolutions, creating an awful racket. Matt handed her a headset, which she donned and adjusted. The headset dulled the whirring and thumping of the blades, allowing Matt's voice to come through loud and crisp. "Ready?"

With a nod of flared dimples, she said, "For sure." The cloudless sky made it a perfect day for a flight. They ascended with ease as she marveled at the breathtaking views below.

Matt's voice came through again. "Is this your first time?"

"Depends on what you're talking about," she quipped.

He chuckled back. "Riding in a helo. The reason I ask is because most first-timers want the security of the doors. My last tour yesterday wanted them off. I'm glad you are OK with it because I didn't want to put them on." Turning toward her, he shot her another of his well-practiced winks. "And besides, like you, I really do like living dangerously."

They took off to the north as Matt began his normal narration. "Up ahead will be the beautiful Wailua Falls, a great place to spend a day."

Amy interrupted him, more interested in *his* story than the routine script. "How long have you been doing this?"

"A few years. Moved here from Texas after my stint in the service. You know what they say about not being able to go back."

"Bad memories?"

"Something along those lines. I try not to dwell on it. Let's just say I needed a change of scenery."

Their conversation remained personal for the next few minutes as she asked subtle questions, getting Matt to drop his guard and open up. He abandoned his rehearsed narrative to pour out his story of returning home early to surprise his long-time sweetheart, Helene. Only to be surprised himself when his unexpected arrival caught Helene in bed with a supposed friend of his.

They were approaching Palihale State Park when Matt said, "Oops. You got me talking and distracted me. We've already passed the Na Pali Coast." Matt moved a lever and explained. "You have to see the cliffs. They are amazing. I'll take you back so you can judge for yourself."

As the chopper made its turn, the glare of bright sunshine bounced off an outcropping of land in the water to the west. Amy pointed to it. "What is that?"

"That is a private island called Niihau." Amy registered it phonetically as *NEE-ee-how*. "Niihau for short," he said, dropping the middle syllable.

"Private?" She questioned. "Who owns it?"

"A family who have occupied it for generations. Eons, maybe. It seems they are in the middle of a dispute with the state of Hawaii right now. I think the state wants part of the island. However, the residents are refusing to give it up, claiming it contains sacred burial grounds."

"Can you show me?"

He gave her a sideways glance and sucked in a breath. "Oh no, not part of the tour."

"So much for *me* telling *you* where to go for *my* hour." Amy challenged, "And I thought you liked to live dangerously? Hmm?"

Shaking his head back and forth, he mumbled in a slow drawl, "My daddy always told me beautiful women would get me in trouble. I guess I'll never learn." He maneuvered the controls. The chopper jolted and veered off toward the area.

After a short flight, the outcropping she asked about peered at her from the glistening water below. Flying at a lower altitude than when they flew over Kauai, Matt asked, "Is it everything you expected?"

"I have no idea what I expected to see. I see a lot of game, which I guess the people here use for food. Also, a lot of beautiful, but empty, beaches."

After clearing a line of rocks that stretched across the sand to the shoreline, a new section came into view. Here figures stood alongside gardens they appeared to be tending. As they came nearer, the islanders pinned floppy sun hats against their heads while staring up in surprise at the passing helicopter.

Amy waved to them.

"Oh sure," Matt said. "Wave, why don't you? And get me fired at the same time."

That ended the tour. The chopper swung away and headed straight back to the heliport.

"I'm sorry," she said when they were back on the ground.

He said, "You didn't have to wave." Then he asked for her number, promising to call.

That was yesterday morning. She still hadn't heard from him.

# Chapter Nine

## Monday Evening

## Kauai Island Hotel Luau

AMY STOOD MESMERIZED, mentally and physically photographing the ambiance of the tropical paradise in front of her. From her position at the edge of a kidney-shaped pond, surrounded by lush foliage, she took in a waterfall cascading down stone steps at the pond's center. Its force sent pink flowers atop lily pads circulating in crystal-clear water.

Leaning in closer to better observe the gigantic koi, she inhaled the sweet smell of her surroundings as the graceful fish maneuvered between and beneath the water lilies, their colors glinting.

A tap on her shoulder broke the trance. Professor Longo said, "It's about to start." They followed an enthusiastic crowd to the back of the sprawling property where the show would take place. A host led them to chairs at the head of a long picnic table. It faced a multi-level stage consisting of three separate platforms.

Longo held her chair before he took a seat across from her. He raised the complimentary Mai Tai and said, "Aloha. It means welcome."

Amy removed the tiny umbrella and raised her glass likewise in a toast. "How do I say thank you?"

"Mahalo."

Amy said, "Mahalo and thank you for inviting me," as patrons continued to be seated down the length of their table. "I could watch those jumbo koi swim around for hours. And this view of the bay, with a fading sun and a rising moon, is so breathtaking."

Their table continued to fill and within minutes, a waiter appeared, inviting everyone to help themselves to the buffet. "We should start with the salads," the professor said, leading her to the first section of the feast. "The Waimea field greens and the baby bok choy are a must." Filling his plate, he asked, "Have you ever enjoyed pig cooked in an *imu*? It's an underground oven where the pig roasts for hours above fire and rocks which are covered by banana leaves. Also a must."

Amy took him up on each of his suggestions, selecting only slices of fresh pineapple for dessert along with a coffee. With the dinner portion over, an emcee parading on stilts in an Uncle Sam outfit lifted a red and white striped top hat high in the air to open the show.

Using the hat as a pointer, he indicated the stage to his right, where three barefoot girls with long and shiny dark hair stood. Each wore a bikini top, a grass skirt, and a lei of colorful flowers. "They always start with what Hawaii is most known for," the professor said. "The hula."

The announcer faded into darkness as the girls became the center of attention. Their hands moved in unison. Their grass skirts swayed from side to side, manipulated by the gentle movements of their hips. Longo leaned forward. "Their movements are a form of storytelling. This one tells the story of a sailor who went to sea and the love of the girl who waited each night by the shore for his return."

When the routine finished, over rapid applause, Longo continued speaking with a greater intensity. "From pictures inscribed on walls in Egypt to the monasteries in Greece, all societies have devised some form of propagating customs, rituals, and things of import to pass on to their heirs. The hula is just that. A simple way of relaying a story that can be taught with ease and passed on."

The emcee reappeared. This time he lifted his arm to a second area where an Elvis impersonator, adorned in a glittery, blue and silver outfit, now stood. The impersonator began belting out a selection from an old movie, *Blue Hawaii,* when Amy's ringing phone made her jump.

She brightened. The number showed up as a local one. *It must be Matt.*

She whispered, "Excuse me. I'll be right back." She got up, crouched low to avoid blocking the view of others, and crept off to the side to take the call.

Far enough away, with the noise of the show fading, she said, "Hey, I wondered if you were going to call."

"Is that right?" The surprised caller said. "This is Detective Palakiko. I have some additional questions for you. I would like you to come in so we can clear up a few things. Are you available now?"

Embarrassed, and even more surprised than him, she said, "No. I'm sorry, I'm not. I'm actually at a luau. But I'm glad you called. I wanted to talk to you. After you left this morning, I returned to my original unit. I noticed a lot of black residue, which I assume is fingerprint powder, around the stove." She steeled herself before saying, "But, if you're thinking they committed suicide, they didn't."

"Why is that?"

"Because I checked in the freezer. I found a carton of chocolate-chip ice cream which I opened. It hadn't been touched. That doesn't make sense. If it was suicide, don't you think they would have celebrated first?"

"Is that so?"

Annoyed at his apparent lack of interest in her news, she said, "Can this wait until tomorrow? I really don't think I can tell you anything more." He didn't respond. During the silence, she pictured him with his dark hair and tanned skin. "Hello. Detective, are you still there?"

After a breath, he said, "Do you know a Mr. Conners?"

"No," she blurted. "I'm only here on vacation."

"A Mr. Matthew Conners?"

"The only Matt I know is a helicopter pilot I took a tour with yesterday morning. But..." She swallowed hard trying to remember his last name. "Is he the one you're asking about?"

"I think we should talk about this in person."

"Is Matt in some sort of trouble?"

"There's been an accident."

His flat, ominous tone frightened her, causing her to shiver. "Is he alright?"

After a long pause, "I think we should do this in person."

She reached out to the trunk of the nearest tree for support, understanding dawning. *That's why he hasn't called.* The Waimea greens and imued pig in her stomach started wrestling, making her stomach feel like she had taken a punch. In a pleading voice, she asked, "Can you at least tell me if he's alright?"

"The address for the station is on my card. I'll expect you here tomorrow. Ten o'clock."

*This can't be happening. First the Plomasens. Now Matt.* Worst-case scenarios, each more morbid than its predecessor, flashed behind her closed eyelids. *Oh God, please tell me he's not dead.* Numb, she didn't respond.

"Miss Pryce, did you hear me?"

"Yes. I'll be there."

She forced herself to calm down enough to make her way back.

In Elvis' place, an elderly Hawaiian was blowing out a foreboding sound from a conch shell.

Longo's focus remained fixed on the performer as he said, "The shell is called a pooh, spelled p-u. It comes from the ocean but sends a sound out across the Aina. Aina means..."

She cut him off. "Can we get out of here?"

IN THE PARKING LOT, standing in front of her rental car, Amy apologized. "I'm sorry. I couldn't stay there." Using the bumper as a step, she plopped down hard on the hood of the jeep.

"I can see the phone call upset you," Longo said. "Do you mind if I ask what it was about?"

"Shock, I guess." Amy exhaled, leaving her gaze fixated on the ground. "A couple died this morning at the resort where I'm staying. I spoke with a detective about it." She glanced up and took in the professor, thinking he so looked the part: left arm folded across his chest, right hand at his face, its thumb digging into a cheek while an index finger covered his chin.

Peering down at her, he absorbed her every word. She smiled in spite of her concern and confusion, finding his interest and intense concentration soothing.

The professor nodded, waiting for more.

Amy let out a long breath. "The detective just called asking me about the guy I took a helicopter tour with yesterday." Tearing her gaze away from the professor, she said, "He mentioned an accident. He wants me to go in and talk to him tomorrow." She shook her head. "I'm so confused."

After a few breaths, Amy said, "I don't believe it. This is so crazy. I feel as if I'm somehow responsible."

The professor scoffed. "Why would *you* be responsible?"

"That stupid island."

"What island?"

"Niihau."

"Now I'm confused," the professor said with a short laugh. "What does Niihau have to do with anything?"

"Because," she said. "I asked Matt to fly over it."

# Chapter Ten

## Monday Night

## The Tiki Lounge, Kauai

"AND DETECTIVE PALAKIKO didn't give you any specifics about the accident?" Longo asked Amy.

She shook her head, "No, professor. The detective wouldn't tell me anything. I have to meet him at his office in the morning."

Because the professor's curiosity had been piqued by Amy's sudden need to leave the luau, he had offered her a nightcap. He brought her to The Tiki Lounge, a local bar with low lighting and a dark interior, hoping it would encourage her to expand on the phone call she received from the detective.

He chose the corner booth. The packed place kept the waiter busy, giving Amy ample time to recount her story of provoking Matt to fly over the private island, before he even noticed them. Longo suppressed a smile at the unrestricted impulsiveness of youth as the waiter approached. He ordered two whiskeys.

"I have my own issues with Niihau," the professor said.

"What's your problem with... What did you call it, *that little rock*?"

"I can relate," he said. "Living here all this time on Kauai, I've met a lot of people, but I only have a few close friends. Some of the dearest are my landlady, Pua Ahuna, along with her two boys. I rent a place from them behind their house. I watched them grow. Abelino, the older boy, couldn't wait to work with his father. He loved fishing from the time he could walk.

His younger brother, Koa, wanted to explore—everything. Including the world. He studied at the university."

The drinks arrived. Amy snatched hers and drained the glass in one quick swallow. Longo pushed his over. "Here. Take this one too."

She downed his as well.

"Now, Pua is all alone. Her boys are gone."

"What do you mean?"

"When I say gone, I mean one is dead, and the other, Koa, doesn't live here anymore."

"Where is he?"

"No idea. He came to me one day at the university to tell me about a terrific opportunity, a job offer he couldn't pass up, even though it would mean he wouldn't finish his last year. He wanted my approval."

"Sounds like he valued your opinion."

"I suppose," he nodded. "I told him it would be a mistake. Told him to finish school. Told him other jobs would come along. I knew his family would be upset if he left, most of all, his mother. But, knowing his thirst for adventure, I always surmised he would leave someday."

The waiter returned and pointed to the two empty glasses. Longo ordered beers for their next round, believing Amy would soon be uncommunicable if she continued tossing them back at her current rate.

With a puzzled look, the professor said, "A few days later, he sought me out again. This time to say that he regretted telling me about the offer and begged me not to tell his family."

"That's kind of weird."

"Then Koa left. But what still nags at me is how secretive he was about the job. Wouldn't give me any details about the job. Nothing. Wouldn't say where he would be working or what he would be doing. He hinted it would begin on Niihau. Since nothing much goes on there, it struck me as odd."

"Mahalo," the professor said to the waiter who had just delivered glasses and two opened bottles to the table. He poured his beer.

Amy grabbed the other one and began pushing down the beads of moisture on it. "That does sound unusual. Did he tell you the name of the company?"

Longo shook his head and said, "No. I guess I should have delved deeper into the details at the time. But I got the impression he exaggerated a little, making the job sound more important than its reality. He gave his mother a story about having to undergo extensive training, implying it could take months, saying she shouldn't worry, just understand."

Amy stopped twirling the bottle, poured her beer, and took a sip.

The professor let out a long sigh as his head thumped hard against the back of the booth. "Here's the worst part..." In anguish-soaked words, he said, "Not long after, his father and brother died in an auto accident. Then, when I contacted Palakiko to locate Koa on Pua's behalf, he couldn't find a shred of information on him. Other than his time here, not a scrap. He simply vanished."

"That's unbelievable," Amy said. "I'm so sorry."

Hanging his head in regret, he added, "I've often thought I should venture to Niihau and tell him how his mother is suffering. That is, if he is still on the island. Or ever was at all."

Amy stopped massaging the bottle back and forth between her hands. She lowered her voice, leaned in closer and said, "When we flew over the island, I noticed people working in a sort of garden. Matt moved us away as soon as we came across the workers. They seemed startled by us. It is possible Koa is involved with something they shouldn't be doing, or, to be more specific, growing."

He gave that some thought. "The Robinson family now gives tours of the island. A beach version for people to collect the island's unique shells and a second geared toward sportsmen, who spend the day hunting the wild game that roam the island."

"If they are doing something illegal, or growing something they shouldn't be," Amy said, "a tour would be great cover for smuggling."

She sat back, straightened, and said, "Well, I'm in. We'll have to find a different way to get there. Any idea how? I don't think we can go in again by helicopter."

Her reaction startled him. "I said I was thinking...." He paused. "Never quite got up the nerve."

LESS THAN AN HOUR LATER, back in the timeshare rental, Amy brushed her teeth, exhausted by the night's events, yet wondering if she would manage to get any sleep.

The disturbing call from Palakiko and the drinks after with Longo left her drained. Her drive back gave her time to analyze the state of her current emotions: baffled, confused, sullen. Scared.

Until now, she had considered herself bulletproof. Confident she could save the world—or at least have a dramatic impact—somehow on it. She still longed to. But, at present, she didn't have a clue on how to accomplish that. The death of the Plomasens—and now with whatever happened to Matt—coupled with the weight she arrived with, had obliterated her self-confidence. Leaving her with an overwhelming sense of helplessness.

*This isn't the vacation I hoped for. My father might be right. Perhaps I do need to talk to someone.*

She shut the bathroom light.

Her cell chimed. She recognized Longo's number. Swiping it open, she forced a little spark into her hello. "Hey. Thanks for the drinks tonight. And the company. I appreciate it. Did you make it back OK?"

"Yes. But it's not why I'm calling." The professor sounded motivated. "After giving it further thought, perhaps you are right. It is time I go and see for myself." He sounded aggressive. "Maybe I do know a way." After a quick breath, he asked, "Are you up for a late-night excursion?"

# Chapter Eleven

## Tuesday Morning

## Stratford Legacy Conference Room

SUSAN ENTERED THE CROWDED lobby of the multi-story office building. She serpentined her way toward the elevators at the back of the foyer. Upset with Mike today, she skipped her normal greeting to the security guard stationed behind the information desk. Her destination, the top floor of the building, held their offices and showcase conference room. The lower levels were comprised of a variety of professional offices and condos. This building served not only to house their offices, but as one of the foundation's many investments, guaranteeing a steady stream of income to ensure their valuable work continued.

"Where is Mike?" She asked Frank as she entered the conference room. "I left him a message yesterday. I said I needed to speak to him and marked it urgent. He never got back to me."

Frank's laptop lay closed in front of him. He cradled its mouse in the palm of his hand. "And good morning to you too," he said, sounding irritated. As he spoke, his hand began rising and settling on the mouse pad in rhythmic fashion, tapping out seconds like a clock. "I didn't hear from him either."

"It didn't hit me until later that Mike said three million for Eunice's request. I'm sure she only asked for two."

"I agree. But I spoke with Becky yesterday, and she told me Mike instructed her to issue a check for three." He locked eyes with Susan and let the mouse rest on its pad for the moment. "It's already been processed."

"What! So fast. Frank, something's going on with him."

Before Frank could respond, the elevator doors opened. Mike strode into the room with half a smile. He took his usual seat at the head of the table and fidgeted with his briefcase.

No one spoke.

When Mike looked up, a smile again in place, he said, "Beautiful day today, isn't it? I hope you both find some time to take advantage of this wonderful warm weather we're having."

Susan did a double-take toward Mike. *He's talking about the weather? What about responding to my urgent message from yesterday?*

Frank and his mouse started keeping time again.

Mike cleared his throat. "Before we begin, I want to expound on our disbursement yesterday. There is a simple explanation. Eunice apologizes for her error. The total needed is five million dollars. She and Joey will contribute two, and she needs us to assist with the balance of three. She simply misspoke when she asked for two."

Susan blurted, "And when did she correct this mistake of hers?"

Mike glared at her. "Does it matter? She made a mistake. We all do, don't we?"

Susan asked, "Mike, why are you so defensive?" She kept her voice steady. "All I want to know is when Eunice explained this to you. Because on Saturday I heard her ask for two."

Mike said, "On Sunday."

"Well, if you knew then, why didn't you explain it to us yesterday before we voted? We were under the impression we were voting to approve that amount. Not an increased one."

Frank cut in. "Where exactly did she tell you this? Was it at the hotel by chance?"

Mike turned his glare toward Frank. "If you must know. Yes, at the hotel. She wanted to explain the error in person."

Frank looked at Susan. "That explains it then. The hotel faxed over a second bill for the suite this morning. I thought it must be a mistake, a duplicate. Now it makes sense."

Mike said, "It's done. Can we move on?"

Frank yelled, "It's a million-dollar mistake."

"That's not even a drop in the bucket when you consider what we have in our coffers," Mike said, undeterred and defiant. "Especially in regard to what we started with. I will remind you again, those children are the direct bloodline of our founder. That makes them deserving." He exhaled loudly. "Of that amount. And much more."

Speechless, Susan rose, walked to the window, and gazed out. At nothing. With each breath, her chest rose and receded with emphasis, opening and closing like the bellows of an accordion. *He's lost it. We have to do something. What?*

"Susan, please take your seat." Mike said, "We have more to discuss."

She turned to him, a baffled look on her face. "There's more?"

"In fact," Mike continued, "the discussion for today is not to clarify yesterday's amount. Rather, I am here to discuss an additional request for five million to provide the children with the best possible care. It is not too much to ask—for *them*."

Back in her seat, Susan looked to Frank to speak. But he appeared dazed. She decided to start. "Mike, you forget I worked with Joey's father, Junior, the same as you did. Junior's beliefs mimicked his father's—the children's great-grandfather. Junior once told me the rule about employees was added on purpose to avoid abuse. I'm convinced he would be furious to learn we are paying out millions for an employee's benefit—and that now you are requesting a second distribution." The bellows expanded wider.

She took a few breaths to wrestle control of both her voice and her words. She hated the position she found herself in, fending off against Mike. "You are also familiar with the rule concerning all-inclusive payouts. It dictates all funds, including necessary future ones, *must* be incorporated as part of the initial request and either approved or rejected at inception."

With a final close of the bellows, she said, "I'm *sure* you recall his often-repeated concern about people believing they'd found a Golden Goose."

Mike took his time clearing his throat. After which he spoke with an effort. "Susan, let me share with you some of the emotions involved here." Looking at her, he said, "Now, I'm not saying this, but... Others on the board who suspect, perhaps you, not having children..."

Susan shrieked, "Mike, you can't be serious." Her Whac-A-Mole reaction popped her to the edge of her chair, nearly jettisoning her out of it as Mike jerked to the back of his. "How dare you? That is so unfair. Not to mention—untrue. And your below-the-belt insult is not the issue. I am as compassionate as you or any of the other directors."

Mike opened his mouth to speak. Her hand flew up. "You made your argument. It's *my* turn."

Susan took a minute to compose herself. Frank sat mute, his mouse stilled for the moment. She softened her tone and continued. "Mike, think about the entire situation from a distance. The normal way we approach decisions. If this request concerned any other baby, in any other part of the world, would we be having this conversation? That is the question you need to ask yourself."

Susan paused, took a deep breath, and said, "I think we all can guess the answer. We wouldn't."

She spent the better part of the next hour arguing, justifying, pleading her case. Even if she couldn't persuade Mike, she required Frank's support to outvote Mike.

When she finished, Mike queried Frank for his thoughts. He waffled a bit, but in the end he succumbed to Mike's further pressure.

Hers was the sole veto.

# Chapter Twelve

## Tuesday Late Afternoon

## Susan Fleming's Condo

*THIS HAS TO STOP. THIS is so wrong.* Susan's hands trembled so badly, she couldn't apply even a light layer of mascara. Shorty observed from a distance as Susan tried and failed.

Twice.

She couldn't fathom why Mike and Frank voted in favor of a second outlay this morning. That second disbursement, the one in the five-million-dollar category, made its way out for the Stratford children in the afternoon. A few hours ago, they learned Baby A passed away during an unsuccessful heart operation. Now Baby B needed additional medical procedures.

Because of these events, Mike once more summoned the team back to the office for an impromptu evening session to discuss a third outlay of money for the Stratfords.

Susan winced at the sudden ringing of her cell. She retrieved her phone, and noted the caller ID. In an instant, she morphed into a nervous schoolgirl about to knock on the principal's door.

Before answering, she exhaled a slow breath to calm herself, hoping to mask her frustration. She wanted to deliver her logic for disagreeing in person rather than over the phone. "Hi Mike. I'm getting ready to leave."

Tonight she would again object, but this time with confidence, bolstered by a series of phone calls with Frank in the afternoon hours during which he agreed with her. The payments did not conform to their mandates.

"Oh. Well then, I'm glad I reached you."

"What's up?"

"You needn't rush." She recognized the familiar sound of him clearing his throat. "Actually, you needn't bother at all."

"Why Mike? Are you canceling the meeting? Has something else happened?"

"Ah, Susan, I initiated a conversation with the other directors today. They agree with me. We think it would be best if you stepped aside and Denise replaced you."

Her knees buckled. She collapsed sideways into a nearby chair, almost missing it and landing on the carpet. "What are you talking about? After all these years, why would you want me removed?"

"Well, you bring up the precise issue." He cleared his throat again. "I checked the addendum left by Mr. Stratford. It dictates we possess the power to impose term limits on the Evaluation Committee participants in the same manner as the rest of the board."

"You checked?" She screamed, "Since when? You never have to check anything. You're the one who's able to recite the rules by heart." Her voice remained loud as she fought to breathe. Her head ached, and an unfamiliar pressure squeezed at her chest. "You know I am scheduled to replace you when you make the move to leave. In the past, you've always been pleased with my work, complimenting me, raving that we do such a terrific job together and make such a great team. And I recall you *begging* me to not ever speak of leaving. What's changed?"

He said, "I'm sorry. It's already done. Denise is replacing you as of tonight. We'll have to continue this conversation another time." The line went dead.

"You can't..." The phone flew from her hand, landing at the far wall, causing Shorty to jump and scamper away. The invisible force at her chest tightened its grip. It took a few moments before she regained the strength to retrieve her cell.

Numb, almost to the point of paralysis, her body wouldn't move—but her mind raced. *Eunice has something on Mike. She must have. Blackmail? What other reason could there be? Frank confirmed the charge for Sunday was valid. Perhaps Eunice's control came from whatever took place in that suite—at the foundation's expense.*

*Replaced. Now. At a crucial time.*

Susan couldn't influence the next vote, but with them tied up in a meeting at the office, it provided an opportunity for her to speak with the three other directors, sans Denise, Mike, and Frank. She wondered about Frank's feelings on the matter and decided she'd speak with him later.

She left a voicemail for the first two. The last one was John Hines. When the recorded announcement finished, she began, "John, I guess you're not speaking to me either. Mike tells me you all agreed to replace me on the Evaluation Committee. He says he held discussions with the rest of you. Care to share your feelings and comments with me?"

A click sounded on the line, followed by an identifiable cough, before a gruff voice came across. "He spoke with us via a conference call. The vote was five to one. Frank voted no." Somehow his last little tidbit made her feel better, although it didn't change things. "Mike informed us it is within the rules to dictate a replacement."

"Not that long ago, when the discussion of increasing our committee to five members to handle the workload came up, none of you expressed an interest in doing the work we do. The vote didn't pass. You all sounded satisfied to sit back and collect your fat payments for just attending the monthly meetings, nodding your heads and not having to do any of the hard work."

"I'd say that's rather harsh, Susan. He also mentioned your indiscretions."

"What indiscretions!" Sputtering, she said, "John, there aren't any."

"Susan, I couldn't say. I can only go by what I've been told." In that instant, she recognized the loss of his friendship. It hit her like a bowling ball barreling straight into her gut. Throughout their working relationship, John would address her as Susie or Susie Q. Sometimes, just 'Hey Sue.' Today she was Susan to him.

She sucked in a deep breath to quell the pain as John continued. "And, you realize, more than anyone, Mike is such a stickler for obeying the rules."

She howled in frustration. "That is precisely the point! We are breaking key ones on an ongoing basis."

"All I can say is you are still on the board."

In disbelief, she uttered, "Did he try to remove me from the full board as well?"`

"In case you're interested, no one wanted that."

# Chapter Thirteen

## Very Early Tuesday

## Niihau, Hawaii

"I CAN'T BELIEVE WE'RE doing this," Amy said. "Thank you for arranging it, professor." They were on their way to the forbidden island—the professor's idea of a late-night excursion—courtesy of Kalani Ahuna, a cousin of the professor's missing student, Koa. The professor picked up Amy mid-way to Kalani's bungalow, before driving them all to the docked boat.

"We are approaching the island, Kalani yelled from the helm." After Kalani heard the professor's story about Koa's strange departure, he didn't need any further encouragement to ferry them there. Moments after securing his craft, the three of them were standing on the sand of the professor's forbidden island.

Kalani asked, "What's the plan, professor?"

Longo took a few moments to orient himself. He scanned the surrounding landscape. In the distance, loud grunts and shrieks echoed. Pointing toward a forested area, he said, "I am guessing the rough area over there is where the hunting takes place." He pointed in the opposite direction. "I believe if we head off this way, we should arrive at the gardens we are looking for."

The professor addressed Kalani. "I think you should remain here with the boat while Amy and I explore. I don't want you to jeopardize your license in case someone spots us."

"Not a problem for me. You be careful."

"Amy, are you ready?" The professor's question interrupted Amy's thoughts, pushing away the memory of the vicious knife attack she witnessed in DC, the one gutting a young man she referred to as Squeaky. The memory she came here to forget. The extraordinary contradiction between that horror and the stunning beauty of this peaceful island couldn't escape her.

Nodding in answer to his question, she and the professor set out, sauntering on shell-covered sand. "Professor, you said they don't have any electronics on the island."

"Not to my knowledge. No TV, no Gameboys, no Internet, no electricity, and no running water." A stillness filled the air as they walked. Other than the sound of water lapping at the shore, the only interruption to the silence came from the crunch of shells beneath their feet. Or, the occasional animal whines off in the distance.

"However," he said, "I do recall a unique tidbit about the island. They have a school that functions solely on solar power. And, as you might have guessed, Hawaiian is the language spoken here."

Although conspicuous in the bright moonlight, visible to anyone in the vicinity, they kept their voices low as they walked.

"God, it is gorgeous here. So peaceful," Amy said. She bent to retrieve a sparkling shell, pocketing the souvenir. As she rose, she spotted an area of land off to her side cordoned off by a two-foot wall of various-shaped cairns. Behind the barrier, strands of shells, in differing lengths, hung by various means of support. A breeze chilled her as she paused to take a better look. Pointing, she asked, "What's that?"

"Cemetery. The hanging leis are grave markers paying homage to those buried in it."

"Well, it appears to be huge. How many people live on this island?"

"It's a small population now." Sadness laced his voice. "I believe less than a hundred."

"I wonder if they appreciate how precious and unique this place is."

"I imagine they do. They are the remaining torchbearers who continue to farm, hunt, and fish as their ancestors did a century ago. They live off the ... " A sudden high-pitched screech made him stop.

Amy asked, "How far away do you think those animals are?"

"Far enough not to bother us," he paused. "I hope. Let's keep moving."

They picked up their pace. Trying to ignore the intermittent animal groans and squeals, they came to a rock formation ahead of them blocking their path, forming a natural barrier across the sand. "You told me the gardens were past a ridge of rocks that extended to the water. Does that up ahead look familiar?"

"It does."

When they reached them, Longo pointed to the water to circumvent the sharp and jagged edges jutting from the rocks. Amy stepped into the warm water, and even at this late hour, experienced another small pleasure—memories of a relaxing bubble bath.

She slowed her gait, enjoying the moment.

"Look over there," Longo whispered as sand again invaded their sandals.

In front of them, a new view hidden by the rock wall emerged. Set back far from the shoreline, an area appeared divided into sections. It looked less rugged than the rest of the foliage, giving it a cultivated look.

Amy hurried forward, eager to examine it. "Let's go see what these guys are growing."

Longo grabbed her arm, pulling her to a stop. "Wait. Did you hear something?"

"No. What? Another animal sound?"

He raised his hand for her to listen. They both recognized the next sound.

A familiar one. A cough.

A human cough.

It made her shudder. *Who? Where?*

Longo pointed toward a cluster of rocks set back in the sand, the continuation of the ones they had just passed. They sprinted to them as fast and quietly as possible for cover.

Sheltered out of the open moonlight, they waited, crouching, using the darkness of the stone to conceal themselves. Amy crossed her arms for warmth. A faint noise in the quiet night sounded like someone breathing.

Longo leaned in next to her, their shoulders touching. He whispered. "We should leave. This is a mistake. We shouldn't have come."

"Let's wait a minute." Her curiosity for the moment overriding the waves of unease coursing through her.

In a sudden panic, Longo grabbed her upper arm and squeezed. "Amy, listen to me. This island is an anachronism. An item misplaced in time. There are no police here. No one to rescue us. No hospital to treat us if we are wounded. We are trespassing. We shouldn't be here. We need to leave."

A loud grunt, followed by a metallic sound, cut short his argument. They both rose, ready to flee, but fear held them in place. The scraping sound implied motion of some sort.

Neither moved. They listened, staring wide-eyed at each other in the shadowed moonlight.

More sounds. This time quieter.

Amy flinched, pulling out of Longo's grip and turning toward what she thought she recognized as the sound of a deep exhalation of breath. It sounded like a breath of relief.

They both froze as the figure of a man stepped onto the sand in the moonlight up ahead.

Longo's hand again gripped Amy's shoulder, indicating they needed to go. They continued to stare from their secluded position. Too surprised to move.

Amy took in his profile, pegging him as a short man, maybe middle-aged. He sauntered forward a few more feet. He took each step toward the water at an unhurried pace. Midway to the shore, he stopped and drew into his pocket, pulling out a cigarette and lighter.

From the darkness behind the man, another voice startled her. It exuded authority and strength along with its warning. "Smoking is bad for you."

Amy turned to Longo in surprise and mouthed, "English?" She wrenched her shoulder clear of the professor and opened her palms, questioning him. He shook his head, indicating he didn't understand either.

The man remained where he stood, his gaze fixed on the sea some thirty feet in front of him. He put his head back and let out a long string of smoke. Returning his focus to the water, the man said, "No. Bad is you keeping me here." He took another drag. "When do I go?"

The stillness of the clear night amplified their words.

"When they tell me you can. Not until then." The firm admonishment came from the unseen person. "I need to take care of something. I'll be back in a little while. Enjoy your break."

Bewildered, Amy dared to whisper. "What's going on here?"

"No idea. Best we leave this to the police. We should go now."

This time Amy grabbed Longo's arm. To her surprise, the appearance of this stranger and his words about wanting to leave replaced her fear with a deep desire to help. "Not yet. It sounds like he's alone now. Let's go talk to him. Find out what's going on first."

"Amy, what about the other man? What if he's armed? We need to go about this the right way." Nervousness filled his voice. "Let's go back. We'll contact the authorities and let them handle this."

"We can't just abandon him," she argued. "What if he's gone by the time they arrive? Then what?"

"I don't think that will happen. The police could be here in a couple of hours. I'd estimate by early morning."

Amy protested. "But you heard him. He said, 'When do I go?' That means he's not free to leave. It sounds like he's a prisoner, or at least being held here against his wishes." She thought about her vow. She couldn't walk away from this. She owed it to Tommy—and herself. "It also sounds like they're getting ready to move him."

Longo reached to restrain her, but she broke away. *If not here and now, then when?*

Her mind made up, her first steps were soft, silent, quick. Then she slowed her gait, straightened, and walked toward the man's back. When she got within a few feet of him, he must have sensed her approach because he turned to her. The man eyed her with curiosity but said nothing.

"Are you OK?" Taking in his features in the soft moonlight, she guessed him to be in his late fifties or early sixties. His unkempt graying hair needed a cut. Thin and shorter than her, he sported a full beard. Eyes of bright blue poked out from sallow skin.

He answered her with suspicion, slowly, drawing out his response into two syllables. "Ye-es."

Amy kept her tone tender. "Do you want to leave? To go away from here?"

"You come for me?" His English was accented, but she couldn't say from where.

"Yes. Yes." Amy shook her head in confirmation. "We can take you off this island. Is that what you want?"

"Where is helicopter?"

"No helicopter. We came by boat. It's not far." Wanting to appear non-threatening, she showed him her most welcoming set of dimples and extended a hand to take his. "Come."

He recoiled. "No. No. Can't go."

Suddenly backing away from her and acting scared, "No. Can't go." His loud objection traveled through the still air.

She raised her finger to her lips. "Keep your voice down."

But it was too late.

From a distant darkness, a surprised voice asked, "What did you say? Are you talking to someone? Is somebody else there?"

Longo surfaced from the shelter of the rocks. Now, at her side, he grabbed her and began pulling her away from the stranger and back in the direction of the boat—with a strength she wouldn't have believed him capable of. He spoke through clenched teeth, but with words clear enough to understand. "Whatever is going on here is not our business. We've got to go."

This time, Amy didn't argue.

Instead, she raised her phone. As Longo continued tugging at her, she snapped a photo of the man already heading back to the shadows from where he had emerged. As she did so, the form of a much larger man came into view. "Hey," he barked, "who are you? What are you doing here?"

"He sees us," she yelled as a run-for-your-life mentality kicked in. Amy ran beside Longo, aware of the heavy breathing behind her. The man's huge bulk handicapped him. When they reached the barrier of rocks, she and Longo splashed through the water to clear them.

Even with the man's huge heft, Amy feared each step closed the space between them. Longo glanced back at their pursuer. Then he began yelling to Kalani, no longer concerned about anyone hearing, hoping Kalani would ready the boat.

Up ahead, Amy recognized the cairns she had asked about and realized they were getting close to the catamaran. When they reached the burial grounds, Longo snatched her wrist and pulled her toward them.

She yelped in surprise.

Panting as he pulled her over the short stone wall and in, she managed to utter. "What are you doing? There is nowhere to hide. These grave markers are too small. Getting by them will only slow us down."

Once they were deep into the cemetery, Longo stopped and turned around.

"Why are you stopping?" Amy sputtered as she ran past him before coming to a halt herself.

Longo remained bent over, hands on his thighs, breathing rapidly, clearly not in the best shape. "Bad juju," he said between raspy breaths. "I believe the man is a native. He won't go into a graveyard or burial ground and disturb the spirits."

Longo took a few more breaths. "And especially not at night."

He was right. Too shocked to move, they stood motionless while the burly bulk of man chasing them stood pat at the entrance. Taking slow steps, he began backing away. After a while, he turned and left them, alone, among the dead, with whatever punishment would befall them for their intrusion and disrespect.

Looking at Longo in shock, Amy said, "You've got to be kidding."

"Nope," he shook his head. "Not joking. But just the same, let's get out of here before he comes back."

# Chapter Fourteen

## Tuesday Morning

## Kauai Police Station

AS THE SUN CAME UP, Amy headed out to the Kauai police station on only a scant hour or two of sleep. Even though somewhat exhausted, she remained grateful the meeting had already been scheduled. It would provide her an opportunity to discuss the trip to the forbidden island and the blue-eyed man she found there.

A responsibility that now fell to her.

Hours ago, nestled inside the cabin of the catamaran for their return trip to Kauai, the professor had a change of heart about having ventured to Niihau. He said, "Reflecting on tonight's activities, realizing we shouldn't have been on the island in the first place, I intend to forget the entire event. Everything about it. And I believe it would be best if we all did the same." Surprised by his comment, and spent from the night's escapade, Amy hadn't responded. Kalani hadn't commented either. He had simply shrugged.

At the police station, Detective Palakiko himself greeted her. He led her down a small hallway, opening the last door they came to. A cold chill snaked down her spine as he said, "We can talk in here."

Amy looked at the barren room, metal table in the center with two stiff chairs across from each other, and shivered. In the tiny space, it was impossible to miss the mirrored wall behind one of the seats.

The detective took the one in front of the mirror and indicated the other for her, saying, "I wanted to clear up a couple of things with you, Amy. Is it alright if I call you Amy?"

"Of course, detective." She said as she sat, wondering if her lack of sleep showed. "What do you want to know?"

"For starters. Tell me about your helicopter tour on Sunday morning."

"There's not much to tell. I booked the tour from home before I got here. It promised a snapshot of the entire island. I thought I would take the tour at the beginning of my stay so I could spend the rest of my week exploring the areas that sounded the most interesting."

"If you were so interested in Kauai, then why were you flying over Niihau?"

"It's kind of a long story. Matt..."

"Do you mean Mr. Conners?"

Exhaustion clouded her brain, weakening her resolve. The anticipated kick from the coffee she downed on her way in hadn't provided the expected caffeine boost. "He introduced himself as Matt."

"Go on." Palakiko sat forward in his chair, his hands resting on the closed file in front of him, his attention on her.

"We were talking, kind of flirting a little. He was acting, you know..." Amy shifted her position. "Kind of macho."

"No. I don't know."

It hit her this detective was not of the same ilk as Mark Peters, who had shown concern for her mental and physical safety back in DC. "Oh God. This is awkward." She sat straighter and stopped fidgeting. Same as him, she placed both hands in front of her, trying to project a confident image, well aware of his unflinching stare. "I guess I sort of challenged him."

"To do what?"

"To live dangerously. I said something like that to him. But you need to understand I only said it because earlier he had asked me if I liked to live dangerously before we began the tour. He meant whether we should fly with the doors on or off."

"What was your answer?"

Her eyelids flickered shut for a moment. She fought to keep them open.

"Well?" The detective asked with more force.

"I said off. We were just kidding around. Look, I'm very sorry if he's in some kind of trouble for deviating from his normal course." Her mind continued its dizzying rotations, like a merry-go-round, with her needing to jump off and not quite sure when to do it. Experiencing a moment of clarity, she said, "How did you know we flew over Niihau?"

"Does it matter how? Are you denying it?"

She bit her lower lip as the carousel kept screaming out a question she didn't want to ask. But had to. "You mentioned an accident. Did Matt fly too close to the side of one of those mountains?"

Palakiko's gaze didn't deviate. He stayed silent for a long moment, intensifying her anxiety. Finally, he answered. "An accident, yes. Although it happened on land." He paused. Amy tried making sense of his words, unsure of what they meant. "Where were you Sunday afternoon?"

She forced herself to recall. "After the tour, I went to the beach and did some snorkeling."

"By yourself?"

"Yes. I came here alone."

"Meet anyone? Talk to anybody who might remember seeing you?"

Her stamina reached a new low. "No."

"And then?"

"Nothing. Matt had my number. I was waiting for his call."

"So, you had plans to meet with him."

"Yes. I mean no. Nothing definite. He indicated we should get together for a drink or dinner. I expected a call from him. That's all." After a few silent breaths, she realized why he was questioning her. When the full implication hit, she couldn't disguise her shock. "You can't think that I..."

"Tell me again about Mr. Plomasen and his diagnosis. Prostate cancer, did you say?"

*Now we're back to that?* An ever-tightening, imaginary handcuff wrapped itself around her waist as she said, "Yes. He had cancer."

"I spoke with his son today. He told me their family doctor assured him at his father's age, the cancer would advance slowly. So much so, he would die from any one of a multitude of different ailments before the cancer. And, because of it, they would not be treating the disease."

Amy sat speechless, believing Palakiko enjoyed delivering that last bit of information.

The detective leaned back and crossed his arms. "So why would they decide to take their lives? When, as you so helpfully pointed out, they were here to celebrate. With ice cream."

"Which never happened," she blurted out as her eyes honed in on his face, memorizing every inch and aspect of it. "I have no idea. Do I need a lawyer?"

"Do you feel you do?"

She hated his annoying trait of answering a question with another. "Why am I here?"

"I told you. To help me fill in a few missing blanks. The issue with their deaths isn't resolved, but the tampering with the helicopter is confirmed to be sabotage. I wonder if you have anything to add to either event."

Even though a figment of her imagination, the handcuff completed its job. Her insides felt so tightly pressed together, they now formed a solid state. It weighed her down. She sat, staring at him, afraid to say anything else.

After an eternity, at the point where she almost asked if she was under arrest, he said, "If you have nothing else to add, I'll take you down to have your prints taken. But don't leave the island without checking with me first."

She gripped the end of the table for support, to assist with her newfound weight, and rose on unsteady legs. "I leave on Saturday."

"No." A brief pause. "You don't. Not unless you check with me first."

# Chapter Fifteen

## Tuesday Early Afternoon

## Kauai, Hawaii

IN RETROSPECT, THE meeting with Palakiko turned out to be a disaster. Amy had intended to discuss the issue of the man on Niihau with him. But, after his interest in her for whatever happened with Matt, she decided her unauthorized visit would only turn his focus more on her.

Somehow, though, she made it back to the time-share rental without a problem. An involuntary shiver passed through her as she entered. The place was freezing. She turned the air off and pulled the sliders open wide, letting in a warm blast from the dazzling sun. Hauling the cover off the bed, she dragged it to the lanai and curled up on the outside chaise. Cocooned in the duvet, the heat of the sun worked its magic.

She slept.

Soon, she was once again in her disguise as a homeless woman known as Lizzie, walking the streets of DC, rifling through a garbage can in front of an abandoned home for food.

A short distance off to her side, two gang members stood face to face, talking in the home's overgrown garden. The one she had nicknamed Lum, for *Large Ugly Man*, held a knife in his hand next to his thigh. Not unusual since the members often displayed weapons.

She returned her attention to the front door of the home. Then came the change in pitch and inflection in Lum's words. They were angrier.

Turning toward them, she heard the sound. The one that now haunts and tortures her every time she closes her eyes to sleep. The horrendous, guttural moan spilling from the one she had nicknamed Squeaky. Then Lum shoved Squeaky's ragdoll body backwards. Exposing his front for a fraction of a second before he fell to the ground.

Soaked in blood.

Lum's knife had gutted him from his bowels to his chest.

Amy screamed herself awake. Soaked in sweat.

Again.

Embarrassed at her scream, Amy thrashed around until she freed herself from the bed covering. She checked the nearest balconies to see if anyone had heard her outburst.

No one had.

Relieved, she headed for the bathroom to shower away the nightmare. Checking the time, she realized she had slept for less than an hour. The refreshing spray of the shower not only cleared away the remnants of the dream, it confirmed to her the necessity of returning to that pesky island. That realization strengthened her resolve. She dressed and hit speed dial for Bonnie.

"Uh-oh," Bonnie said after hearing Amy's hello. "What's wrong?"

"You're not going to believe me." Amy filled her in on the trip to Niihau with Longo and Kalani, explained finding the stranger, and ended with the morning's meeting with Palakiko. "Bonnie, I have to go back." Amy's logic told her she couldn't have stopped Lum. Or saved Squeaky. It all happened so fast. But now, having been on Niihau, seeing the man there, she felt convinced she could help the blue-eyed man in trouble on that island. She couldn't walk away from him.

"You're scaring me," Bonnie said. "Why does it have to be you? Let the authorities handle this. If you're not happy with this detective, find someone else. Contact the FBI. They have jurisdiction in all fifty states."

"I can't let this go. I'll never forgive myself if I don't get involved. I can't believe I didn't even ask him his name."

"You said you took his picture?"

"Yes, but it's not great. Longo was dragging me away at the time, and even with a full moon, it was still dark. It's only a side view."

"Amy, listen to me. This is not your responsibility. You can do so many other things to make a difference in this world."

"Bonnie, I know you don't quite understand how I feel. But Tommy died. Squeaky died. What if this guy dies? When am I going to do something... If I don't, then why am I here?" Amy took a few calming breaths. "I'm texting you his picture now. I also posted it, asking if anybody knows this man."

Bonnie gulped. "You didn't!"

"Already done. I knew you wouldn't want me to. I need to go. I have to figure out how to convince Longo that we, or at least I, have to go back. I'll call you later."

Amy hung up from Bonnie and dialed the professor, still curious about his sudden change of mind about informing the authorities. She pegged him as a straight-laced, law-abiding, by-the-book kind of guy. *Guess I was wrong about him.*

When he answered, his voice sounded detached. "How did your appointment with Palakiko go?"

"Well, considering he thinks I'm somehow involved with Matt's accident, I guess I would have to say not too well."

"Why on earth would he think that?"

"I haven't the foggiest." She decided to get right to the point. "Longo, last night has been replaying itself in my head."

He interrupted. "I should warn you. I'm short on time." Yesterday's camaraderie nonexistent today.

"Longo, I am troubled by the man, or should I say captive, we met on the island. I can't stop thinking about him. I am wondering..."

Interrupting again, he said, "My class starts..."

"Stop trying to get out of this conversation. We both witnessed the same thing. The man is in some kind of trouble. He is being held against his will. You know it. And I know it."

"That may not be true. He has consumed my thoughts as well."

Irritated by the professor's excuses, she said, "I'll bet."

"He may not be a prisoner. Do you realize how erratic he sounded? Agreeing he wanted to leave and then backing away from you like you intended to hurt him. This may simply be a case of voluntary incarceration.

It might be for his own benefit. He may suffer from some level of mental incapacity. Perhaps he is being restrained to prohibit him from doing some damage to himself or others."

Further irritated with his flimsy explanation, she scoffed, "Who are you trying to convince? Yourself or me? That's not the case, or else the other monster of a man wouldn't have chased us."

"You forget. We were not supposed to be there. He wasn't aware of what we were trying to do. He may have believed..."

"Just stop, will you? Believed what? What we were attempting to do was talk to a man who wanted to leave."

"Did he? I'm not so sure."

Frustrated, she said, "Right. And you can't, or won't, help. I'm sorry, but I'm not going to drop this."

"Before you go, let me ask, out of curiosity, what did Kimo, uh, I mean Detective Palakiko, say when you told him?"

Amy sensed her answer was important to him. "Nothing." She decided not to let him off the hook. "I didn't tell him yet. But I intend to."

# Chapter Sixteen

## Tuesday Late Afternoon

## Kalani's Bungalow

"I WANT TO THANK YOU for taking us to Niihau yesterday," Amy said to Kalani, who she found lazing in a hammock in the backyard of his house. Below him, an empty beer bottle sat at the base of a tree. Uncertain of how she would convince him to take her back, she had approached him slowly, stopping beside the oscillating net near his feet.

Kalani raised his tilted head, shielded his eyes against the late afternoon sun, opened them, closed them again, and resumed swaying. He didn't seem surprised to see her, but his lack of welcome destroyed any hope she had that he would help.

After her phone call with Longo, Amy realized she was on her own. She couldn't count on the professor to help her return to Niihau. She had also considered informing Palakiko, reasoning: *He's an officer of the law. He wouldn't be allowed to ignore what I tell him. Would he? But how would I explain why I went there again?*

She dismissed that option and decided to reach out to Kalani herself.

Without a phone number or address, she needed to find his bungalow. Logic had her start where the professor had picked her up. From there she drove the narrow roads at a snail's pace, searching for landmarks, trying to retrace his path. Her slow speed required her pulling off at times to allow others to pass. After several wrong turns, she finally succeeded.

"Kalani, I couldn't sleep last night. I imagine you overheard us talking about the strange thing that occurred while we poked around the island."

His gentle swaying didn't stop, but his eyes opened in question. "You mean about disturbing the spirits?"

"Well, that too. Please understand, though, we had to do it. We were chased, in fear for our safety. We didn't intend to be disrespectful. But a man is being held there against his will. I spoke to him. I asked if he wanted to leave, and he did."

"That's not what the professor said." His words were flat, emotionless.

"I can't explain why." She shook her head, confused by his reaction as well. "At first, he was happy someone had come for him, but the professor is right. After saying yes to me, he changed his mind and said no for some reason. But, Kalani, if you believed someone was being held captive, wouldn't you want to help?"

She let the question hang in the air, staring down at him, wondering what argument would motivate him. "I need your help. Please. I want to go and talk to him again. I need to at least try. I think the professor wants you to believe, for some ridiculous reason, the man is there for his own benefit. I don't buy his argument. Even if he is right, I must find out for myself. Can you understand that?"

Kalani didn't answer. She tried a different tact. "Did you speak to Longo today?"

The voice from behind made her jump. And turn. "No, he hasn't," Longo answered for him.

"How long have you been standing there?"

Longo stepped closer. "A little while."

Amy said, "I take it you're here to try and convince him not to take me back."

"On the contrary." Amy's jaw dropped. "I am here precisely to talk to him about going back. I, too, have been reconsidering the events of last evening. I am now convinced the man chasing us last night was Koa. My missing student," he nodded toward the net which had stopped moving, "and Kalani's cousin."

At hearing those words, Kalani finagled his way out of the net. "You didn't say anything last night, professor. Why not?"

"Because I couldn't be sure." The professor drilled his finger back and forth across his mustache. He put his hand down and said to Kalani, "His voice sounded familiar. He spoke very little, and I only caught a quick glimpse of him. He's heavier than when I last saw him." Amy imagined the professor was wrestling with his own regrets surrounding Koa. "Later, in the burial grounds, I turned around and took a halfway decent look at him. It was still from a distance, but I'm pretty confident it was him. I think he recognized me too."

In disbelief, Amy plunked down on a rotted stump beside the hammock, her mouth still open wide.

The professor said, "I also wondered if that was part of the reason he let us escape—in addition to us being on sacred grounds."

"So now you're on board with going back to rescue the poor man?"

He turned toward her. "No. I'm sorry. I'm here to talk to Kalani for another reason."

"What other reason?"

"About going back to talk to his cousin. To tell him of his brother's and father's deaths and the heartbreak his mother is going through." Longo shook his head. "If she realized where he is. How close."

He stood silent for a breath. "By the way, thank you, Amy, for not mentioning our activities last night to Palakiko."

Kalani spoke up. "Alright, professor. We'll go talk to him."

"Sorry, Kalani. I can't."

"You're not coming?"

"I've got too much invested at the university. He doesn't need the two of us. You're family. He will either listen to you or he won't. Me being with you won't change a thing."

"But you could help me talk to him, reason with him, convince him. He had a great deal of respect for you, professor."

Longo lowered his gaze to the ground. "I'm sorry."

Amy stood. "Well, *I'm* going with you!"

The native Hawaiian shook his head no.

"Please, Kalani."

He held up his hand. "We go nowhere until my boat gets fixed. I told you on the way back, something didn't feel right. My friend is working on her as we speak. He'll be finished tomorrow or the day after."

"But the man could be gone by then."

Kalani plucked up his empty beer bottle and shuffled toward the bungalow, his shoulders slumped as if he carried an invisible load of twice his weight. He called back to them, "If you're able to work on boats, you can go help. Otherwise, tomorrow at the earliest."

*Tomorrow...* Amy left dissatisfied but hopeful. Kalani would take her back— although it wouldn't be for another day or two. *Maybe it's for the best.*

The delay would allow her to get some much-needed rest. Then she would be better equipped to deal with the issue of the man with the piercing blue eyes. As she drove back, she fought a drowsiness threatening to take over. Relieved when she arrived safely, she started to hum, *Tomorrow, tomorrow, you're always a day away ...*

At the base of the stairs, she paused, considered the elevator for a moment, but climbed instead.

Reaching the fourth level, she stopped to exhale. *Made it back. Now for some rest.*

She teetered down the walkway to her door and unlocked it. She was still humming when the push from behind forced her inside, catching her completely by surprise.

# Chapter Seventeen

## Home of Eunice and Joey Stratford

## Tuesday Night

JOEY STRATFORD LAY stiff as a corpse in his king-size bed, staring at the coffered ceiling. The President and CEO of Stratford Industries counted his lucky stars each day that he found and married this wonderful woman. The one next to him, stroking him, comforting him, encouraging him.

Just trying to relax him.

Earlier, after an evening out for dinner, at Eunice's coaxing, they stopped for a pousse-café. As the bartender poured layer after layer of liqueurs to make the rainbow concoction, she teased, promising to share exciting news with him. But, per her usual tactic, it required him to wait until they were alone—and usually in bed—before anything would be divulged.

"I told you it would work, darling." Eunice snuggled in closer to whisper in his ear. "You need to have faith."

Joey appeared transfixed, as if under a spell, rendering him unable to comprehend what she had just revealed. After some time, he said, "I do. I'm amazed. I can't believe you went ahead and met with them."

As he listened to her, his gaze fixed on the ceiling, she described the meeting with the members of the Evaluation Committee. Explaining in detail how she justified her reasoning to them for abandoning their restrictive rules governing the distribution of funds from the foundation.

At first, Eunice floated the idea of both of them approaching the committee together. For a short time, Joey agreed. After reconsideration, he backed out, pleading with her he couldn't. He wouldn't survive another taxing and, even more embarrassing, battle.

Not after just completing the recent one with his board.

After backing out, he thought the subject ended there. In his wildest dreams, he never envisioned Eunice taking up the charge and approaching them on her own. But obviously, he still didn't recognize the full potential of the power this woman could wield.

Even over others.

It shouldn't have surprised him. He already realized the overwhelming influence she held over him.

"And you believe they are going to go ahead with the request?" He asked, still doubting. "Against all the rules my father and his father put in place to prevent something like this?"

"What have I been telling you?" With a devilish smile, she said, "You need to have faith. Faith in me. In us."

He rolled to his side and began to return her affection, kissing her gently on the forehead, her cheeks, down her body, mumbling as he did. "You're right. You always are. I should, and I will from now on, believe in you. I don't know why I ever doubted you. You are my Wonder Woman."

# Chapter Eighteen

## Tuesday Early Evening

## Rented Time-Share

SHOCKED BY THE UNEXPECTED shove, Amy's shrill scream pierced the hallway's silence as she turned to face her attacker. Her tired eyes struggled, before blinking with recognition. "You're not dead!" The sudden revelation snapped her out of her lethargy.

"Is that what you were hoping for?" Matt stood before her, a scowl across his face, his hands planted on his hips.

"No," Amy managed to say. "I thought you were, but oh God, no. Of course not. Why would I want you dead?"

"Well, someone did. I just wasn't expecting that someone to be you."

"That's because it wasn't me," she said with genuine surprise. "How could you even think I could do such a thing?"

"I have my reasons. What makes you think I died?"

"Because of Detective Palakiko," she said. "He told me you had an accident. He wouldn't give me any details. He..." She stopped, her lethargy returning. "I *think* he said you were dead. Right now I don't recall what his actual words were." Her tired brain struggled to remember. "But, because of the way he talked, I guess I assumed the worst."

"Did Detective Palakiko question you about this?" Matt maintained his stance in front of her, blocking her path further in.

Amy said, "Yes, he did. Matt, I am so happy to see you. You have no idea. I feared something dreadful had happened."

"Something did," he said.

Amy surveyed him. Her focus settled on the left side of his face, taking in the inflammation, bruises, and redness of his cheek and ear. It looked as if he had contracted a bad case of poison ivy. Amy reached to touch the pus-filled blisters. Matt grabbed her wrist, pushing it away. His abrupt action caused her to recoil. "Hey, I'm glad you're alive. I have no idea about whatever's going on with you, but I had nothing to do with it." She raised her voice. "So, if there's nothing else, I'm exhausted. I didn't get any sleep last night, and I really need some."

"I'm not leaving until I get answers."

"Fine," Amy said, "but can we sit?" He tilted his head to the side, indicating she could. He let her pass. She moved into the sitting area dropping onto the end of the couch. Matt followed, taking a seat on a swivel rocker across from her. "Why do you think someone tried to kill you?"

"Somebody poked a hole in the chopper's fuel line. A nice little tactic to bring down the bird and kill everyone aboard."

"But you're here, so nothing happened?"

"I didn't say that." He sucked in a quick breath. "I saw the stain on the ground yesterday morning. I fuel up at night, but I always check her again the next day. The wind would have whisked away the smell, but I caught sight of the spillage. I went to the office to contact my boss about canceling the day's flights. As I did, a disappointed customer walked over to check for himself. I waved out the window for him to come back, which he did, but not before tossing away the butt of his cigarette. The bird went up in flames."

He paused for a moment. "We grabbed fire extinguishers and managed to put out the fire. But before we did, a breeze blew up a lick of flame, which caught me before I managed to extinguish it."

"So, those are burns on your cheek?" He didn't answer her. They sat in silence for a long moment. "Matt, I'm happy you're OK," she smiled at him, her dimples blooming. "But trust me, I wouldn't even know how to find a fuel line, let alone put a hole in it. I'm sorry it happened, but I didn't do it. I'm dead tired. Can we talk about this another time?"

"No. I need to know if you played any part in this."

"I had nothing to do with it." Her face sagged, which made her dimples disappear. "Why would I? And why would you even ask me such a question?" *Boy was I wrong about this guy. I thought he would be so much fun to be with. Now he's here thinking I tried to kill him?*

"I need to ask you another question, and I need you to tell me the truth."

"What is it?"

"Why did you take the tour with me on Sunday?"

Her frustration skyrocketed. "Not you too! Palakiko already asked me about this. I wanted ideas for the week. That's all. I didn't come here to hurt you. Or anyone else, for that matter. That's not who I am. It was bad enough having to answer to him for something I had no involvement with, but I don't have to answer to you too."

"I'm not finished."

"Well, I have nothing else to say, so no more questions. You can just leave."

Matt hesitated, but after a moment, he got up, moved to the counter, and wrote something. At the door, he flicked on the lock and pulled it closed behind him.

Amy sat stunned. *What had all that been about? Someone sabotaged the helicopter. Why?*

*More to the question, is why does he think I did it?*

This new and unexpected puzzle piece made no sense. She no longer felt drowsy. Adrenaline surged through her. She pulled a cold drink from the fridge, determined to make sense of it. Determined to fit the unconnected pieces together, and see what the full picture looked like.

Now was no time for sleep. And there wouldn't be any—at least not for a while.

# Chapter Nineteen

## Wednesday

## Kauai, Hawaii

AT THE STARBUCKS COFFEE shop, Amy ordered a drink, found a seat, and reflected on Matt's sudden appearance last night. Although happy he was alive and pretty much unharmed, she didn't appreciate his intrusion. He had left a note with a number on the counter asking her to call so they could talk further. He seemed to be a decent enough guy, but any amorous interest in him vanished yesterday.

It resolved one issue for her. Her focus now re-centered on the man on Niihau.

And Kalani's boat repair.

After Matt's visit and a late-night conversation with Bonnie, Amy managed a few hours of sleep, and awoke refreshed. The bright sunshine streaming in through the sliders alerted her to the fact that she had reached a milestone: sleeping for several hours straight.

A young blonde snapped her head in the direction of the door as a strong, confident-looking Matt blew in. A good deal of the inflammation had subsided. A light covering of salve shone across his cheek and ear. His clothes were casual: jeans and a golf shirt.

Those few hours of sleep must have done her good because for a moment her thoughts drifted to the more physical. She had to admit, if other issues weren't distracting her, this could have been a very enjoyable week.

Matt settled onto a stool across from her. "Let's go somewhere where we can talk."

"I haven't finished my drink yet."

"Take it with you." He threw her one of his trademark winks. He got up and held the door for her as the blond eyed her with envy. "Have you eaten?"

"Not yet."

"Me either. I think I owe you. Come on."

In the parking lot, he indicated a Ford F150. "I'll drive," he said, hopping into the black pickup.

"How did you find me?"

"Don't have to be Sherlock Holmes. You told me where you are staying. I recognized the jeep, but I didn't know which unit you were in, so I waited in the parking lot until I saw you leave. I tailed you to the small house up in the hills, hid until you left, then followed you back and up to your door."

"Then it was you I moved over for on my way to Kalani's bungalow."

"Guilty." He took his hands off the wheel in mock surrender. "What were you doing there?"

"You first."

As he drove, Matt recounted his anger at finding the sabotage done to the helicopter. Even though he didn't own the chopper or the business, he still viewed it as a personal attack. It helped her understand his roughness and rude behavior last evening, although it didn't quite excuse it.

By the time they reached the restaurant, her attitude toward him had softened. With nothing to do until she heard from Kalani, she decided to live in the moment, and enjoy his company in the meantime. A hostess in a bright red and blue muumuu seated them at an outdoor patio. Colorful flowers, including Birds of Paradise, surrounded the tables. Their seats faced a wide swath of glistening water. The ambiance mellowed her even further. "But you practically accused me of being responsible yesterday when you shoved your way in. How could you even think I could do something so vicious?"

"Because by the time the police arrived, the fire was out. Our mechanic had examined the bird and determined the puncture was man-made. The detective started asking me the expected questions. Does anyone have a gripe with the company? Or me? Any other vandalism? Do I have any enemies? No to all of them."

A server arrived and took their drink orders. With him gone, Matt said, "Then Palakiko asked for the tour log. He took one look at it and jumped on his phone, asking someone at the other end to run a complete background check on you. He must have recognized your name. If he was so interested in you, well then, so was I."

"You're talking about Monday morning, right?"

Matt nodded.

"I spoke with him then."

He raised an eyebrow.

"A couple died at the complex where I am staying." Amy sighed heavily before filling him in on switching with the Plomasens. As their drinks arrived, she said, "I think Palakiko believes they committed suicide. By blowing out the pilot light on their stove."

"What stupid idiots. The entire building could have blown up, just like the chopper. They could have taken out a lot of innocent people with them."

In a voice full of conviction, she said, "They didn't do it. They would never do such a thing. They were too nice." Suddenly the idea of sharing a meal with him didn't appeal to her. She pushed her chair back and placed her napkin on the table.

Matt snatched her wrist, pinning it against the placemat. "I'm sorry. I didn't mean to be so blunt. I'm often too direct and have a bad habit of blurting out my thoughts. Not always the smart thing to do." He winked at her. "Let's talk about something else."

With his hand still restraining hers, he began stroking it with his thumb. "You said you flew in from DC. Is that home for you?" She cast her eyes to his massaging finger, and he moved it away as their waiter appeared.

The Plomasens weren't forgotten, but they had been relegated to a back burner because of the man on Niihau. Realizing her reaction to Matt's comments came from her own frustration with both issues rather than him, she relented. After ordering pineapple pancakes, eggs, and sausage, she said, "Funny you should ask."

"Why funny? It's a pretty normal question."

"Yes, I guess it is. DC is where I grew up. But I didn't grow up normal. My mom and dad sound weird to people. They are not your typical couple.

I spent my childhood living with two pleasant, but very different, people—who happened to be my parents."

For the first time, Amy found herself discussing her home life with someone other than a close friend. It occurred to her she might be settling with it, instead of being embarrassed by it.

"My mother is a professional in her own right, and my dad is more the matriarch of the family. He is the one who did all the chauffeuring around while my mother concentrated on her work projects. He lives for weekends and holidays, always planning what we would do or where we would go. If my mother was available, not tied up with work, she would join us. If not, it was me and my dad."

"I've heard of them before," Matt offered. "Househusbands, I think they're called."

"Yes. But what about bi-coastal couples? My mom lives in Seattle and has for the last several years. She's a forensic accountant for an international firm. Most of their clients are in that area or further west of it."

"Got to admit, that's a new one on me. Unless, of course, they're divorced."

"Nope. No divorce."

"And you're happy with the situation?"

She paused as the waiter brought their food along with a pot to refill their coffees. "I've accepted my life a long time ago. They're still married, not even separated. They both carry on as individuals, are amicable to each other, and neither sees any reason to make it official. You could say I'm their only connection."

"It doesn't bother you she wasn't there for you? For your first big heartbreak? I thought girls always run to their mothers?"

An uncomfortable flush struck her at his words and the truth in them as she cut into her pancakes. "It's the way she is. She's happy, and I'm happy for her." She took her first bite, which included chunks of fresh pineapple, and paused for a moment to savor it before changing the subject. "My mother paid for my entire college education, leaving me as one of only a handful of my peers who graduated with a degree and no student loans hanging over their heads."

"Does that make up for her not being around?"

Wanting to avoid Matt's remark, she pivoted the conversation to her dad. "My father, for his part, decided to offer me what he calls freedom, so I could *experience* life instead of just *living* through it. He bought me a used car and agreed to pay my housing expenses for five years after college until I turned twenty-seven, which I did a few days ago."

Matt stopped attacking his meal. "Why did he do that?"

"I think my dad regrets not doing a lot of things himself, much earlier in his life. By the time he decided to, he was too close to retirement, and Mom wasn't around."

"What did you do with all that free time?"

"Anything I chose to. Travel, which I did as part of what I call my hands-on education. Instead of just taking courses in an area, I apprenticed in it. I learned enough carpentry to build a small home in Africa, did a stint in traditional marketing, then another which relied entirely on social media. I would work as a waitress or a maid in a variety of places to earn extra money. I taught school for a semester. Went through outdoor survival and EMS instruction, then volunteered as a firefighter for a while. I worked for a vineyard for several months. Along the way I learned other skills—like making cheese and baking breads. I chose my activities based on unusual subjects that I found interesting. Speaking of which, it's part of why I'm here. I'm researching Hawaiian culture."

"So, five years. What's at the top of your list for most memorable?"

His question stopped her for a second. She never thought to prioritize them. "They were all wonderful in their own unique way. So many things intrigued me. They were all different. The last two weeks I've been living on the streets of DC posing as a homeless woman." She smiled at his abrupt halt in sending food down his throat—plus his unasked question of why.

"Wow," he said. "Didn't see that one coming."

Amy's phone chimed. She read the text and said, "Terrific," before typing in a response.

"By the way, congrats on the birthday."

"Thanks." She said, showing off her dimples, happy to accept his birthday wishes. "When I get back, I start work on a temporary assignment at the company where my best friend works, which should last for the next few months. It will be my first stab at complete independence, pulling my own weight." She raised her coffee cup to him before taking a sip.

He toasted back. "Are you ready for it?"

"Not sure yet, but I think so. God knows my father is. Everybody thinks he is such an ultra-liberal man because of his gift, but they haven't seen his other side, where he can be as steadfast and unmoving as the Rock of Gibraltar. My *new* life starts when I get home."

Her words brought her back to the current issue pressing on her. "Right after I go find out what's going on over on Niihau."

"Niihau?" He swallowed a mouthful before asking, "Why would you want to go there again?"

Amy explained meeting Professor Longo and the trip to the island with him.

"You're telling me a man is being held there against his will?" Matt put his silverware down. "Well, that's intriguing."

"I have proof." Excited, Amy unlocked her phone to show him the photo.

Matt frowned. "Hmm. A blurry side view of a man. Could've been taken anywhere. Of anyone. I don't see any cuffs."

She stopped playing with the remnants of her pancakes. "A skeptic, eh? I can't tell you why he's not in handcuffs." She put her fork down, defiant. "All I can tell you is I'm clear on what I saw. And I'm going back now that Kalani's catamaran is repaired."

"Kalani?"

"A friend of a friend."

He rolled his eyes.

"He just texted me to say his boat is fixed. You're welcome to come and judge for yourself."

"I have to admit, I'm curious. I'm not sure I believe you, but... I just might tag along."

# Chapter Twenty

## Wednesday Evening

## Kauai, Hawaii

"HE SPOKE ENGLISH," Amy said to Matt. "But it sounded rough, like it isn't his first language." Inside the cabin of Kalani's catamaran, Matt was stretched out on a bench with his arms across its back. After Amy told Matt about the man on Niihau, he not only agreed to travel with her back to the forbidden island, he even offered to pick her up.

Amy stood next to Kalani at the helm, marveling at the ease with which he pulled away from shore, and maneuvered the vessel in general. "I believe he understood me when I asked if he wanted to leave, because he said yes."

She glanced at the clouds hiding the moon and grimaced. Tonight's weather was cooler than the first trip over with Longo. It meant she and Matt would remain inside tonight. On the ride to the boat, for a breath, the thought of enjoying a moonlit evening on the bow of the catamaran, this time with Matt, had crossed her mind. Having to remain inside ended that idea.

It probably worked out just as well, since Amy and Kalani each had their own mission to complete. Kalani wanted to bring his cousin back to speak with his mother. Amy wanted to find out the story with the man she had spoken to last time.

Next to her, Kalani grunted as the craft began picking up speed. "That's not what the professor said." Spray slapped at the windshield forcing the wipers on.

Amy said, "At first he did. But you're right. For some reason, he changed his answer to no. He also said something like where is helicopter. He didn't exactly phrase his question in the proper form, but he did ask. That must be how they brought him to the island."

Strong waves began splashing over the bow of the catamaran. Without diverting his attention from piloting the boat, Kalani said, "Or, he's aquaphobic."

Amy looked to Kalani. "What did you say?"

"Aquaphobia." Kalani laughed. "Fear of water. I had a family who hired me once for a private cruise. The husband hated the water. Paid me extra so I would return whenever he wanted." He pointed to a portion of the bench seat with two grab bars. "For the entire trip, he sat with a life jacket on, both hands on the holds and his eyes shut tight. Didn't eat a thing. Craziest tour I ever gave."

"Well, a fear of water would explain things," Amy said. "When I told him we have a boat, that is when he changed from yes and began yelling no."

Matt said, "Amy, if that's the case, and he still wants to leave, I suggest you don't mention the boat until we're closer to it, or we can figure out how to persuade him to climb aboard. Speaking of persuasion, Kalani, how do you plan on convincing your cousin to come back with you?"

"I'll remind him of what his name stands for."

"Which is?"

"A warrior. A valiant one. Someone we should all look up to. And that is not what's happening now. I won't let him forget what he had in Kauai—where he belongs." After a brief silence, "And if I can't convince him," he shrugged. "I have another option."

He removed a small leather pouch from a hook and placed it on a shelf next to him.

Matt reached forward and snatched it.

"Better be careful with those," Kalani warned.

Matt pulled the flap back, spread open the sack, and carefully withdrew two metallic hooks with his thumb and index finger. Each had a spear at its head.

"Lures?" Matt questioned.

Kalani answered without turning toward Matt—he needed both hands since they were approaching the shore. "They are soaked in a solution that will relax him, but they will only work for a short time. I think an hour at most. I brought a few. I'm not sure how many I might need."

"Better be careful you don't use too many. You might kill him."

"I do not want to harm my cousin, but I will see that he returns and honors his family and his name." Kalani sounded firm and confident, having the power of ancestry behind him. "First, he will pay respect to his dead father and brother. Later, after he makes peace with his mother, he can do whatever he wants. I won't try to stop him."

Amy exhaled a strong breath of relief at hearing that the lures were only meant to incapacitate. She didn't think she could handle another death.

# Chapter Twenty-One

## Late Wednesday Night

## Niihau Island

WHEN THEY REACHED THE island, Matt helped Kalani secure the catamaran before helping Amy off. The three of them headed out under a blanket of clouds, with Matt and Amy leading the way, Kalani lagging a bit behind.

Matt asked, "The first thing we are looking for are the grave markers? Is that right?"

"They are set deeper in," Amy said, "but I'm sure I'll recognize them."

They hugged the coastline, walking in silence, each consumed with their own thoughts. Matt's were on Amy, fascinated by her, yet unable to figure her out. After their long brunch, he had shown her around Kauai while she filled him in on how she had spent her last five years *experiencing* life. Expounding in detail on her portrayal of a homeless woman known as Lizzie, where she'd witnessed the murder of a gang member.

He tried to picture her as an *elderly* woman. He couldn't quite conjure up an image, even though she had explained how she completed the ruse. Friends in LA, working for movie studios, provided her with props. A wig, as well as a skin-like facial mask and elbow-length gloves, to hide her youth. Then they trained her in applying makeup to blend the items in. Taught her how to walk and gave her a warning not to speak. To use hand motions instead, because aging affects voice, and it is a dead giveaway.

Matt's thoughts were on an image of an elderly bag lady when he noticed the cairns. "Are those the burial grounds?"

"Yes. We should come to the rocks soon."

As they continued, the night took on a deeper hue, and the clouds thickened. When they reached the rock wall, Amy said, "It's just on the other side. Once we cross, we should all head further in from the shore so no one sees us."

She led the way through the water. When they were back on sand again, she and Matt abandoned the shoreline and headed inland. Kalani didn't alter his course. He stood out in the flickering moonlight.

Amy called to him. "Kalani, they might see you. Come over here."

"You take care of your business. I'll take care of mine."

"Leave him alone," Matt said. "Let him get a little ahead of us. And, from now on, no talking. Give me a signal when we are at the location where you saw the... Man." He didn't say prisoner or captive because he didn't believe a man was here and being held against his will. After that far-out story about a couple committing suicide after switching apartments with her, he started questioning her mental status.

But then he thought about the destruction to the helicopter and knew it was real.

Amy stopped short and pointed. Up ahead, light spilled onto the sand. Kalani must have seen it too. He cupped his hands to his mouth and started wailing strange sounds that echoed through the still night.

It didn't take long.

From the shadows beyond, Matt gasped as a broad-shouldered male appeared from behind the rocks and headed toward Kalani. For a moment he worried a fight would ensue, but he soon recognized the greeting of *mahalo*.

Amy said, "That must be Koa. He looks like the guy who chased us away the other day. The one the professor said he recognized as his student."

Matt and Amy waited and watched as Kalani and Koa continued speaking. They soon reverted to their native language. Matt said, "It certainly looks like they know each other." Whether intentional or not, Matt couldn't tell, but as they spoke, Kalani edged further away from where he and Amy were hiding, leading his cousin away with him. *Good deal, Kalani. I owe you one.*

Matt motioned Amy down with his hands. They inched closer toward the light, careful to remain hidden in the shadows. Steps later, Amy pointed to a piece of metal affixed to the front of an opening in the rocks, shuttering a small cave.

The metal resembled latticework with a multitude of diagonal and diamond-shaped holes cut into it. The heads of large bolts, secured into the surrounding rock face, protruded from the metal barrier. It contained a functional door at its center with a simple gate latch to secure it.

*Latched on the outside.* Matt recognized a restraint when he saw one.

*It is a prison! One point for the lady.*

The cut-out areas cast flickering shadows across the sand, indicating movement from within. Amy whispered, "The light is coming from those open spaces."

"Yeah. I see. I'm going to lift the latch. Stay behind me and poke me if Kalani or Koa notice us or start heading this way. Are you ready?"

They crept forward. The amount of light increased. Peering inside, Matt could identify the silhouette of a man's back. Kalani and his cousin were off in the distance. Judging it safe, Matt moved the metal lever up, to the side, and down, into the unlocked position.

Trying to minimize any noise, he gripped the handle and began pulling open the door with a slow movement. The sound of metal scraping against some type of plate at its bottom made him stop.

Behind him, keeping watch on the two Hawaiians, Amy said, "I don't think they heard it."

He resumed pulling on the door until it passed over an area of sand where the scraping ceased. With the quiet, he yanked the door fully open.

Taking an urgent step inside, a wide-eyed man turned to face him. Matt said, "It's OK. I'm here to help you. Do you understand?"

"Yes."

Amy stuck her head in. "That's him. He's the man in my photo."

Matt asked, "What's your name?"

The man beamed with pride. "Wilhelm Van den Berg."

Matt scanned the natural horseshoe cave, altered to function as a prison cell. He judged the space to be about eighteen feet deep by twelve feet in width, with an entrance of a little under seven feet. The roof portion descended downwards the further back it went.

The inhumanity stunned him, flaring up an anger he hadn't experienced since his time in the service. His body reacted, placing him back on the battlefield in an instant: his breathing deep and forceful, his heart beating at a staccato pace, every molecule on high alert, ready for action.

Now in full combat mode, he said, "Wilhelm. Are you here of your own free will?"

The man shook his head no.

"Are you ready to leave?"

"I want to go. A minute."

As Wilhelm began gathering his belongings, Matt surveyed the makeshift prison with its natural vaulted ceiling. A glance around revealed a sleeping bag atop an inflatable mattress, a portable flush toilet, and a folding table.

He said with disdain, "All the comforts of home," as his anger increased to rage, incensed at the thought of this frail, elderly man being confined in this manner.

Picking up the battery lantern and shining it around the cave, he realized the holes in the door provided the man's only source of air. He focused the light on a bucket being used as a trash bin—and the needles discarded within.

Amy, still keeping watch at the door, said, "Kalani is coming. He's alone."

Wilhelm began gathering up papers lying on the folding table.

Kalani arrived at the doorway, huffing. "We have to go. He won't be out for long."

Matt said, "Amy, go give him a hand. But make it quick."

Matt and Kalani waited as Wilhelm piled papers into Amy's extended arms. It appeared to be some sort of journal, although, Matt noted the script didn't look like English.

With her hands full, Amy turned to say something. "No!" she screamed.

But it was too late.

# Chapter Twenty-Two

## Early Thursday Morning

## Kauai, Hawaii

"YOU DIDN'T HAVE TO do that!" Amy lectured Matt. Safely back on the boat, heading back to Kauai, she and Matt were keeping watch over their two subdued passengers, Koa and Wilhelm, while Kalani once again manned the helm. "It wasn't necessary to drug him. We could have explained what we had planned."

"If Wilhelm had a fear of water, there wasn't enough time to try and convince him that we were friendlies," Matt argued back.

"But we didn't know that," Amy said, "did we? You didn't even ask him. You only thought he might because of the story Kalani told us on the way over."

Kalani interjected, "Doesn't matter. I agree with Matt. Once I knew Koa didn't want to come with me, I did what I had to do. And then I needed to leave. I told you I didn't know how long the drug would last. There was no time to argue."

"OK. OK. You guys win." After a few breaths, Amy said, "By the way, Kalani, that was a great idea to use a raft to bring Koa back." Back on the island, Kalani had come prepared. When it became clear his cousin would not return with him of his own free will, Kalani used one of his tranquilizers before pulling the cord on a compressed item he had brought with him. The ripcord inflated the raft, and a few seconds later, Koa dropped onto it.

With that accomplished, Koa returned to Matt and Amy, ready to leave. There, as Wilhelm handed Amy the items he wanted to take, Amy witnessed Matt use one of Kalani's lures to subdue him. After he collapsed into Matt's waiting arms, Matt hoisted him over his shoulder in a fireman's carry while Amy and Kalani used the raft to drag Koa back to the catamaran.

As soon as they reached the Na Pali coast on Kauai, Matt called Detective Palakiko, saying. "I know it's very early, but you're going to want to see this for yourself."

After that phone call, it required Amy's help to get Koa off the boat, onto dry land. There, like a fawn learning to walk, Koa managed to stand on shaky legs. Kalani appeared determined to complete his mission. He began, at alternate turns, nudging and pulling his cousin forward as they trudged across the beach.

The two cousins held Amy's attention as they staggered away, disappearing into the first rays of early morning light.

Inside, Wilhelm dozed on a bench, still drowsy. He slumped into a dangerous position, at risk of falling to the floor. Amy took a seat next to him and propped him up. His limp head fell to the side, resting on her shoulder.

Matt remained on land waiting for the detective. He arrived, and Matt updated him on what transpired on the island. Then Palakiko climbed aboard to witness the woozy Wilhelm for himself.

Noticing Amy, he said, "You again?"

"Let me explain," she tried.

"Oh, you will. But for now, I need to see if he is alright." He placed two fingers on Wilhelm's neck, causing Wilhelm to quiver from the touch. "He's alive."

Amy was spent after another night without sleep. But her dimples bloomed. Her inner peacefulness came from a profound sense of satisfaction at accomplishing something so positive. Elation ran through her at the thought of the rescue, confident her brother would be proud.

"Wait here. I'll call an ambulance and have him checked out."

*I'm not going anywhere,* she thought to herself through a comfortable haze, leaning her head back, resting it on the wall.

The medics arrived. Asleep beside Wilhelm, one of them took hold of her wrist to take her pulse, rousing her. "No. Not me. Just him."

As a medic began checking him, Wilhelm began coming out of his drug-induced oblivion. They strapped him on a gurney, then loaded him onto an ATV to get to the ambulance.

With him gone, Matt asked, "How about some breakfast?" He didn't wait for an answer. "I know a place."

At the all-night cafe, coffees in front of them, they ran searches on their phones for his name.

"I found a Wilhelm Van den Berg who is reported missing in Paris," Amy said. "He was on his way to a clinic but never arrived."

"Yeah, I have a similar article. Says he's Dutch and lives in Switzerland. What do you think a Dutch man from Switzerland, missing in Paris, is doing here on a Pacific island?"

"Well, it would be a great place *not* to look for him," Amy said. "It wouldn't be my first choice. Sounds like he might have been kidnapped. Did it say anything about that?"

"No. Nothing. Just that he is missing. If he was, I guess it would be for ransom. Isn't that what most people are kidnapped for?"

"Is there anything about a ransom?"

"No."

"Do you think Palakiko will tell us anything?"

"I don't think he knows," Matt said. "It sounds like he's as much in the dark as we are. I'll do some digging, though. If he was choppered in, I can nose around and get my hands on the flight logs to see who's been flying in and out of Niihau."

"Great. With any luck, it will at least give us a lead."

"Us?"

"You owe me. You have to fill me in on whatever you learn."

She put her cup down and changed subjects. "Any idea which hospital Wilhelm would be in? He should be pretty coherent by now. And after all, we did rescue him. I don't see why he wouldn't talk to us."

Matt raised his coffee cup to her. "Lady, I like the way you think."

# Chapter Twenty-Three

## Friday

## Kauai Police Station, Hawaii

AMY AND MATT SAT ALONGSIDE each other in front of Palakiko's cluttered desk, in an office not much larger than the interrogation room, although the chairs were a bit more comfortable.

They had tried to visit Wilhelm in the hospital, but without success. The detective forbade it, having given strict orders that Wilhelm could not have visitors—especially the two of them. Although they didn't get a chance to speak with him, the detective promised to fill them in after they provided their statements—-which they just did.

When Palakiko finished reading them, he dropped them on his desk and said, "Wilhelm is on his way home. He asked me to convey his thanks. He also wondered why he suddenly passed out back on Niihau. Any ideas on that?" The detective's question came with a raised eyebrow.

"I guess it was the excitement at being rescued," Matt said.

Amy cut in. "We wanted to speak to him ourselves," her disappointment apparent. "After all, we did rescue him."

"I'm sorry, but orders came from above my pay grade, straight from Europol."

"Europol?" She and Matt both questioned in unison.

"Yes, they operate in conjunction with Interpol to fight crime in Europe. The abduction occurred in their jurisdiction."

Amy said, "I've been trying to figure out how Wilhelm wound up on the island in the first place. All types of possibilities played out in my mind over the last twenty-four hours, but none of them made any sense."

"Amy, I did speak with Detective Peters as you suggested. He doesn't believe the gang you mentioned has connections here. His thinking is this is unrelated to the events in DC."

Palakiko shot her a concerned, almost fatherly look. "You do realize what this means." She stared at him in silence. "The supposed accident in 401 may have been intended for you." With her attention so focused on *blue eyes,* her nickname for Wilhelm, the deaths of the Plomasens seemed worlds away.

The detective must have sensed her malaise. He remained quiet a long while, allowing his words to penetrate. "My guess is when you two took your detour over Niihau, Wilhelm's captors somehow found out. They responded to the threat you posed by trying to get rid of you. You at the rental unit, Amy." He nodded toward Matt, "And sabotaging the chopper for you."

It took a few beats for his words to register with her. "You might be right. Somewhere in the back of my mind, I suspected the flight over that crazy island started all of this, but I couldn't accept it because it just seemed too outrageous."

"You should be out of danger now, though. Wilhelm is safe, and there is a lot of pressure on this case coming from several different sources. But I would still advise you to be careful and take precautions at least until we manage to get a better handle on what went on here." He paused. "I'll need your contact information on the mainland. When are you headed back?"

"Tomorrow."

"Where will you be staying?"

"I share an apartment with my best friend. Why?"

He took down the address, inserted their statements into a file folder and closed it. "I've filled in Peters, sharing what I know here on my end. He asked you to keep in touch with him and advise him when you arrive back. Otherwise, since there's nothing else I need from you, you're free to go."

The detective turned to Matt. "The same goes for you, although I know where to find you if I need to. But I am curious about something, I know the island doesn't have electricity. How did they restrain Wilhelm?"

"They blocked up a small cave and used camping products with long-life batteries."

"Interesting," Palakiko said, "And I guess, if they needed more or to recharge, it would have been easy enough to ferry supplies over from here. I'll look into that. Thank you both for your statements."

"Not so fast," Amy spoke up. "You promised to tell us what the story is with Wilhelm."

Leaning back in his chair, he took a quick breath. "Here's what I can tell you. A little more than a week ago, Wilhelm traveled from his home in Switzerland to Paris to visit a health facility. On the train ride over, he mentioned feeling woozy to a fellow passenger. The working theory is he was drugged via something he consumed."

Listening to him speak, Amy noted how familiar his face looked to her. After staring at it so intently the other day, memorizing it, she realized she could sketch it from memory, even though the one thing she couldn't do was draw.

"Europol has CCTV video of him exiting the train. Someone helped support him off, holding him up as if intoxicated. Both heads were down. Although they couldn't confirm his facial features, they suspect it was him based on several factors, including the clothes, his height, gait, and a few other key metrics. The only other possibility is he got off mid-route, which they can find no evidence to support. The train never stopped. That's all they have. He never arrived at the clinic, and when he didn't return home as expected, his wife reported him missing."

"That's terrible for her," Amy said, "But how did they manage to bring him all the way here? And why?"

"People find ways. Boats for one, and we have plenty of private jets landing here on the islands. A false passport, who knows?" The detective shrugged. "Everything is being checked out now." He sounded stressed.

"Sorry for causing you more work, but I can't say I regret rescuing him."

Giving her a slight nod, the detective said, "You did good." Those words of praise made her cheeks go bright red. Ones she would never have imagined hearing from him.

Palakiko opened a desk drawer and slid the folder inside. "Not sure I'll come up with many answers, but I'll keep at it here. Since the abduction occurred in Paris, I doubt I can do anything to help with their investigation. Definitely out of my jurisdiction."

Matt asked. "So, it *was* a kidnapping. How much ransom did they want?"

"No ransom. They wanted him in the flesh."

"For his brain?" Amy asked, "Is he some kind of genius? A scientist or a mathematician?"

"Nope. Nothing like that. It's a new one on me." The detective shook his head. "They wanted his blood!"

# Chapter Twenty-Four

## Friday - Mike Shore's Townhouse

## Toronto Canada

"BLOOD!" SUSAN SPAT out the word, her disbelief so profound she found herself incapable of anything else except uttering the word.

The former evaluation team of Susan, Mike, and Frank was reunited, nestled in a comfortable nook off the kitchen of Mike Shore's townhouse overlooking the shimmering water of Lake Ontario. After Frank relayed Susan's concerns about the clinic and her intention to go to the media with them, Mike invited Frank and Susan to his home to discuss the matter in private.

It took a few breaths before she could ask, "You're telling me this is what we've paid out millions of dollars for? Are you serious?"

"I am," Mike said, resembling a sad beagle, his hands clasped on the table they surrounded. "And if you will calm down, I'll explain."

"Alright. I'm listening."

Mike steepled his hands in front of him. "When Eunice first told me, I didn't believe her. She showed me the lab report and gave me some insight into blood types. I never realized so many existed. We are all familiar with the common ones, A, B, AB, and O, either negative or positive. However, those are just the more common ones. Entire categories exist that are documented but not often discussed since they fall into the classification of rare. I don't understand the details. Frank has been delving into them."

Frank shifted his view from outside Mike's bay window back to them. "I'm sure you are aware we need red blood cells to live. But did you realize all red blood cells carry antigens on them—up to 342 on each—which control the production of antibodies we require? As Mike indicated, we don't all possess the same blood type. The presence or absence of these antigens determines what your blood type is."

Opening the folder in front of him, Frank selected a sheet and passed it to Susan. "Here are the 35 blood group systems. Our genes determine which antigens our blood cells carry and which blood group system we are in. There are in the neighborhood of 160 *high-prevalence* antigens on the red blood cells of most people. If one of those antigens is missing from your red blood cells, then you are *negative* for the blood group. Which means..."

Frank glanced at Susan, who appeared rapt with attention. He forged ahead. "For example, the Rh system consists of 61 antigens. If the *D* high-prevalence antigen is missing, you are considered Rh D-negative."

He handed Susan another sheet, which she laid alongside the first. "I wasn't aware of this until I started my research. It surprised me to learn that if you are given the wrong blood type, in an emergency or, for example, during surgery, the incompatible blood could *kill* you. Your antibodies could react with the foreign blood cells, triggering a further response from your immune system, which can be lethal."

Frank selected another paper, slid it across the glass tabletop, and said, "About 15 percent of Caucasians are in the Rh D-negative blood group, making them rare."

Frank paused as Susan studied a familiar summary format of facts and figures he had uncovered. When she looked up, he emphasized his words. "Eunice and Joey's babies *contain no* antibodies on their red blood cells. *None.*"

Their eyes met. He held her gaze. "This makes them rarer than *rare*. They carry the rarest blood in the world. One so scarce, fewer than a hundred people *on this planet* share their blood type. It's called *Rhnull*."

He gave her time to consider his words, then raised his hand to forestall her question. "Now, of those few, less than *ten* are available to donate their blood. The agencies that track uncommon blood types only maintain records of six or seven people who *do* donate, making Rhnull blood *EXTREMELY* rare. A most precious commodity. You could say *it* is *the* most priceless thing on earth."

Frank closed his file. "And those life-saving operations, they required blood."

Mike exhaled and shrugged as if exhausted. "You realize what this means. Without the blood, it was a guaranteed death sentence. I tell you from the bottom of my heart, I am at ease in having approved those expenditures."

Susan sat numb, seeing Mike in a new light, shaking her head in disbelief. "I still don't see why you couldn't have shared this with me earlier. We've always been a team." Directing her focus at Mike, "Or, at least I thought we were, with the same goal in mind even if our opinions differed."

"I may have been a bit pushy," Mike said. "That's on me. Still, I stand by my decisions and hope you can now understand enough to drop all this foolishness about going public to expose some sort of subterfuge you presume is taking place. At least for Joey and Eunice's sake. They are contending with enough. With their first boy gone and the second one so critical, their focus must remain on him."

Her mind spun in so many directions; a space capsule circling the Earth would have been an easier ride. But, somehow, she managed to ask, "So, if this blood is so rare and so difficult to acquire, how do you go about finding it?"

Frank answered. "There are a few agencies around the world that track this kind of thing. They notify a donor when their blood type is requested. But they don't collect or store the blood. The donor would be required to go to a blood bank—at their own expense—and donate a vial of theirs. It's the only option *unless* they already have stored their blood for their own use. Some do this in case they need a transfusion themselves. If that is the case, the blood bank holding the priceless fluid for the donor's use can release it to someone else if needed. It's a condition of storing your blood with them."

"I see. And how much does a pint of this unique blood cost?"

Mike wouldn't meet her eyes. Frank shrugged.

Oscillating between them, Susan said, "Well?"

Appearing uncomfortable, Frank said, "The blood bank has precious little in storage and charged a reasonable price. That first batch was easy to come by." His expression morphed into concern. "Mike, do you want to carry on from here?"

Mike stiffened, sat straighter, and pulled his shoulders back. "That's all they had in storage. At this point, we aren't aware of where the blood is coming from. An opportunity extended itself to the Stratfords to provide them with a supply of blood. But, as you would expect, it came at a very high price."

Susan smirked as both men squirmed. "How much?"

"When you consider the worth of the product..."

"How much?"

Mike looked at her. "As you know, the first came with a five-million-dollar price tag. Each subsequent one has increased."

"And now?"

"For the next one, they are asking twenty million."

"Asking? Really? You mean extorting, don't you?"

Mike returned her stare.

She shook her head watching Frank fold and unfold a paper clip. "This is crazy! We need to find out where the blood came from and do something about this. What is wrong with you and the staff at Devereux? They must realize this isn't normal."

Anger made its way into Mike's words. "At this point, they can't track where the blood is coming from. Whoever is supplying it is careful at covering their tracks. Eunice and Joey do not want an official investigation yet, because if that happens, the blood will stop, and their second child will die."

He took a long time before continuing. "Afterwards, they have assured me, they intend to turn everything over to the police and cooperate once he is in stable condition. For now, their only thoughts are on saving him. They further informed me they are already having the matter pursued with their people. At this point, they don't want to rock the boat. Plus I gave them my word we wouldn't."

# Chapter Twenty-Five

## Susan Fleming's Home

## Toronto Canada

*ARE THEY OUT OF THEIR minds! After all those years working with me, do they not know me? At all?*

Susan left the unofficial meeting at Michael Shore's home enraged, knowing she couldn't ignore this abuse no matter how much the Stratfords wanted to wait and keep this shakedown quiet. Rare blood or not, someone is extorting the Stratfords, the clinic, and her life's devotion, the Stratford Living Legacy Foundation.

In her home office, she poured herself a whiskey neat, took a sip, retrieved a lined pad, and began a checklist of things to do. She wrote: *Conduct an interview with the man in charge of the organization, Dr. Zoric.*

She printed his name. Then, seeing her shaky letters which were the result of the tension she was feeling, she took a calming breath and rewrote it in neat cursive, still proud of her penmanship.

"What do we know about him?" She asked aloud, causing Shorty to leave his bed and tiptoe to her, moving between her feet. "Not much. I guess I'll start with Frank's research on him." She bent down to administer a few loving strokes to his head. He tilted it toward her, softly purring.

Experiencing a newfound drive, she rose and added the names of two investigators who they had used over the years to do deep dives into the backgrounds of people.

Mike had fired her, taken everything from her. What he didn't realize is that when you have nothing, there is nothing left to lose. She never imagined herself a whistleblower. But if that's what she needed to be, she would rise to the task.

Frank mentioned the blood arrived via courier. A different one each time. She jotted a note. *Need to talk to the clinic's employees.* "Oh," she said, "and we need surveillance at Devereux to determine who delivers the blood and track where it comes from."

Mike's news stung her to the core. In every waking moment, in one way or another, her life revolved around work. Her focus always involved the foundation. *Nobody has the right to extort those funds. Money that would otherwise be put to such fruitful use.*

She wouldn't allow it!

Susan caught sight of her housemate beside the sliding glass door, waiting to be let out. Shorty considered himself an outdoor animal, at least to the extent of Susan's deck. She slid the door open and walked out after him, taking a seat on one of the lounge chairs, making another notation: *Need to contact the blood-tracking agencies.*

Frank mentioned two. One in the United States and one in Filton, England.

*Also need a list of people with this type of blood.*

Her mind drifted to Mike and his recent actions as Shorty groomed himself.

*Mike would never have gone along with this before. He's changed. What's happened to him?*

Thinking back on her past interaction with him, she realized she had placed a high value on Mike's opinion and leadership. At times, even abandoning her own judgment. "Why did I do that, Shorty? Do you have any idea?" He meowed at the sound of his name.

Susan watched her cat lick himself, twisting into what looked like an impossible position with his shortened paw. "Do you know you are different, my dear?" She asked, recalling the words the girl at the rescue used to describe him—*A feline who would otherwise command a hefty price, except for a small deficiency.*

Shorty didn't answer. He finished his grooming ritual and curled up for a nap. Susan added a few more items to her list. She took her last swig, put the empty glass on a table next to her, and closed her eyes to contemplate.

Her mind returned to Mike—and the critical question.

*Does he still deserve to be the chair? Or, more to the point, even on the committee?*

Evaluating him now, she declared him unfit. His performance with regard to the blood issue highlighted his incompetence. He not only permitted the extortion to take place; he contributed to it by encouraging approval for the payments.

Her eyes flew open at the irony. Mike and Frank must have believed that their efforts today in explaining the details of the extortion would dissuade her from making a stink.

*I'm just getting started. If they think I am going to keep silent, they are mistaken.*

# Chapter Twenty-Six

## Stratford Industries Headquarters

## Toronto, Canada

"I SEE YOU ARE STILL babying your plants," Susan said to a surprised Eileen Olsen. Eileen was the Accounts Payable Manager at Stratford Industries, the role Susan had enjoyed before accepting the position at the foundation.

Since Susan no longer served on the Evaluation Committee, she now found herself with available time. After setting in motion as many things as she could into her personal investigation of the blood issue, she decided to take some time for herself.

Eileen sprang up as Susan entered her flora-filled office, encircling her with a hug. "Can you stay for a coffee—or tea?"

Eileen's former boss gazed in amazement at the abundance of plants filling the windowsill and covering the tops of filing cabinets. Susan took in a deep breath, the fragrance reminding her of stepping into a florist's shop. She had only planned on dropping in for a quick visit. But, in that instant, she realized how much her dedication to the foundation had cost her in terms of time spent with friends. "Yes. I think I will."

In the company's break room, Eileen shut off the quick-shot pot for Susan's water. "Is English breakfast OK?"

"Sounds lovely." From her seat at one of the long picnic tables crowding the room, Susan surveyed the surroundings with melancholy, noticing the familiar Formica countertop. "I see the old hundred-cup coffeemaker is gone. Did it finally die a natural death?"

Eileen approached with the hot tea in one hand and a slice of lemon on a napkin. "No. Joey got rid of it." She grimaced. "This isn't the same place anymore. Do you recall how Junior used to supply us with those delicious sweets from Ned's bakery each morning?"

"Do I ever," Susan said, her eyes widening as she dunked her bag up and down. "I can still picture the clear plastic dome covering the mounds of donuts, crumb cakes, and muffins drawing us in to have a better look. And oh, how I tried to resist."

"Joey got rid of that, too. Do you also remember how Junior himself would come in here and join us? Always making us feel he was one of us." Eileen retrieved her coffee, taking a seat next to her old friend. "How he'd take an interest in how things were going. How he paid attention when anyone brought up an issue, no matter how small."

"I certainly do."

"Well, things are not what they used to be. To put it in polite terms, Joey is nothing like his father."

"You sound disheartened," Susan said.

"He's bad enough. But that wife of his." Eileen shuddered.

"Yes," Susan said, "I've met Eunice."

"What a piece of work. She barges in here whenever the mood strikes her, parading through the department as if she's the boss, feigning needing a place to handle some business. She commandeers an empty desk and makes phone calls."

"Does she help out?"

"Oh, God. No. Her calls are all personal. To her hair stylist or masseuse. Nothing for the company. My employees are courteous to her, but I find her needy and disruptive. Believe it or not, at her age, when things don't go her way, the tears come out."

Susan reflected back on the crocodile ones that appeared during her meeting with Eunice. Even though they were alone in the room, Eileen lowered her voice. "If they only knew how vicious and vindictive she is."

"What makes you say that?"

"Susan, I trust you, but this must remain between us. A few months ago, I hired a woman who turned out to be a fantastic worker, diligent, confident, and secure in her own skin. One day I walked in at the end of a discussion between her and Eunice. I could see they didn't agree. I didn't think much of it, but a day or so later Joey, her husband, calls me in to give me a heads up that we need to cut staff, and he suggests I let *her* go."

"Did you?"

"I had to. Six weeks later, we're ready to beef up personnel again. I told Joey I intended to reach out to her, asking about her availability. He shut me down. Despite my raving about her qualities, he suggested I go through normal protocol and post the opening with the agency handling our staffing. I knew then. I have no proof, Susan, but I would bet most anything her dismissal came about because of Eunice."

"I'm sorry," Susan said, unhappy to hear about her friend's difficult situation. Susan had intended to fill Eileen in on her own problems at the foundation, but after witnessing the stress Eileen was suffering, she decided not to add to her troubles. She did, however, make a mental note to stay in closer touch in the future. "Is there anything I can do for you?"

"No. I've decided I can't work here under these conditions. Not for him. And not with her. My resume is updated. I'll be out of here soon, but it frustrates me that people believe whatever comes out of her mouth. She is very clever at disguising the manipulative, conniving woman she is. I wish I could warn my staff about her, but I can't share any of this with them. Her new thing is she tells everyone to call her 'E' for short. I do. But when I say it, I'm thinking it's short for evil."

"You sound harsh, Eileen. It doesn't seem like you."

"I'm telling you that woman is. Take my advice. Stay far away from her. I don't trust her. And you shouldn't either. You would understand if you dealt with her. I value our friendship too much to repeat how derogatory she is about you and your committee."

Susan repressed a shiver at Eileen's dire warning. Before she could comment on how extreme Eileen sounded, Eileen's phone buzzed.

Eileen glanced at the ID and said, "I need to take this. Thanks for stopping in. Stay and finish your drink."

With Eileen gone, Susan continued sipping a lukewarm cup of tea, contemplating her friend's unhappiness, when her phone lit up with a text from Frank. *Call me when you get this. I have some interesting news to share.*

# Chapter Twenty-Seven

## Susan's Home

## Toronto, Canada

"I SEE HOW THERE COULD be a connection," Susan said to Frank. Earlier, he had given her the name of a man who could be a possible source for the blood. After querying him and finding several interesting articles about the man, she called Frank back to discuss it further. "How did you find him?" Frank's lead also gave her a sliver of hope that he was not giving up on pursuing the extortion.

"I did some research on people who carry that rare blood." The fact that he had done further research heightened her spirits.

"Well, the timing coincides with his abduction and his return home. Without knowing about the blood, the whole story of being taken then released unharmed sounds a bit off."

"It makes sense they wanted him for his blood," Frank said. "To sell it. Then, I guess once Baby B died, and they realized his blood would no longer be valuable, they let him go. In either case, whether he was the source of the blood or not, there will be no further payments. I thought you'd be happy."

"I am happy. Happy the extortion will stop. Happy the abducted man is back with his family. But unhappy with the concurrence of the two events. They bother me. They are suspicious, to say the least."

"I agree with you."

"Well then, Frank, what about the possibility of Wilhelm himself devising this scheme once he learned about the need for his blood?"

"From what I understand," he said, "the clinic storing the blood never releases the name of the requesting person or agency, only divulging that they received a requisition. So he wouldn't be told who is asking. The entire transaction is confidential. One of the articles I read indicated someone found him in the US on a private island. I got the impression it was by accident they stumbled onto him."

"I didn't read that," Susan said. "Consider this. He traveled by himself and only *claimed* to be held. Took a little vacation. With all the money we've sent him, I would say the idea is more than plausible."

Silence filled the air for a few moments. "I guess anything is possible. Interpol reported the abduction. It must have been verified. I don't think they would let the story fly if it wasn't factual."

"Then who, Frank? Who would be aware of the need for the Rhnull blood and, at the same time, be knowledgeable about the donors? In addition, they would have to be aware of where Wilhelm lived and his schedule. Who would possess the entirety of all the information and have the connections to pull off this elaborate scheme? Any thoughts on that scenario?"

"No. But that's why you always play the role of Devil's Advocate."

"Used to," she said, correcting him.

"Sorry. I'm thinking you'll be back soon. Denise isn't happy with the work, and I'm not sure she cares for the position."

Susan's head began pounding, a migraine forming at the thought of being reinstated, knowing she would have to abandon her solo investigation. The weight of continuing to follow up on this alone also grated on her. She longed for Frank's support. "We can't let this go, Frank. This is immoral. What's more important, it can happen again. I'm betting you're not giving up on this. Tell me if I'm wrong. I need your input. My guess is this is gnawing at you the same as me."

A long silence ensued while Susan clenched the phone to her ear, hoping and praying all those projects they worked on together had cemented a union that Mike couldn't shatter.

"I agree with you," he said. "It could be his blood. But I don't think he concocted a scheme. He could have been upfront about wanting money for it. The next question becomes, if not him, who? Devereux, of course. They reached out to the blood banks, citing the circumstances."

As Frank continued to speak, sounding interested in resolving the issue, Susan's throbbing head began to slow, adding to her growing hope that he would help in her investigation. Although Mike wanted to ignore the issue, Frank appeared interested in pursuing it. She could hear it in his voice. He said, "Anybody at either of the blood banks would be familiar with the requisition. Who the request came from and if they had any in storage. I recall the first bag came from a legitimate outfit in England. I would start there. Not sure where the subsequent ones came from."

"I'm with you so far, Frank. Here's what baffles me. Let's say you or I work for one of them and we find out about the requirement for Wilhelm's blood. I'm sure this has occurred before; some agency must have requested it. By the way, I tried contacting Wilhelm myself, but I couldn't reach him. I'm guessing he's being hounded by reporters and is avoiding phone calls."

She took a breath. "But, back to what I am wondering, a requisition comes in, and they oblige, sending out the first batch. What happens next? How would anyone anticipate more would be needed? So much more, that they decide kidnapping him to supply the additional quantities makes sense? What if the twins didn't require any more blood?"

"Yeah. You have a point. It does seem rather like a long shot. They would be taking a huge risk, possibly for nothing."

"I can't let this go, Frank. I could use your help."

When he didn't answer, she exhaled loudly. "Where is Mike on this? I remember he promised the issue would be looked into once the babies were out of danger. With them both gone, now would be the time to expose the scheme."

"He wants to drop the whole subject. Mike's position is we have enough on our plates to keep us busy. He says whoever made contact with the Stratfords to provide the blood, it's on them."

"Right, and extort us." She snickered.

"Do you want me to finish?"

"Yes. Sorry."

"Joey and Eunice are trying to move on with their lives. They want to put this behind them. They just lost two children. Now, Joey has a lot of pressure because of the company's upcoming IPO. Highlighting the fact that the blood was for Joey's kids will turn an unnecessary critical eye on them and the company. He argued the business is at present being investigated upside down and backward because it's about to go public. He begged us to please let it go."

Susan's head hammered again as her heart sank. "And are you going to?"

"I've got two kids in high school, soon on their way to college. It's not that I don't care. It's rather I've analyzed the situation and, realizing how strong Mike is in ensuring this stays quiet, I've decided to accept it and move on."

"Well, I can't. And I won't."

# Chapter Twenty-Eight

## State Park

## Island of Kauai

"THE BIRDS HERE ARE so pretty," Amy said to Matt, focusing on a circle of white that surrounded the eye of one of the scavengers. "I don't see any seagulls."

"Don't have any here," Matt said as he continued flinging out fries. They had picked up a takeout lunch after providing their statements to Detective Palakiko. They decided to eat it at one of Kauai's many parks overlooking crystal blue water. Matt broke a long fry into smaller pieces and tossed it out. A loud shriek came from one of the birds with a golden yellow breast. The bird hadn't reacted fast enough to grab a morsel.

"Interesting. We are overrun with them on the East Coast." Sitting on one of the benches, Amy angled her head back, took in the blue sky above, and inhaled a deep breath of the salty air. "Do you ever get used to how beautiful it is here?"

"You do. Not at first when all of it is new. But you settle into a routine, like anyplace else. You work, eat, sleep, and repeat. I don't take time out like this unless someone comes to visit."

Amy thought his words summed up her dad's life. *Work, eat, sleep, and repeat.* It called attention to the *new* life she would be embarking on when she returned home. It made her shiver despite the heat. "I wonder if *I* would?"

"You would," he said, nodding with an unnerving assuredness.

Birds continued to attack the fries as she pushed those thoughts away and reflected on their meeting with Palakiko. "Our pictures looked like mugshots," she said.

"It was voluntary. You didn't have to comply."

"Sure, but when he mentioned Europol would like photos of us, I assumed I would stand next to you and he would take a nice shot. I didn't think it would be in front of a background with lines on it."

"I guess they wanted our height too," Matt said. He dusted off his shorts and threw away the empty container. A bird with a bright red head above a snow-white and gray body landed close to Matt's feet, vying for a morsel. "Sorry, no more. All gone."

Amy asked, "That didn't bother you?"

"Once you've been in the military, you learn to adjust. They are aware of everything about you. Every mole and secret tat you have." Glancing at her, he said, "The ketchup in your lap is running away."

She wiped it up and wrapped up the balance of her lunch. Putting the wad in Matt's waiting hand, she teased. "Really, a hidden tattoo?"

After discarding her trash, he took a seat next to her. "Believe me, if I had one, they would know."

Small waves collapsed and disappeared on the sand as Amy reflected on her time with him. An attraction at first, then an intruder. At present, they were edging toward a friendship as a result of their combined exploit to free Wilhelm. "So, just back to work as if nothing happened when the new helicopter arrives?"

He turned and gave her a curious stare. "I didn't say that."

"Then what?"

"I did a little digging. I know who choppered Wilhelm to Niihau. Don't know much more than the company's name. They signed in on the log as SSI, but the charge went to Security Services for Industry. At least it's a start. They're based in Canada, Toronto, to be exact. Since Palakiko is done with us, and I'm out a job for the time being, I'm thinking of paying them a little visit. Nosing around a bit and trying to figure out how Wilhelm being on Niihau is connected to someone *messing* with my bird."

Amy brightened when it occurred to her she might be able to obtain more information on the company. "You say you only have their name and where they're located, but I may be able to provide you with additional background on their business."

"Thanks. I would certainly appreciate anything you can find. And you? Your flight home is tomorrow."

Amy watched the last holdout for Matt's fries give up and fly off. "Yes. I'll be on my way back to DC. Then, after taking care of a few things at home, I'll be reconnecting with you in," she faced him, "where did you say we could find them? Toronto, was it?"

"I don't remember inviting you."

"Don't forget, I was the registered occupant who would have been asleep in 401 when someone *messed* with it." She had just made a conscious decision that required putting the start of her new life on hold for a while longer. "And I wasn't asking," she said.

# Chapter Twenty-Nine

## Dad with Ben and Sam

## Washington, DC

LESS THAN TWO BLOCKS from his home, Amy's dad hunched over a half-empty coffee cup, waiting for his friends, Ben and Sam, to arrive. Seven days a week, these three retired government workers started their day here unless the weather prohibited it or one of them was away.

From the doorway of Lottie's Coffee, Sam yelled out, "Hey, Dad, you're in luck today. I see they have the cinnamon bun with the cream cheese icing." Nick was his given name, but everyone called him Dad, a cherished moniker bestowed on him by friends and associates because of the endless talk about his Amy.

Bringing his coffee and bun to the table, Sam said, "You're not indulging?"

Dad noticed the selection when he arrived, but after the morning's phone call from Amy, his appetite disappeared.

Taking a seat, Sam took in Dad's expression. He asked, "Is there a war going on or something? I haven't seen you looking so bad since..." He paused. "Well, since I can't remember when."

The aroma of cinnamon invaded Dad's nostrils as Sam took a bite. "It's Amy."

"Is she ill?"

"No. She's not sick." Dad pushed his cup away and leaned back. "I think I owe Ben a coffee today. And for the next month. I believe that was the bet."

"For those of us who weren't here when the bet took place, care to fill me in?"

"You're well aware of the deal I had with Amy. The *freedom* I wanted her to experience and enjoy for five years after college, before life's everyday responsibilities became her primary focus. What I considered my contribution to her education."

"Yeah. I remember all the..." He cleared his throat. "Shall we say *unusual* things she participated in while you footed the bill?"

Dad absentmindedly rotated the bottom of his cup, forming rings of circles from the few drops of spilled coffee lingering on the table. "It ended last week when she turned twenty-seven. I thought that at this age she would be mature enough to understand and respect its limit. And my generosity." Abandoning his cup, he sighed. "I guess I may have been kidding myself, just as Ben predicted."

Dad rose and pulled back his shoulders. "Here he is now. Let me find out what he wants."

When he and Ben returned, Sam was wiping away the Olympic ring logo Dad had made. "Thanks for breakfast," Ben said. "If my guess is right concerning what you are about to tell me, I hope you realize this is a bet I never wanted to win."

Dad's forlorn look required no explanation. "Well, here's the story. Amy called today and told me she wouldn't be starting work with Bonnie, as expected, when she gets back. She also asked to borrow some money."

"What for?" Ben managed to ask before digging in.

Dad said, "She wants my support to spend time on a final project. A short one. It will only be a week or two. For sure, less than a month. Afterward,..." He shrugged. "She promises this will be her last. When she returns..."

Sam interrupted him, "Returns from where?"

"Canada."

"What's so important there?"

"She wouldn't tell me. She said this time it's of real importance. But she won't tell me why."

Ben theorized, "Sounds like Amy being ill might be easier on you than this. I'm sorry. What did you tell her?"

Dad wouldn't meet their eyes. "I told her no." He resumed twirling his empty cup. "Broke my heart. But I said no."

Then he sat back and exhaled a long stream of air. "But it gets worse." Ben and Sam exchanged worried looks. "Last night, Detective Peters called asking if Amy was back yet. I told him she should be home later today. When I asked why, he claimed he was just checking in on her because of something that took place in Hawaii. Now this, after I gave her the week in Hawaii to recuperate because she wouldn't let me pay for the counseling I think she needs."

Ben said, "Did he tell you why he is concerned?"

"He didn't say much, except not to worry, which to me means that's exactly what I should be doing. I'm scared. I think she's delving into things she has no business getting into. Whatever's going on, she won't share it with me. I'm frightened for her, and at her age, I can't stop her." Shaking his head in defeat, he said, "I couldn't bear to lose my only other child."

Sam said, "Let's talk about something else."

Somehow, the hour passed.

As Ben got up to leave, Dad's phone lit up, displaying a smiling picture of Amy. "Sorry, man. I know it hurts."

Sam said, "Dad, I'll see you tomorrow. Ben, I'll walk you out." The two men retreated toward the exit as Dad slid open his phone.

"Dad, I have a question. The car I'm driving, it's in my name. That makes it mine, right?"

"Yes. It's yours." His words sounded drained, as deflated as he felt.

"Well, I checked. The car is worth several thousand dollars. I understand what the terms of your gift to me were, and I really do appreciate it. I don't expect you to just *give* me anything more. I want to tell you, though, I'm planning on using the car as collateral and borrowing against it."

*What have I done? Have I created a monster by giving her all those years of freedom?*

Dad sat back and closed his eyes as years of memories flew by at breakneck speed in comic-flip-book style.

*What do I do about it now?*

"I found a company that will loan me the money. I've checked with Mom. She says their interest rate is *outrageous* and advised me I should search elsewhere for a better rate. The great thing about this company is they will consider all credit scores, especially since I don't have a great one. I wonder if you would consider giving me the loan instead?"

He massaged his temple and forehead as he pondered whether to applaud her cunning or recognize it as a delaying tactic. "When do you need an answer?" He asked, stalling. His only relief lay in the knowledge that his wife would support him by not providing Amy any further financial assistance after the five years. By then, she had agreed with him, Amy would need to succeed on her own.

"The sooner, the better. Let's say tomorrow morning?"

"Fair enough. I'll call you then."

"And Dad, if you say yes, I expect a very low interest rate, comparable with current market APRs."

He whispered a silent thank you to his wife. "I see you've been talking to your mother."

"Yes. She said to say hello."

# Chapter Thirty

## Hotel Room

## Toronto Canada

THE BRISK KNOCK ON the hotel door startled Amy. After using the door's peephole to confirm it was Matt, who had arrived in Toronto yesterday, she flung the door open. She refolded the pocket transit map for the city of Toronto in her hand. Amy had been familiarizing herself with the transit lines that crisscrossed the city before Matt arrived.

She needed a distraction from the stress she brought with her. It came from the devastating reactions she received from both her father and Bonnie when she returned to DC and made her announcement. Instead of starting her job with Bonnie, she would be traveling to Toronto to delve further into the blue-eyed man on Niihau. Her attempt at justifying it to her father ended when she looked into his sad, chocolate brown eyes. In Bonnie's case, a rare explosion from an ever-positive friend spelled out her disappointment and disapproval.

Amy asked, "How did the meeting go?"

"Odd," Matt said, tossing his jacket on the bed. "I met Joey," he made air quotes at his name.

Back in Hawaii, after providing their statements to Detective Palakiko, Amy and Matt had spent the remainder of her time there together. They researched the owners of SSI—the company that brought Wilhelm to the forbidden island—aided by information from Amy's mother. The euphoria of rescuing Wilhelm bound them together romantically. Albeit for only her final day there. They both knew it wouldn't last. But, for Amy, it did end the trip on a high note.

That euphoria also drew them here to Toronto to track down his captors, and for Amy, it opened up an interaction with a too-long-absent mother. She and Matt were looking into Wilhelm's abduction for different reasons. Not as a couple. They arrived at separate times, registered at the same hotel, joined and motivated only by their common interest in Wilhelm. They were each on an unsanctioned, unpaid mission. One that drove them both as if it was the most important thing in the world. Which, to them, it was.

"He told me everyone calls him Joey," Matt said. From Amy's mother, they learned SSI, Security Services for Industry, is a company that was formed a little over a year ago, and Joey Stratford is listed as one of its four partners. Matt contacted him and the other three owners concerning the flight they authorized to Niihau. Only Joey returned his call. Not only did he return the call, he also invited Matt to Toronto, dangling the possibility of a job offer to him. It sounded weird, but Matt checked and had verified that Joey was the CEO, the person in charge.

Amy said, "You didn't get a good feeling from him?"

"I can't put my finger on it. I think he's a phony." Matt walked to the window, pulled back the curtain, and peered down at the streets of Old Toronto. "He's the president and CEO, and he takes time to hustle me through the offices and warehouse himself."

"That makes him sound like a decent guy."

Matt shrugged, letting the curtain fall. He turned to her. "I'm not sure. He showed me the skis they sell and told me how his grandfather started the whole operation. He went on and on about a new venture he's going into. Making snowboards. The man kept bragging about how the boards are going to," Matt made air quotes again, "increase their numbers. He's talking about doing an IPO, whatever that is."

"So you two didn't hit it off?"

Taking a seat at the edge of the bed, he said, "Joey didn't give me a warm and fuzzy vibe. He peppered me with a lot of questions about how we got to Wilhelm. Wanted to know who else was with him. I didn't give him a name. I told him I didn't know, but he did appear to be a native. The entire conversation felt off somehow."

Matt reached over, opened the little fridge, and asked, "Are these waters yours?"

"They were by the coffee maker. I put them in. Help yourself."

"Joey asked a lot about the police. Stinging me with questions about how much they know. Asking me to explain how I made the connection to SSI. I told him I saw the flight logs. What struck me, though, was he asked me if I mentioned the logs to the police. Told him if I found out so easily, they would too."

He opened a bottle and took a long drink. "I'm beginning to think this whole job offer is just a ploy to drag me up here so he could find out how much the cops in Hawaii are aware of." He capped the water, returning it to the fridge. "By the way, he doesn't think anyone at SSI is Hawaiian. I almost asked him what Hawaiians look like."

"Did you see Koa anywhere?" Before leaving Kauai, Amy had called Kalani to thank him and discovered Koa never spoke to his mother. He must have high-tailed it after Kalani left him alone on his mother's front porch to deal with the situation in private.

"No. Today I only spent time with Mr. Personality. Tomorrow I'm supposed to meet with someone who's going to talk to me in more detail about the job he has in mind. When I asked about SSI, Joey brushed it off, saying he and some fellow businessmen started the venture to provide security to their respective businesses as a cost-saving measure. Nothing more. But he would arrange a meeting with them if I still cared to. I told him I would."

"How about you? Did you go for the interview?"

Amy had done her research back in Hawaii. In researching Joey, the majority owner in SSI, she came across an article in which he raved about a clinic where his wife gave birth to twins. Amy linked to the clinic's website, found an employment tab, and completed an application. She thought it would give her some plausibility for being in Toronto and might also be able to shed some information on the man from a different angle.

She fist-bumped the air. "I'm in. Sort of. I told them I'm working on my master's here at the Toronto Film School and am only interested in part-time work. They seemed fine with it. Stacey, who interviewed me, explained they have a lot of college kids working for them."

"Film School?" Matt asked. "Where did you come up with that?"

"Remember the friends in LA I told you about? The ones who helped me with the disguise for Lizzie and provided the elbow-length gloves replicating real skin. Well, they do an awful lot of work here. I understand quite a bit of film production takes place in Toronto because it's cheaper than the States."

"Interesting tidbit. So when do you start?"

"Tomorrow."

"So soon?"

"I almost didn't start at all. When I went for the interview, I didn't have all the necessary papers I needed, including a valid work visa. Since I didn't plan on staying here long, I never applied for any of them. She said they needed someone to start immediately. I told her I would get them in order and asked if we could work something else out in the meantime. Maybe act as an outside contractor or consultant on a temporary basis. She left for a little while, then came back and said we could work out a deal off the books for cash until I get my papers in order. I told her that would be perfect."

Matt lifted a brow in surprise. "That's interesting."

"I'll be working for a woman named Hillary Whitley. I believe she is the person in charge at the clinic."

"Nice job. Are you up for a little research?"

"What kind?"

Matt grabbed his jacket. "I want to check something out, but I would like to change first. I'm also famished."

Amy followed Matt to his room one flight up. As he stripped off his dress shirt, replacing it with a snug black turtleneck, his bare chest, firm and taut, reignited memories of their time on Kauai, rekindling a tiny spark.

"I could swear I closed this," Matt said.

"What did you say?" Amy asked, her thoughts off in a different direction.

"Nothing. Never mind." Matt drew out a pair of jeans and tossed the bag into the closet. "I thought I zipped this duffel up when I left. Maybe not. I was in a hurry."

# Chapter Thirty-One

## Streets of Toronto

## Toronto Canada

"AND WHAT ARE WE DOING here?" Amy asked Matt after stepping out of a cab in a desolate residential area of Toronto. The street sat empty. Sidewalks and porches were devoid of people.

"Looking for the main office of SSI. I didn't want anyone to see me being dropped off right in front of the building." He glanced at her. "But I did want to see where I would be heading tomorrow."

She scanned the area, spinning completely around. Homes sagged on narrow lots, almost touching each other. Most needed repair. "Based on what I'm seeing, you can go casual." Alarm company signs poked out between overgrown shrubbery. "Are you sure about this? I'm not sure the driver got it right. I don't see any commercial buildings here. What is their address?"

Matt handed her a slip of paper. She plugged the address into her phone's GPS. Amy pointed to her side. "It's a couple of blocks this way." Heading in the direction Amy had indicated, they allowed the blue line zigzagging across her screen to direct them for their next few turns. Close to their destination, Amy's phone rang. "It's Bonnie. I'll get back to her." She sent the call to voicemail.

A short time later, the GPS announced their arrival. Their destination turned out to be an empty, cracked asphalt parking lot across the street. The house next to it had a tattered sign advertising chiropractic services. "Either you have the wrong address or this is someone's idea of a joke," Amy said.

A single-car garage sat at the far end of the property, behind the parking area. Amy glanced left and right. "I'm going to take a wild guess here, and say we are in the seedier part of town."

"Oh yeah? What was your first clue?" They took a few long strides and stepped into the parking lot, heading toward the pull-down door ahead. Amy pointed out a sign attached to the side of the adjacent home, which read: Patient parking.

Matt tugged on the door. Finding it locked, Matt said, "Let's try the back."

At its rear, weeds reached halfway to the roof. The windowless back door was locked. Positioning himself at a rear fence a few steps behind it, Matt pounded forward and, using his foot, kicked it open, breaking off its lock in the process.

Amy stepped inside and activated her phone's flashlight, brightening up the dingy area. Racks of discarded household items rimmed the upper portion of one wall. Broken picture frames filled a corner.

Matt surveyed the junk. "There's nothing here."

Before leaving, Matt managed to prop the back door into its original position—almost. No small feat considering the lock had torn away a portion of the wood. Amy complimented him on his work. "Not bad. Do you think they will notice?"

He smirked. "Don't think anybody ever comes here."

"I agree. Which is why I'm a little concerned about them sending you here."

"They didn't."

"Then how?"

"I got this location off the papers your mother emailed. Joey told me he didn't have the address at hand and would get it for me." He winked, "I guess they must have moved since filing the original paperwork."

They left the desolate area, walking until they reached a busier street where they were able to hail a cab.

Once settled inside, Amy listened to Bonnie's message. *The apartment was broken into yesterday! I spent the night at Jeff's. I saw it when I came back today. I called Detective Peters. I'm not sure what's missing. The place is a mess. Call me.*

# Chapter Thirty-Two

## Devereux Clinic for Health

## Toronto, Canada

HILLARY WHITLEY WAS bent over, riffling through a drawer in the center of a U-shaped formation of three desks when Stacey from the HR Department led Amy to her. Straightening, Hillary said, "Ah, here they are."

The Devereux Clinic occupied a three-story building at the edge of town. Amy had arrived early for her first day of work. She met Stacey in the HR Department, and even though she would be working off the books until she could provide the necessary paperwork, she needed to listen to an introduction about the facility. Stacey then led Amy to the third floor to meet Hillary Whitley, the director of the clinic, and the person she would be working for. After making the introductions, Stacey left.

Hillary indicated the other two desks. "You can use either. I'm very pressed today. Are you ready to get started?"

"Yes, Amy said. Whenever you are." She placed her bag on the desk closest to the door. Four filing cabinets and a printer lined the wall behind it.

Hillary flipped through the found documents, culling out several sheets. She handed them to Amy. "I need these handwritten notes typed up and this list of categories entered into a spreadsheet. Are you familiar with Word?"

"I am. Stacey mentioned I will also be taking your calls," Amy said.

"Mine is the first button on the top row." A sleek multiline phone sat alongside a terminal. "As a general rule, please try to take a message. Tell callers I'm tied up, and I'll get back to them. If they persist, text me." Hillary pointed to the base of the phone, where a sticky note held a phone number. "That's my cell."

Sudden movement at the door caught their attention. They turned in unison as a petite woman strode in and came to a quick stop, a few steps short of reaching Hillary. Amy recognized her from the social media pictures she and Matt had pored over. Eunice Stratford, the wife of the man Matt met with yesterday.

"Can you spare a minute?" The woman asked Hillary.

"Of course. Take a seat in my office. I'll be right in."

Hillary turned to Amy. "This should be enough to get you started."

With Hillary gone, Amy poked around. The top drawers of her desk contained the usual office items. Nothing of interest. The lower ones were bare. Across the room, a matching phone and monitor sat on a similar desk with only a bare wall behind it and a door off to its side.

Pulling open one of the drawers in the cabinet behind her, she discovered neat file folders arranged in alphabetical order. Each with typed headings. She found nothing for Stratford or SSI under the section marked S.

A gunmetal keypad on the door's jamb near the opposite desk caught her attention. Its twelve keys protruded from the faceplate in the same layout as her phone. She strode to it and tried the knob. It didn't budge.

Amy returned to her seat and switched on the terminal. She opened up Word. In another window, she tried accessing the Internet but couldn't. It required a password. She began typing in Hillary's data, pausing between sentences to concentrate on how next to proceed.

It was a stroke of good luck to be assigned to Hillary. Since the Stratford children were born here, and Joey Stratford is a part owner of the company that shuttled Wilhelm to Niihau, Amy had reasoned Hillary might be the right person to provide some additional information about the man.

However, after seeing his wife and Hillary together and sensing something more than a business camaraderie between them, she decided to kill that approach. Amy was considering how best to snoop around Hillary's office when, as if Hillary could read her thoughts, her door opened.

Eunice headed straight to the elevator. Hillary returned, stopping in front of Amy, carrying a folded document in her hand. "Any questions?"

"Word is working. But will I need any other codes or passwords for the work I'll be doing?"

"You will for the Internet. We each have a separate user name. It's some anagram of our names, but I don't know what yours would be. You'll have to ask Stacey later, but for the time being, you won't need any."

"I also see a lock on the door behind the other desk. Is there a code for it?"

Amy witnessed a flicker of fire behind the woman's dark eyes. Hillary's face froze. "It's a confidential filing area," Hillary answered in a calm voice, belying the blaze burning in her optics.

"Will I be doing any filing there?" Amy asked, trying to soften the gaffe.

"No. That won't be necessary."

"OK. I just thought I might need it." Amy lowered her head and resumed typing after witnessing Hillary's reaction, realizing how much her question had aroused suspicion. She made a mental note to be more covert with her curiosity.

Hillary lingered a few seconds longer than necessary before moving across the room. At the locked door, Hillary positioned her body in a purposeful manner in front of it in order to obscure the keypad. That convinced Amy she intended to enter the room. Amy feigned typing, keying in pure gibberish, as she stole glances toward the woman.

Amy sensed, more than saw, the cautious look from Hillary as her cell rang. Taking a step back, she answered it. "I'll be right there."

Repositioning herself in front of the door, Hillary drew her left hand back, reaching into a rear pocket to replace the phone. That action angled her shoulder outward and back, away from the lock. It exposed both the keypad and her right index finger while entering the code.

*Got it. Easy one.*

Amy's heart pounded faster than her fingers were keying. Hillary left the door open, but from where she sat, she couldn't see into the room. Amy did, however, recognize the sound of a drawer being pulled open and then slammed shut.

In mere seconds, Hillary emerged, closing and tugging on the door to ensure it locked. "I'm expecting a call from Dr. Zoric. If he calls, tell him I'll get back to him soon. I'm just going down the hall."

Amy's curiosity raged. But with Hillary in the area, it would be too dangerous. For now, she would have to content herself with deleting the garbage she had entered and resume with the valid entries.

Her curiosity would have to wait.

# Chapter Thirty-Three

## Devereux Clinic for Health

## Toronto, Canada

AMY'S FIRST MORNING had already proved interesting. Before lunch, she returned to the HR Department, asking Stacey for an Internet password. Stacey supplied her one. Then invited Amy to join her for a sandwich in the cafeteria.

Unlike the room where Amy had spent the morning working, framed artwork hung on these walls. The surrounding areas were painted in either bright or subdued colors meant to highlight the paintings. No hospital white in sight. In line, Amy made her selection, noting that the portions were small and the prices large. The cafeteria mimicked the clinic's foyer and waiting areas. They smelled of money. Stacey pointed to a pedestal table with two swivel-armed chairs. When they were settled, Amy said, "I'm kind of surprised to be working for the administrator."

"Her assistant is sick," Stacey said. "She should be back in a day or two. So this won't be permanent for you. Hillary needed some work done for tomorrow. She told me she'd do it herself, but she's giving tours today. You turned up at a perfect time."

"A petite dark-haired woman met with Hillary today, but I don't think Hillary gave her a tour."

"Was she tiny, designer-dressed, with every strand of hair in place, along with a great makeup job?" Stacey asked, sounding envious.

Amy thought back to Eunice's arrival and realized, with the shock of seeing her in person, she hadn't paid attention to what she wore. But she did recall her makeup and hair made her appear ready for a photo shoot. "Yep. She is the one."

"Eunice is one of our most important clients. Her husband is the CEO of Stratford Industries. Are you familiar with them?"

Amy glanced away, shaking her head as if trying to recall. "No. I don't think so," she said.

"Well, she gave birth to twins here with special circumstances. Even though we specialize in a variety of difficult areas, their situation was rare and unusual."

Amy continued chewing, trying not to show her interest. After a long swallow, she asked, "What was so unique about it?"

"They required a specific type of blood for their procedures. Hillary took a personal interest in their case. Her background is in nursing. And she scheduled herself in for all the procedures with the twins. Unfortunately, as is often the case with preemies, the babies didn't survive."

"That's so sad, but I find it interesting that the administrator would have time to participate in their care." Mindful of how Hillary's suspicions were raised when she asked about the code on the locked door, Amy asked her next question with an air of indifference. "Does she participate in procedures often?"

"No, but they are very high-profile clients. I think Hillary wanted to guarantee they got the highest level of service."

Stacey spent the remainder of their lunch highlighting the benefits of working for the clinic.

When they were done, Amy said, "I'm so curious. This unique blood the children needed, where were you able to get it from?"

"I'm not sure." Stacey stood. "I'm just glad we did."

WITH LUNCH OVER, AMY peeked into Hillary's office before heading back to her desk. She believed whatever Hillary filed behind the keypad must have come from her meeting with Eunice Stratford. Something important enough to be kept under lock.

With Hillary's office empty, she ignored her uneasy stomach, deciding now would be her chance. She'd deal with the indigestion to come later. She rushed to the keypad and depressed each key with extra care. The code was a straight line up the center, from bottom to top, 0852.

*I hope Hillary's taking a long lunch today.*

Grasping the handle, she glanced behind her before twisting and pulling open the door. Inside the small area, wide enough only to have served as a closet in the past, stood two four-drawer filing cabinets with barely enough space to pull the drawers out.

Finding one labeled S-Z, she yanked it open. She thumbed through the folders until she found a thick one labeled Stratford. She extracted it and spread its contents wide atop the others in the drawer. Unsure of what she would find, she picked through the documents, most of them meaningless to her, recognizing only invoices for services.

The first item in the file, an off-white, 8 ½ by 11 sheet of paper in the same shade as Hillary had been holding, stared up at her. The fold marks still visible. A large label affixed to the sheet appeared to have been removed from something else.

*This must be what Hillary filed.*

Amy tried to snap a picture with her phone, but the crinkled label would not lie flat. After a few precious seconds wasted trying to straighten it, she raced out, placed the sheet on the glass of the copier, and hit the button.

It took almost a minute. The possibility of Hillary entering at any moment, along with her frayed nerves, made her realize she wouldn't be able to risk any further copies.

The moment the machine finished, she pulled the original and its copy out. Scurrying back, she replaced the original in the folder. As she was shoving the folder into the drawer, a voice from behind made her flinch and slam the drawer closed.

She folded the stolen copy in her hand, stuffing the paper into her side pocket before turning to see who had spoken.

"Oh. You scared me," Amy said, trying to disguise her nervousness, which morphed into relief when she realized it wasn't Hillary. And she hadn't been caught. "I didn't hear you come in."

The older, heavyset blonde woman stood only a few steps away, at the edge of the open door. "I'm here to speak with Hillary."

Amy took a slight step forward, now an arm's length away from the woman, hoping she would likewise step back.

The woman stood firm.

Amy said in a brusque tone, "If you don't mind, this area needs to remain locked."

SUSAN FLEMING FOUND Hillary's office with ease from the directions the guard downstairs had given her. In her quest to uncover the source of the blood, she had settled on speaking with the clinic's administrator, Hillary, before having a conversation with Dr. Zoric, whom she suspected of being complicit in the extortion.

She wasn't sure how forthcoming Hillary would be, but decided it was worth a try.

Hillary's office sat empty. Susan peeked into the adjoining space, hoping to find someone who could tell her when Hillary might return. As Susan entered, she caught sight of a young girl rushing to an inner area.

She strode to its doorway, where the young woman turned to her and complained that the room needed to remain locked.

Susan took her time retreating from the doorway. "As I said, I would like to speak with Hillary."

After closing and jiggling the door handle to guarantee it was locked, Amy returned to her desk. "She's not here."

"Will she be back today?"

"I guess she will, but I'm not sure when. Can I take a message?"

Having been a manager for years at Stratford, Susan's *Spidey Sense* kicked in. Instinct told her something wasn't right. The sudden fear in the young girl's eyes and the snarky reaction to her inquiry about Hillary confirmed for Susan that something felt off.

"Yes. Please tell her I stopped by." Susan handed a card to Amy, scrutinizing her. "This is my number. Please ask her to call. Tell her it's of the utmost importance."

"No problem. I will."

Susan had her own issues to investigate, but she couldn't resist giving Amy an I-know-you-are-up-to-something smile as she walked out.

# Chapter Thirty-Four

## Hector Lopez

## Outskirts of Toronto, Canada

RECOGNIZING THAT GOING up against Mike and the foundation's board would be no easy task, Susan found herself sitting in her idling car, awaiting her secret weapon.

As she waited, she focused on an open field in front of her, imagining the number of apartments or condos that could be built if its location were in town, instead of here in the suburbs. It seemed to her every meter of space was being scooped up to hold a high-rise building of some sort in Toronto, with no apparent end in sight.

Hector Lopez opened the passenger door and slid in, along with a cool breeze. A flash of a long-ago memory—of their initial meeting—blew through her before he greeted her as he always did. "Hello, Miss Susan."

The meeting had been set for early evening at a McDonald's, a public space where they could discuss the broad outline of the job she wanted done.

After twenty minutes, she phoned him, leaving a message. Forty minutes later, without receiving a return call, she labeled him a no-show and headed to her car.

Nearly there, keys in hand, she heard the low voice from behind. "Just keep walking. No one gets hurt." Her heart stopped for a beat.

In less than a microsecond, the voice pivoted. It became louder, non-threatening, accommodating. "Can I get the door for you, Miss Susan?"

Earlier, she had questioned him about his ability to operate in secret, apparently too much, forcing him to provide a live demonstration.

He wasn't a surprise to her anymore.

"Hector, I need you to check out someone." She hesitated. "No, make that two people who work at The Devereux Clinic."

She handed him a slip of paper with the address and a phone number. "I need everything you can find on a Dr. Zoric. He is the one who operates the place. I'm also interested in a girl who works for the administrator, Hillary Whitley. I'm sorry. I didn't get the girl's name."

"What type of information do you want on them, Miss Susan?"

She had long ago told him to drop the *miss*, but it was like telling a career soldier to skip the *sir*. "Everything. And anything."

What Susan wanted defied description. She didn't always know what to look for. He did, though.

He was so perfect for the job, ferreting out the little details, sometimes seemingly meaningless, that she had urged Mike and Frank to retain him as a full-time investigator. She only relented when Frank pointed out a potential problem with the idea. Working for them as an independent, no one would be aware of his assignments. However, as an employee, his involvement would be known. With that knowledge, others could, and very well would, have his movements surveilled.

After hearing Frank's logic, she acquiesced. Although not employed by them, his workload from her kept him busy.

"He's the doctor running the clinic. I already have what he presents as his credentials, but I'd like to see what you can come up with. On his background. Where he's from. Where he's studied. Where he's traveled. Or anything else on his family. As for the assistant to Hillary, I'm not familiar with the girl. Something felt off with her. That's all I can tell you."

"I would expect the doctor, but something's not right about the girl, Miss Susan?"

"Something, yes. I'm not sure what, but something is going on at the clinic, and I think she's involved. Whatever you can find."

"OK, Miss Susan. How important is this?"

"Make it top priority."

She thought, and not for the first time, his native Puerto Rico had lost a valuable resource when he left. "You can drop everything else. Dr. Zoric and her are the things I am most interested in."

"I will take care of this, Miss Susan."

And she knew he would.

# Chapter Thirty-Five

## Italian Restaurant

## Toronto, Canada

MATT WAS LOOKING FORWARD to the meeting with SSI, eager to hear an explanation for their ridiculous garage headquarters. However, an early phone call from Joey doused his anticipation. Joey's plan for today included two other Stratford employees for lunch—and nobody from SSI.

Matt and Joey arrived at about the same time. Joey held the door for Matt. The moment Matt stepped inside, an aroma greeted him that made his stomach growl. Joey entered, pushed past the hostess station, and headed straight for a table where two suited men were scanning menus. Matt followed.

Joey said, "Matt, this is Will Cavanaugh and Jim Turner." Joey pulled out a chair and took a seat at the cloth-covered table, saying, "Gentlemen, meet Matt Conners."

Matt shook hands with both of them as he took in the abundance of shiny silverware at each place setting. "I hope I'm not underdressed," he said, referring to his shirt and casual slacks.

"Not at all. What we concentrate on is getting work done." Motioning for him to sit, Jim said, "I work from home in my pajamas at times. Results are what count. How you dress, well, that's secondary."

A waiter, introducing himself as Angelo, appeared and took their drink orders.

Matt said, "I like the sound of that." He added the smile he imagined they were expecting. "But can you fill me in on what exactly I'll be doing?"

"Matt's an ex-soldier," Joey cut in. "I'm sure his talents will be of great use to us."

Matt chided in silence. *Once a soldier, always a soldier. Never an ex.*

Ignoring Matt's question, Joey leaned toward Jim, saying, "I need to reschedule this afternoon's meeting." The two men opened their phones and began scrolling through their calendars. They huddled in quiet conversation as Will and Matt waited.

After a while, Jim looked up and said, "I think Mr. Stratford here," he paused as the drinks were delivered to the table. "I think Mr. Stratford here," he nodded toward Joey. "I hate calling him Joey. It seems so disrespectful since he's our boss."

Joey lifted his glass in an appreciative gesture to Jim and took a long drink, downing most of its liquid. "As I was saying, Mr. Stratford has huge ideas on where the company can grow. He's brought on a new line of boards. Several other campaigns are in process, waiting, and ready to go once we go public. Let's just say we are ready to spread our wings."

He turned toward Will. "Wouldn't you say it's a good way of putting it?"

"I wouldn't put it in those words. I would say we are ready for other markets. The States are ripe for us. Someone like you could help us make that happen."

Matt asked, "In what capacity?"

Before either of them could answer, Joey finished his drink and stood. "Gentlemen, I'm sorry, but I must get back. I'll leave the rest to you to finalize." He extended his hand. "Matt, I hope I'm not jumping the gun here, but welcome aboard."

Matt laughed in disbelief, hoping it came across as friendly. *Is he for real? Ignores my question and just assumes I want to work for him.*

With Joey gone, they ordered lunch. The conversation revolved around Jim's interpretation of sales territories and strategies for achieving their earnings. Matt glanced at Will several times, noting he didn't join in, guessing him not to be a numbers man.

Over dessert and coffee, Jim ended with, "Everything we've discussed today is common knowledge. However, once you begin working for us, you will be exposed to more detailed, future, forward-looking plans for the direction of the company, and they will all be confidential."

Matt shrugged. "Of course."

"Great."

Will, who had been mum throughout much of the lunch, reached beneath the table, pulled out a document, and placed the paper in front of Matt, his role now apparent.

*Lawyer.*

"It's a standard confidentiality agreement."

Matt began to fold the agreement in half. Will slammed his hand on top of it. "I'm sorry, but you have to sign in our presence."

*So the quiet member of the team is the more lethal one.*

"And why is that?"

"We ask all of our key associates to sign one. I'll provide you with a copy after I sign and have it notarized."

"I thought I would take it with me so I can read it over. See in more detail what I'm getting myself into."

Will removed his hand. "That's not possible. And it would not be the smart thing to do. This opportunity is only being extended for..."

Jim cut in. "Matt, don't play games with us." His cordial mealtime attitude now as cold as the remaining ice in his glass. "You seem interested. We've just spent a great deal of our time helping you understand what the position entails. As I've already said, until you tell us you're in, we can't disclose any more to you."

Jim folded his napkin and laid it on the table. "If this is how we're starting, without your trust, then I'm guessing it's not the right fit for either of us."

"I see," Matt said, giving Jim a knowing smile. "You mean it's now or never?"

Jim said, "I guess you could say that."

# Chapter Thirty-Six

## Matt's Hotel Room

## Toronto, Canada

"YOU SIGNED IT!"

Matt was in no way prepared for Amy's reaction to his lunch story: her shriek about signing it, her collapse onto the loveseat, and then her foot banging against its ottoman. "Relax. It's not that big a deal," he said.

Amy had joined him in his hotel room after completing her first day of work at Devereux. With a hand massaging her knee, she said, "And you have no idea what you agreed to?"

"I glanced through the paragraphs. It had all the legal mumbo jumbo you would expect." Still surprised at her reaction, Matt said, "They made me feel like I had to. Right then. I'm sure it contains something about me not disclosing anything I might discover while working for them."

"Like what? What exactly do they want you to keep quiet about? Can they make you stay quiet about things that happened before you started working for them? Like finding Wilhelm?"

"I wondered the same thing." Matt moved to the windows. He pushed the curtains aside and stared out at the people walking about on the sidewalk below. He thought for a moment. "Could be that's their game. I won't be able to discuss anything concerning Stratford or any company working for them, like SSI. Which means I can't discuss the connection I found between them and Wilhelm. Other than that, I haven't the foggiest."

"I'm sorry, but what did you say?" Amy put her hand to her ear, feigning a hearing problem. "Who did you say found Wilhelm?"

His lips tightened as he turned serious. "At this point, Amy, it's better if they believe I found him alone. I don't think you want to be in their crosshairs. These men sound serious and smell dangerous."

Amy shot up. "Thanks, but I found him, and I'm going to follow through until I get some answers. I don't need you to protect me. I can take care of myself." She moved past him and leaned against a chest of drawers with a TV atop it. She gave him a serious look. "But *you*, on the other hand, should be worried. What are the repercussions of signing that document? What can they do to you if you somehow break one of the rules of this contract? Didn't you even wonder about the consequences?"

"Of course. They can sue me for everything I own and then some. But lots of luck to them getting anything out of me."

"What about putting you in jail? Did you ever consider that?"

"I'm an American citizen. Not Canadian. Do you think they can arrest me because I break a contract over here? I think I'll take my chances."

"Matt, you're ignoring the obvious. The most important thing is if you find out something, anything at all, I'll bet you are required to stay silent. I'll bet there is a clause precluding you from reporting, or even discussing, what you find. To anyone, including the police."

Matt caught himself thinking how attractive she looked when she got riled up, deciding he might need to do more things to generate this sort of reaction. "I don't care what the document says. I'll tell whoever, whatever I please." He paused. "If I even manage to find out anything at all about them."

"Why? What do you mean?"

He moved to the loveseat, sat, leaned back, and crossed his legs. "Amy, they're bringing me on as a representative of their company who will be based back in the States. Nothing to do with security, as he implied on the phone, baiting me to come here. I'm going to be hawking their skis and a new line of snowboards. I'll be nowhere around here to find out anything to tell anyone."

"Why? Where do they want you to work?"

"From home."

"Home? Hawaii?" Matt laughed at her expression. Her eyes opened so wide they threatened to explode out of their sockets. "Do they know it doesn't snow in Hawaii?"

Matt patted the seat next to him. "Come over here." She gave him a strange look, hesitated for a moment, but complied. Wanting her complete attention, he leaned in and put an arm around her, placing them in an intimate position.

"This whole lunch meeting was a sham. Something felt way off. I couldn't put my finger on what. Then, their whole deal became clear to me. They were buying me off. They knew it, and I knew it. I'm still not sure why, but I am confident that is what they are doing."

At this close distance, he resisted the urge to close the few millimeters between them and draw her in for a kiss, but his concern for her safety surfaced. Needing to maintain the seriousness of the conversation, he removed his arm. "For a fraction of a second there, I wondered if that would have been my last meal if I didn't sign their agreement. Crazy, I guess. So, when I realized they wanted to take the legal route to silence me, I went along."

"But why? Why do they need to?"

He inched further away from her, still grappling with his urge. "Got me, but let's face it, I have no more experience selling their products than the man on the moon."

"Really?" A playfulness found its way into her voice. "Did I just hear a man admit he may not be good at something?"

He chuckled before turning serious. "Do you see? Because I really do need you to." Wanting her complete attention, he grabbed her shoulder. "During this lunch ruse, Jim joked that my working from home would give me lots of time to spend with my *girlfriend*. I never mentioned having one. I tried to pin him down after he made the comment, but he danced around it, saying he just *assumed* a guy like me would have one. Not a fiancé or a wife. A girlfriend. I'm concerned they somehow know you are here with me."

Amy tried to shrug his hand away, all playfulness gone. "Well, I'm not leaving."

He tightened his grip. "Great. Because I'd rather have you close until we make it back to the States. One more thing. Since your mother dug up the names of the men who founded SSI, can you ask her to dig deeper into this Joey Stratford guy and this IPO he's talking about?"

"Of course."

He gave her arm a squeeze before standing. "And last, I don't think you can stay here. We've got to find you another place."

"Find *me* another place," she said, sounding annoyed. "What about you?"

"I told them I wanted to spend a few more days here and take in Toronto." Matt picked up his key and headed for the door. "Come on. I'll walk you to the elevator."

"Where are you going?"

"Downstairs. To talk to the concierge to see if we can find you a safe place to stay."

# Chapter Thirty-Seven

## Amy's Hotel Room

## Toronto, Canada

AMY'S HOTEL ROOM DOOR stood ajar while she waited for Matt to return. Its lock protruded out, preventing the door from closing shut. In his absence, Amy had given serious consideration to Matt's concern for her safety. Her carry-on now sat alongside the door, packed and ready to go. She had also fired off an email to her mother requesting further information on Joey Stratford and his company.

Matt pushed open the door, juggling a carrier with two hot drinks in his other hand. "Were you not listening to me?" He reset the lock and kicked the door closed as he entered.

"Oh, great. Are one of those for me?"

Matt stood in place for a long minute—making his annoyance clear. "You can't just leave your door open like this."

Amy didn't answer. Instead, in an excited burst, she said, "I didn't get a chance to tell you what I discovered at the clinic. I know what the connection is."

Matt took a seat alongside her on the loveseat. "Not sure you deserve this for leaving the door open—but here." He handed her a coffee. "I'll bite. What's the connection?"

"Wilhelm. I found a link between him and the clinic. The Stratford twins had a very unusual type of blood. I'm pretty sure it's the type Wilhelm has. I asked, but Stacey, the girl I had lunch with, didn't know the exact type or where it came from. Only that it is unique and she was happy the clinic managed to secure it."

"So, you're thinking the blood they took from Wilhelm, Rhnull blood, was for the premature kids? If you're right..." Matt shook his head. He whistled when comprehension seemed to set in. "If he's no longer having blood drawn from him since he's home with his family, what are they doing now?"

"The babies didn't make it. They died."

"Well, that's convenient." He placed his coffee on a side table, sat back, and locked his hands behind his neck, staring at the ceiling. After a while, he asked, "Chicken or egg?"

Amy rolled her eyes. "What do you mean?"

"What came first? Did the babies die because Wilhelm is free and isn't supplying any more blood? Or, because the babies died, they didn't need Wilhelm anymore?"

With a faraway expression, he asked, "If they didn't need him any longer and we hadn't rescued him, what would they have done? Kill him because he is of no further use? Maybe just let him rot there on the island? Or, after seeing the prison they devised, do you picture them as the sort of nice guys to somehow let him return home?"

"Oh, my God," Amy said. "What a horrific thought." She got up, retrieved her bag, and began rummaging through it. "I found out they didn't die together. The second one just died. There's more." Pulling out the photocopied sheet, she handed it to him. "Take a look at this. What do you make of it?"

"It's a label. Looks like it came from somewhere else. It has a batch number and a control number. I see tracking numbers as well. What am I looking at?" He asked.

"I'm not sure. Eunice Stratford came in to meet with Hillary today."

"That's Joey's wife."

"Yes. They met in Hillary's office. When their meeting broke up, Hillary came to where I'm working and entered a locked filing area with what I believe is *that* sheet of paper in her hand. That's not the original. It's a copy." Amy observed Matt, waiting for his comments.

When he didn't say anything, she continued. "She entered the code and I saw it. I couldn't tell what she did there, but I'm guessing she filed the paper in the Stratford folder. She only stayed inside for a few seconds. After lunch, when I found out the babies required a unique type of blood and suspected it came from Wilhelm, I snuck in and pulled this out of the Stratford File."

Matt stared at the sheet, his expression blank. "The date is recent, but it doesn't contain a name. Are you sure this came from the Stratford File?"

"Yes. I'm sure I took it out of the correct folder. It was the top document when I opened up the file. I saw other papers in the folder referencing Baby A and Baby B. Do you remember the article we found saying the babies were never named, only referred to as Baby A and Baby B?"

"Yeah. I do." He considered the document. "Maybe she filed something for a different account than Stratford. It could be a coincidence she decided to file it at that particular moment. Or, it's possible she put this sheet in the wrong folder."

Matt analyzed the copy in his hand more carefully. He twisted it around and held it up to the light. "Appears to be a label of some sort. This code at the bottom is a registration number of some kind. It's a little blurry, but it also contains a collected and processed-by address, which means it can be tracked. But I don't believe this is the one for the Stratfords. This has the letter B and Rh POSITIVE in bold letters on the label. Palakiko told us Wilhelm's blood is Rhnull."

"Yeah. That bothers me too, but Matt, I don't believe Hillary misfiled this."

"Only one way to find out. We need to get another peek inside that file."

# Chapter Thirty-Eight

## Home of Eunice and Joey Stratford

## Toronto, Canada

JOEY STRATFORD LOOSENED his tie as he entered his kitchen. He found Eunice seated at the island in its center with an open tour book and a glossy brochure alongside a glass of wine.

"How about a drink?" She asked. He took off his jacket and leaned over to kiss her.

"Yeah. Sounds great."

She retrieved a bottle, knowing his preference, poured in the liquid, and handed the glass to him. "How did lunch go?"

Joey pulled out a stool and took a seat. "Just like I predicted." Joey gave himself a perfect score when it came to people, imagining himself an excellent judge of character. "The guy's greedy, just like everybody else. Looked at the offer as easy money. The guys told me when they mentioned he could work from home, his eyeballs almost flew out."

"He didn't ask you about anything else? Wasn't curious about why you wanted him to work for you?"

Joey swirled the liquid around in his cut-glass tumbler before taking a long drink. "Not a thing. I told you he wouldn't be a problem." He credited his perceptive ability to the years he spent in sales, watching and analyzing people, observing their actions. It was how he knew Eunice would be his before they even spoke.

She sidled up next to him and wrapped her arms around his neck. "We are so perfect together. We are going to be so blissful. So happy. You will paint to your heart's content. You will create the most beautiful pictures. We'll relax and enjoy life as we were meant to. Soon, this will all be behind us."

He gave her a long kiss. "Have we found a destination for our paradise yet?"

"Working on it. I did narrow our choices down to a few. I think we should spend some time in each of the locations first, though. We need to ensure the place will work for us."

Joey got up and refilled his glass. "Work faster, sweetheart. It's going to happen very soon. I need you to be ready."

Eunice was back in her seat, turning pages, as he walked out. "Don't worry. I will be."

# Chapter Thirty-Nine

## Somewhere on the Streets of The City

## Toronto, Canada

SUSAN HAD JUST PULLED into the parking lot of a local grocery store when her phone rang. With her newfound time, she had decided to try her hand at cooking again, a passion she had enjoyed, then abandoned with the workload from the foundation. "Hello, Hector. I think I can guess why you're calling. It's because of Frank's call to you. Isn't it?"

After Mike removed her from the Evaluation Committee, she had no further contact with him—except for the meeting at his townhouse about the blood. Frank, however, continued to stay in touch, checking on her and relaying information about the committee's actions. He had just shared with her Mike's request for an update from Hector on his work for the foundation.

"Yes, Miss Susan. He needs me to resume my work on the other cases I have open. The ones I was working on before you asked me to do the research on the doctor and the girl from the clinic." He paused for a moment before saying, "He also seemed surprised when I told him I am doing something for you, Miss Susan."

She sighed and shut off the engine. "I'm sorry, Hector. That's my fault. You were doing that on a personal basis for me. As a matter of fact, you should know I've been asked to step down from the committee. So, I won't be dealing with you on behalf of them anymore. Frank or Denise, the woman who replaced me, will be interacting with you."

"Then I should drop this and go back to working on what Frank asked me to do for him, Miss Susan?"

"Yes. Of course." She hated to lose his valuable support, but she couldn't involve him in her efforts. His livelihood, as well as Frank's, depended on the foundation. She couldn't ask them to give that up. "But before you do, I'd like whatever you have compiled so far on either or both of them. Also, can you recommend anyone else? Someone I can trust. The work would be for me alone. I'll take care of paying them."

"I'll get back to you, Miss Susan."

"Thanks. And thanks for all the work you've done for me in the past. I have to say, it truly was a pleasure working with you."

"Goodbye, Miss Susan."

She hung up, tore up the paper containing the list of the necessary food items to purchase, and shoved it in the cupholder. A deep sadness surrounded her. One she wouldn't have believed possible. Because her job was her life, the people she interacted with because of it were her family.

She couldn't employ Hector on a constant basis the way the foundation could. He needed to look out for himself, and she understood. But Hector had become more than a working associate. Over time, he became a confidant, and she would miss the frequent, almost daily, interaction with him. Without his valuable assistance, she wondered how much she could accomplish on her own.

Susan sat numb, exhausted by the trinity of psychological pain.

Mike had fired her, slicing open a deep wound.

Frank's continuing friendship, even though more distant, functioned as a constant reminder. One that wouldn't allow the cut to heal.

Now the loss of Hector's talents—a major blow—sprinkled a heavy dose of salt on top of the sore, all but ensuring it would fester.

*How long do I have until the gangrene sets in?*

She started the car and drove away, no longer having an appetite.

# Chapter Forty

## Stratford Legacy Foundation Offices

## Toronto, Canada

SUSAN ARRIVED AT HER office early the next day, eager to delve into the research Hector had dropped off for her. It concerned Dr. Zoric and Hillary's assistant. Unlike the extravagant conference room with its elaborate and unadorned windows, their offices made use of traditional blinds. Susan opened hers wide, hoping for a little sun to brighten her spirits. Glancing outside, she noted gray clouds moving quickly over the city. Even the sun wasn't helping today.

Settling into her chair, she lifted the yellow envelope with her name written in bold on the front. The word *CONFIDENTIAL* in bold italics caught her eye at the bottom. She tore into it. Reflecting on her personal mantra—*Always find the silver lining*—she realized one positive side effect of not having the responsibilities of the Evaluation Committee. She now had time to pursue this.

Spreading the contents across her desk, she separated Hector's two packets. Picking up the one on the doctor first, she scanned its contents.

It contained information on his schooling, degrees, and accomplishments covering three pages. On a personal basis, he had a wife, a daughter, and put in long hours. She put the analysis of the man aside, finding nothing unusual. *For what he gets paid, I would expect such a high level of dedication.*

Susan picked up the single typed page on the girl, Amy Pryce. She guessed it was all he had gathered thus far.

*Graduated college. Traveled a great deal in the following years. Lived with a father during her adolescent and grad years. No mention of a mother or a divorce.* In the margin, Hector had written the word *dead* along with a question mark.

*Involved with the death of a gang member in her hometown of Washington, DC. Listed as a prospective witness in a case against Luis Rodriguez.* In red, Hector noted: *Looking for a plea deal? Possible protection program?*

Hector also included a printout of a newspaper story concerning a drug raid in the area that happened around the time of the gang member's death. Susan assumed it concerned Amy somehow, although her name didn't appear in the article.

*Last travel for her: a return trip from Hawaii back to Washington before entering our country.* After circling Canada several times, he jotted down the word *why?* Susan wondered about the reason for her being here, too.

At the end, as he always did when providing a report to the foundation, Hector included his assumptions.

*She appears to have some association or connection with illegal activities. To what degree, I cannot determine. However, the ease with which she travels with no apparent source of income makes drugs the most likely conclusion. Her travel also allows for the movement of product. In addition, a known occurrence of a connection to a drug raid and/or gang affiliation can't be explained any other way.*

*There is no record of her being enrolled at university here, as she noted on her job application to the clinic. I could find no relatives or close friends here. This appears to be her first trip to our country.*

*Still, a caution, more work is necessary to confirm these assumptions.*

Susan copied the report on Amy, put the copy into a small envelope, and checked the time, realizing she had taken more time analyzing Hector's reports than she had intended. She still wanted to brush up on Frank's findings on the clinic before leaving for today's appointment with Hillary. The one she had requested when she stumbled upon a nervous Amy.

# Chapter Forty-One

## Student Housing

## Toronto, Canada

AMY LED MATT TO THE third floor of a fourth-floor walk-up. She opened the door at the top of the steps. The key lay inside on top of a dresser. Seeing the double bed in the center with two pancake-flat pillows, Matt whistled and said, "Home, sweet, home."

Amy gave him a do-not-say-a-word warning look. After taking in the multi-colored, tattered duvet with frayed edges, she dragged her carry-on inside. "It'll be fine." She pulled open the single drawer on the nightstand to find nothing but a few restaurant flyers. "It will have to do."

The concierge at the hotel had been of no help. Concerned that her name might pop up on some type of registry if she booked into a different hotel, Amy had considered how else to stay hidden.

Recalling students doing work on laptops in most locations where they ate or drank, she asked one of them at a Tim Horton's coffee shop where to find a place to stay. It led to a student-housing application that she downloaded to her phone and registered on.

A simple glance allowed her to take in the full room. Her focus landed on a small dresser with one of its four drawers jutting out, screaming black and blues.

*Lizzie would be happy here—maybe.*

Matt separated the two pieces of cloth covering the single window, turned to her, crossed his arms, and stood without saying a word.

Taking his silence as disapproval, she said, "I won't be here long. I spoke with Detective Peters this morning about the break-in at Bonnie's. He's thinking it might have something to do with my time in DC. Maybe because I agreed to testify. I didn't want to tell him it's more likely connected to my time in Hawaii. He's on my case enough as is. I assured him I'd be back in a couple of days."

Amy shoved her suitcase next to the dresser, annoyed at having made the promise. She hated the thought of having to leave without learning more here first. She had delayed calling Detective Peters for as long as she could, well aware he would have questions about why she left for Toronto.

Matt said, "Right or left?"

Amy took her annoyance out on the protruding drawer. With some force, she lifted it and tried to shove it into place before discovering the track for the drawer had been ripped off. Amy snapped at him. "What are you talking about? Right or left? On or off? Do you even know how to conjugate full sentences?"

He seemed unfazed by her outburst. "Which side of the bed do you want?"

Feeling bulletproof, she said, "Why? You're not staying here. I don't need you to babysit me. Besides, there's only one bed."

"Did you think I was just going to let you hang out here alone?"

"As a matter of fact, yes. I did."

Seconds later, realizing she would be grateful for the company, she said, "I thought you were going to keep your room at the hotel."

He shrugged. "I didn't check out. Let them think I'm still there." He slid closed the white, almost translucent curtains and switched on the light.

"And where do you intend to sleep?"

"On the other side of whichever half you tell me you want. We can both be adults about this. Can't we?"

His words made her realize the source of her irritation. It was the promise to return to DC that gnawed at her. It limited the amount of time she could remain here. Time, that precious commodity she needed more of.

In a conciliatory tone, she said, "Either side will be fine."

"We need to be smart about this," Matt said. "From now on, no more open doors. We need to be careful when we're out. Check around to see if anyone's following us before we return here." His words were firm, authoritative, like when they were on Niihau. "Did you put my number on speed dial?"

"Yes. I removed the others. At least for the time being. I'll reset my favorites when I get back home."

"I'm heading to the hotel to pick up a few more things. I'll be back in a little while."

"You can take the key," Amy said. "Don't worry. I'll be fine, and the door will be locked."

Before leaving, he grabbed it and said, "Don't wait up."

Hours later, Matt entered a room in total darkness: the shade down, the curtains closed, and the single light off. Amy was in bed, but awake. He stripped off his jeans and shirt and crawled in quietly beside her, their backs to each other. Matt's breathing slowed seconds after he settled in. A minute later, she heard him snoring, apparently possessing the rare gift to be able to sleep on demand.

With his return, Amy slipped into dreamland and back to the streets of DC as Lizzie. In front of her stood Luis Rodriguez. His knife in his hand. The blade glinted in the bright sunlight. Fear paralyzed her.

She knew what came next.

The blade would be thrust into her, and she would be gutted like a deer.

# Chapter Forty-Two

## Student Housing

## Toronto, Canada

MATT SPRANG OUT OF bed. He flew to her side, shaking her awake before her blood-curdling scream ended. "Wake up. Wake up. Wake up!"

Amy's eyes opened to find him leaning over her, his hands gripping her shoulders. Dazed and trembling, she said, "Sorry. I must have been dreaming."

Straightening, he stared down. "I wouldn't call that dreaming."

Amy fumbled to untangle the twisted sheets. Still twitching, she managed to maneuver to a sitting position at the edge of the bed. Her tank top and pajama shorts were soaked with sweat.

Matt retrieved his duffel, picked through it, and drew out two rolled items. He brought them to her. "Here. Take these. They're clean. More importantly, they're dry."

She rose and extended an unsteady hand for them. Seeing her shivering lips and chin, he pulled her close, surprised at how her earlier facade of grit and bravado had evaporated. She reminded him of a lost child in a refugee camp. He held her in a bear hug of an embrace until her trembling stopped.

He moved his hands to her shoulders and took a step back. His t-shirt now dampened, he attempted to meet her downcast eyes, which wouldn't rise to meet his. He squeezed and gave her a shake. "Listen to me. The sheets are soaked. Take a hot shower. Then come back and use the other side of the bed."

Releasing her, he added, "That's what I do."

She gave him a silent nod. With a lowered head and slumped shoulders, he watched her walk away like an athlete in defeat.

When she returned, Matt lay spread out in front of the dresser, his pillow on the floor and his hands behind his head. His curiosity about her nightmare at a fever pitch. "So, do you want to tell me what that was all about?"

"When I posed as Lizzie, the homeless woman I told you about... I witnessed two gang members talking one moment and then... They were off to my side when... When I heard a horrific sound. A sound I'll never forget. I turned toward them. I saw one of them pulling out a blood-soaked knife, and the other falling to the ground covered in blood. I don't remember much else."

Neither spoke for a few minutes. He watched her spread out her wet clothes atop the nightstand before stepping around him, smelling of flowers. As he had suggested, she rearranged the bedding, moving the wet section of sheet aside before crawling in on the side he had occupied.

"Thanks for the suggestion. The shower felt good." After a long silence, she said, "Move to the other side. Is that what you said you do?"

After another long silence, Matt spoke in a quiet voice. "Danny. A gentle soul I served with. He always talked about *his girl*. How he missed his girl. Loved his girl. How he couldn't wait to get back and see her. He loved her. And horses."

Matt smiled, touched by the memory. "I asked him her name. When he told us *Thunder,* we realized his girl *was* a horse. We showed him no mercy. Couldn't let that one go. Teased the life out of him. One day, he received a letter from home saying his girl was pregnant, about to give birth to a foal. You would think he was having a kid of his own."

Matt stopped.

"Please," Amy said, "go on."

It took a while before he said, "We were at camp in an area considered friendly. We started taking sniper fire. The first shot hit our cook, who was dumping water a few steps away from camp. Danny scurried to him to pull him back. The next shot hit what looked to be a rock."

The quiet in the room sounded deafening, not even the tick of a clock to break it. "What happened?"

"It exploded. Sending shrapnel in all directions, a large piece sliced away a portion of Danny's head. For a few moments, the force of the explosion had him hanging in mid-air—minus the top of his skull. The whole thing took place in slow motion. The frantic expression on his face is immortalized forever in my brain. I don't think I got any sleep for months. Pictured his face every time I closed my eyes. Soaked sheets became a standard nighttime ritual for me."

"How did you get over it?"

"You don't. You've got a busy day tomorrow. What do you say we get some sleep?"

# Chapter Forty-Three

## Student Housing

## Toronto Canada

*I THINK WE SHOULD TALK in person about this.* Amy stared at her mother's cryptic response to her email request for information on Joey Stratford and his company. Although she found it odd, she appreciated having something else to take the focus off her embarrassment at last night's outburst.

After reading it aloud to Matt, he said, "Give her a call. There must be a reason."

Although early on the West Coast, Amy knew her workaholic mother would answer. "Hi sweetheart. How is Canada?"

"Fine, but before we go any further, you are on speaker. I'm here with a friend who wants to listen to this too. His name is Matt."

"Well hello, Matt. Amy, I don't understand. I got the impression from your father that you are in Toronto for a job. I didn't realize you're vacationing."

"Not a vacation mom. We're here trying to..." Amy gave Matt a perplexed look.

He took over. "Mrs. Pryce, it's a pleasure to speak with you. We're here because..."

"Mrs. Pryce? Well, Amy, he sounds polite. I'm guessing I won't need to worry about you this time." Those words struck an awkward chord with Amy. They didn't talk often, and with the geographic and emotional distance between them, she never considered that her mother worried about her. Living apart all these years, Amy assumed her mother wasn't invested in her—or her dad.

"Mom, you don't have to. Everything is fine. We are following up on something we found in Hawaii. Nothing dangerous. Just some research." The expression on her face told Matt she intentionally wanted to downplay the situation.

"Well, sweetheart, as you asked, I dug into Stratford Industries. They are a well-established company and are indeed planning on issuing an IPO."

Matt asked, "Can you explain what that means?"

"Of course. an IPO stands for *An Initial Public Offering.* It indicates they will begin selling shares of the company they own to the public. The company will then be listed on a stock exchange. Private companies take this route—go public—when they need to raise a great deal of money, most times for expansion or to start a new line. Something major where they need to bring in a large amount of additional funds."

"I had lunch with the CEO," Matt said, "and he talked about starting to sell snowboards in addition to the custom skis they now make."

"The offering says as much. A new product line is a safe bet on what they want the money for. IPOs bring in millions of dollars, sometimes hundreds of millions, depending on how many shares are sold and the price they go for."

"Excuse me," Matt said, "but he made it sound like they are already rolling in cash."

"I'm sure you realize you can't believe everything you hear. They exaggerate in more ways than anyone can imagine." She laughed. "I'm OK with it, though, because they keep me busy trying to figure out what they are saying, or, more likely, not saying."

"But Amy, here is why I wanted to talk to you. I dove into the offering as if I were researching this for a client who intended to invest. I'm involved with an audit at one of the banks they deal with, so I procured some of their actual records in addition to the information in the IPO."

Amy said, "Is that legal, Mom?" Amy surprised herself with her question, realizing she didn't know the full extent of what her mother's job encompassed.

"Yes, dear, it is. I'm surprised you're asking, but think about this: if you do an audit, you must have access to everything. How else could you verify that what they are reporting is accurate?"

"Mom, I'm only teasing. I would never challenge your integrity."

"I know, sweetheart."

The phone went silent. Matt raised his eyebrows as the silence lingered. Amy shrugged and asked, "Is everything OK, Mom?"

"Yes. Of course. I got off track for a moment. I had a bout of melancholy talking with you, but professional mom is back now." She cleared her throat. "I was going through the data, and I applied some filters as I always do, scanning for the atypical item. Well, I didn't find anything unusual until I filtered the data by SWIFT codes. Then I picked up an anomaly. Some of the company's larger payouts, which I assume were payments for purchases, were returned."

"Mom, I have to stop you. What are you talking about? What's a SWIFT code?"

"Oh, a number each bank is assigned for transferring money to different countries. Think of each bank as having an identifying ID. Does that make it easier?"

"Yes. I got it. So, from the code, you can follow which banks the money goes to. Is that what you are saying?"

"Yes. However, the anomaly I found in the filtered data is that the same SWIFT codes were being used in reverse transactions soon after. That's very odd."

"I don't understand. In English, please."

"I found several recent transactions of millions of dollars transferred out. A short time later, those exact, or similar, amounts came back to the same bank. For example, if they prepaid for raw materials and if the order got canceled or the product didn't arrive up to spec, the money might be returned. But it wouldn't happen so soon."

"I'm not sure I understand," Amy offered. "But, are you sure?"

"Sweetheart, are you doubting your mother?"

"Me, Mom? Never." Amy's confidence came from her youth, when the three of them still lived together as a family. Memories of missed meals, school events, and being picked up on time solidified the level of her mother's dedication and investment in her work. To the exclusion of most everything else—including them.

"It's not normal, which is why I find the data suspect. Why I wanted to point this out and alert you to the fact that something isn't right. I don't have the entire picture yet, but something is strange. I'll dig some more and get back to you. I can tell you this, though: if this were for a client, I'd advise them to be cautious."

"Thanks, Mom. We'll talk soon." Years' worth of conflicting feelings flashed through Amy. Now was not the time for the long-overdue career-over-family conversation. But she promised herself it would happen soon.

Before clicking off, her mother said, "And don't forget to call your father. He's been asking if I heard from you."

After promising she would, Matt said, "I didn't sense any of the stress you implied your mom is always under. She didn't sound abrupt or distant or uninvolved. Not at all the picture I got from you."

"How did you picture her?"

"A no-nonsense taskmaster. Aloof, self-interested, narcissistic."

"I never used those words."

"No, but an absent, workaholic parent with sporadic phone calls and infrequent visits, and only when it fit her schedule, says the same thing."

His description further cemented the necessity for the long-put-off call about her mother's nonpresence in their lives.

Matt had moved to a reclining position, lying stretched out on the bed, staring at the ceiling. "More and more, I smell skunk with everything surrounding this Stratford guy. Including the clinic. I realize you want to dig deeper into this, but I think it's getting a little too dangerous."

"Well, I'm not stopping. I want to get a better look at the file."

"Amy, I'm not asking you to quit. I'm in your corner. But I think you should call in sick today. I'll make you a deal." He propped himself up on his elbow. "Spend the day with me, and I'll help you retrieve the copies tonight."

"Oh, really?" She asked, "And how do you think you are going to do that?" He flummoxed her. On one hand, he could be kind—loaning her his dry clothes last night.

"I'll explain when I get back."

Or, he could be cocky and confident—like now, delaying her efforts to find the answers to Wilhelm's captivity.

"First, I'm going to grab us some breakfast."

She couldn't decide whether she welcomed it or resented it. She had come this far and wasn't ready to quit. But she realized she couldn't remain here too much longer.

With him gone, Amy gathered up all the damp clothing and headed down to the basement, where she had access to a communal laundry area. As she waited for the wash and dry cycles to complete, she reflected on Matt's story about Danny, again warming toward him.

With the laundered items dry and folded, she returned upstairs, culled hers out, and lifted his duffel to replace his. The zipper snagged as she yanked to close it. She tore away a piece of paper that had lodged itself between the teeth, freeing the jam. She pulled out the balance of the torn sheet, straightened it, intending to replace it, when a word caught her eye.

A word she had only become familiar with on her first day in Hawaii. Sandwiched between others in a long column that ran down the edge of the sheet, she spotted a word she would never forget.

She unfolded the sheet to reveal a flight log. One similar to the one she had signed for Matt for her tour. Amongst multiple entries for Kauai, Oahu, and Maui, the word Niihau stood out like an unwelcome virus.

The column's caption: *destination*. She checked the other headings, finding one labeled: *pilot's signature*. Amy scanned across the sheet and recognized the scribble immediately—as her world catapulted into a tailspin.

Matt never checked with the other pilots to determine who ferried Wilhelm to Niihau. He knew who it was.

Because it was him.

# Chapter Forty-Four

## College Room-sharing House

## Toronto, Canada

MATT CONNERS WAITED in line to pick up breakfast sandwiches for himself and Amy, pondering ways to get rid of her. Amy had followed him to Canada to investigate the unexplainable on Niihau. He had no doubt her interest was as strong as his.

But for different reasons.

Which meant she had to go.

But first, he wanted to see the contents of the Stratford File. He'd need her help to get it. Which meant he had to keep her occupied until he could retrieve it along with her.

Returning with the food and coffee, Matt laid out his plan. "Yesterday, you told me the clinic is open twenty-four hours to handle emergencies for Devereux clients. We'll head there tonight, after hours, go up to where you're working, and get a better look at the file."

Amy said, "That might be a problem. I don't have an identification badge yet. Stacey said she'd issue me one today. I also had to be escorted by a guard to her office. I couldn't go up alone."

"My guess is it was because you were new and not familiar with the place. Not as part of a normal routine. Don't forget, I'll be with you. If that's the case, I'll find a way to distract the guard. Let's not worry about it until tonight. My meeting with Andy, the person at Stratford who is to connect me with their contact at SSI, isn't until tomorrow. What do you want to do today? I don't think we should hang around here."

"Fine with me. I'd rather be outdoors. And moving around always helps."

Matt thought for a while. "Well, I told Joey I wanted to stay and take a couple of days to tour Toronto, so how about we take in the sights? We can start at the CN Tower."

# Chapter Forty-Five

## Home of Eunice & Joey Stratford

## Toronto, Canada

"WHY DO WE HAVE TO WAIT for the IPO?" Eunice was rubbing Joey's arm with long strokes. "I thought you said everybody you needed to talk to and everything you had to put in writing was finished. What's left to do?"

Joey crossed to the refrigerator and pulled out a soda. He raised the bottle in the air, checking if she would like one. She nodded. He withdrew two and handed her one.

He removed the cap, poured it into a large glass, and watched it form a foamy head. "It won't be long. I promise you. I just can't leave before Monday morning. I need to make an appearance at the stock exchange when it opens and then attend a breakfast that follows. Then I'm free."

He took two sips of his drink and went to the sink, spilling the balance down the drain, leaving the empty glass on the counter.

Eunice observed him, confused. "Darling, why do you always do that? I'd be happy to share one with you. You know I'm careful about my weight."

"Because, my love, I can. As a kid, my father always kept soft drinks in the little fridge behind the bar. I wasn't allowed to take anything from it." He crossed to her, encircling her in his arms. "So, if I wanted one with dinner, or for whatever reason, I would have to ask. It was a rare occasion when he would let a request pass without a lecture on how soda is a special treat and should be viewed as such. He said I needed to be aware of and understand someone had worked to obtain the money necessary to purchase it."

Joey snorted. "My father would repeat the same speech each time. Then he would add that his father had impressed this important lesson on him, and he was passing it on to me. When he finished, I couldn't even enjoy the whole can. He would split the drink with me."

Eunice leaned into him, their noses almost touching, her arms resting on his upper chest.

"I doubt he even wanted the stupid drink. I hated having to beg while all my friends had soda whenever they wanted."

She nestled in closer, very aware of his need for affection. Something she guessed he had been denied as a youth. She knew his insecurities well and catered to them.

"Now, it's a reminder to me. I am my own boss, and I can do whatever I want."

Staring into his eyes, she snuggled closer, agreeing and reassuring him. "You can. Of course, you can. And I aim to see you get to do just that. We both will for the rest of our lives together. Consider it a promise."

# Chapter Forty-Six

## Downtown Toronto

## Toronto, Canada

A SKY FULL OF GRAY clouds greeted Amy and Matt as they stepped out of the cab at the base of the CN Tower. The pall over the area matched Amy's dreary mood. This morning's discovery about Matt walloped her, shaking her to the core. It had her analyzing and questioning everything about him.

And herself.

*What am I doing here? I'm disappointing my father. My best friend, too.*

*I'm in a foreign country, where I don't belong, planning on copying, or, to be more accurate, stealing records.*

*With a man who's lying to me. Why? Because I was duped by him? By what? His friendly wink?*

*Is he part of this? Whatever this is.*

*I need to confront him about Wilhelm.*

*I need to go home.*

At an empty ticket counter, Matt dished out his usual charm to a young female attendant. "Do we need reservations for lunch?"

She responded with a wide smile, revealing perfect teeth. "Yes. Although I wouldn't recommend it today. The view won't be great because of the weather."

"What about the observation area?"

"Not great on a day like today either. But it's worth seeing if you've never seen it before."

He purchased two tickets. In the confined space of the elevator, Amy stood on the opposite side—as far away as possible from him. She bit her lower lip, suppressing a scream, finding it difficult to be in his company.

When it reached the top, she let him exit first, then headed in the opposite direction. Amy meandered around the two-level observation deck for a time before pausing at a spot where the railing brought her almost level with the low-lying clouds.

Matt found her staring at the miniature-looking city below. "It's a shame we couldn't have lunch today. It would have been nice to see the whole thing from the same seat at the restaurant while the building did a full 360." He leaned over and stared down.

"It's not that we couldn't have lunch," Amy countered, keeping her focus on the world below. "It's just very overcast today, and the view wouldn't be great. But thanks for the offer." Unwilling to look at him, she continued wrestling with how to approach him about the log she found in his duffel.

"You should never pass up an opportunity," Matt said, straightening and sounding disappointed. "Who knows if we'll ever be here again?" He stepped back from the railing. "I'm going to check out the wall with the heights of the world's tallest buildings. Interested?"

"No. Thanks. I'm fine here." Amy returned to the self-analysis raging within.

*I had a fantastic gift. Five years of freedom.*

Her thoughts returned to the irony of her father's gift. He had intended to provide her with memorable experiences at a young age when she would derive the most from them. Those five years had given her a lot, but they had cost her, too.

Her first dose of reality hit when Bonnie explained that she had to plead and vouch for Amy—even to secure a temporary assignment with the company. The HR Department there deemed her unacceptable, questioning why a college graduate could show no period of steady income for the five years after graduation.

During those years, her peers had begun their careers. Several had advanced in their chosen professions. Once, if not twice. Most had married or were involved in long-term relationships. Many had started families. There was a race to be run after college. She had been given a pass at starting. A good thing at the time. For the moment, she wished she had not waited and had instead entered the race with her peers.

Matt returned, interrupting her thoughts. "It's early. There's an aquarium next door. What do you think?"

"Sure," she said, stalling, not quite ready for the necessary conversation.

After a few hours of wandering separately through the aquarium's exhibits—which only extended the awkwardness between them—Amy found Matt waiting for her at the exit. "What do you say we head back, grab something to eat, and go get that file?"

AS THEY WALKED TO THE transit station, their path led them past the Metro Toronto Convention Centre, their silence deafening. When they turned onto Lower Simcoe Street, Amy's pace reflexively slowed.

Pointing up, Matt said, "Look at that. We could've walked inside from the Metro Centre. It looks like it takes you right to the station." Above them, the Metro Centre's enclosed walkway spanned the length of the busy street and sidewalks below. Huge pillars supported the walkway.

Amy stopped, taking in her surroundings with shock and surprise.

On the sidewalk, between the pillars, a four-foot concrete guardrail connecting the pillars formed a wall, separating the sidewalk from the street on either side. The shelter from the weather above and the security of the wall—which acted as a barrier from the noise, exhaust, and danger of the passing street traffic—drew in the homeless. They occupied every available bit of space between the pillars. Their meager possessions were tucked in behind them, positioned against the guardrail.

Amy stood transfixed, watching as a young girl, no older than ten, unzipped a pop-up tent and got out, along with an older man. The youngster asked, "Can I give it to Grandma when we see her?"

Matt had not stopped walking. He had reached the end of the block. Noticing that Amy wasn't with him, he hustled back and said, "It's sad. But there's nothing we can do about this."

An unusual, yet powerful, confidence ignited in Amy. She didn't respond.

"Amy, you have that faraway look in your eyes. Forget about this. This is not our problem. I know you want to, but you can't fix the whole world."

"Cover me."

"Cover you? What are you talking about?"

"Stand in front of me so they can't see me if they turn around."

"Who?"

"Them." Amy pointed to the man and girl who, by now, had reached the corner Matt had just returned from. Amy bent down and unzipped the U-shaped arc opening for the tent. She pulled the flap down and peered inside.

"What are you doing? Take your hand out. Yuck. Don't touch anything."

Amy knelt, pressing her hand inside, fumbling through items at arm's reach. "I'm surprised you're so squeamish," she said. Ignoring his advice, she stuck her arm in further, fingering items tucked into the farthest corners.

"What are you doing?"

"Practicing for tonight." Inside the tent, her hand locked on a small flat item. She pulled out a notepad. Flipping through the pages, she saw drawings of buildings, wondering if they were places where the young girl had spent time. She closed it, ready to put it back, when it slipped from her fingers. It landed with the back cover splayed open. It contained a name and address, printed in childlike lettering. *Mrs. Sherry Winters and an Ontario address. Grandma?*

Amy snapped a picture of it and replaced it as near as she could to where she had found it before zipping the tent closed and standing. Finished, she scurried away, not waiting for Matt, requiring him to hustle to catch up to her.

When he reached her, she turned and glared at him. "You're right, Matt. I can't fix the whole world. But I can fix the wrongs *that I* come across in it. Wilhelm wasn't my problem either, but now he is safe at home with his family. What would have happened to him if I had not pursued it with Kalani? And now, before I leave here, I want to know what the connection is and why they did that to him."

Matt knew when to keep quiet. They continued in silence to the station. When they reached it, she grabbed the door and held it open for him. "If this winds up being a waste of time... So be it. At least I tried."

# Chapter Forty-Seven

## Devereux Clinic

## Toronto Canada

"I'M SORRY IT'S TAKEN me so long to stop by and check out the work you do here. I've planned on it for a while now, but we've been so busy," Susan said to Hillary Whitley as she entered her large and spacious office. Susan wondered how much information she would obtain from the woman, and how aware she was of what had taken place right under her nose.

Hillary stood to greet her, coming around the desk with a hand extended. "It's a pleasure." Motioning Susan to the far side of the office toward a small table with inlaid ceramic, Susan registered how at ease Hillary appeared. She took it as a positive sign. That helped lessen the migraine, which had been her constant companion the last few days.

Before leaving her office, Susan learned Dr. Zoric is Croatian. He had migrated to Canada as a student. He stayed to further his education, completed all the necessary steps, and graduated as a specialist in heart surgery. He practiced for two years at Toronto General before opening up Devereux, a private facility catering to those who could afford him. The clinic concentrated on facelifts, tummy tucks, and other elective procedures. Apparently, the doctor found rearranging people's faces more rewarding than fixing hearts.

Taking a seat, Hillary said, "Well, you're here now. Tell me what I can do for you."

Susan chose one of the swivel chairs, settled in, and said, "I would like to follow up on the bills we received from you for the care of the Stratford children."

"It's so sad, wouldn't you say?" Hillary glanced away. Susan waited as Hillary took a needed moment. "We are so sorry we couldn't save them. At least one of the boys." She stayed silent for another few breaths, then shrugged and stiffened. "But regardless of how trained our staff is, or how advanced medicine is, some things still don't work. The Stratfords are handling the whole situation quite well, I think. Don't you?"

Wanting to avoid a discussion of them, but not wanting to appear rude, Susan said, "I'm not sure, but I understand they are. About the charges..."

"I'll have to dig into the matter. You should have received a detailed list, an item-by-item explanation." Her hands went up with flared palms, appearing astonished at the oversight. "I'll check with accounting and make sure you receive one."

"What I'm specifically questioning is the largest of them, the ones for the blood. I also want to follow up on how it arrived. Who signed for the delivery? How you paid them? But, most of all, who provided the blood?"

"Who provided it?" Hillary fell deeper into her seat as if blown against its back. "We don't know. I'm shocked Michael Shore hasn't shared the story of how we procured it with you."

Susan held her disappointment in check as Hillary's wide eyes stared back at her. "I overheard Joey tell him he received a text, which Joey opened and showed us. The gist of which said the person had the blood the boys required and was willing to provide it for a price. If he agreed, Joey needed to respond YES to the message, and he would receive further instructions."

Hillary shrugged as if what she just described could be considered routine behavior. "Once Joey agreed, he received the specifics. We received a sample, analyzed it, and the blood turned out to be legitimate. My understanding is he paid for a portion and asked you for the additional funds needed."

The woman's cavalier attitude elevated the dull throb behind Susan's forehead to a full-blown pounding. She made it sound as if millions of dollars being doled out for a pint of blood was as common as someone being short the necessary change for a candy bar. Susan couldn't stay quiet with that.

"You must recognize extortion when you see it. Few people would have the resources to cover the blood's exorbitant cost. That's extortion, and I intend to discover the source."

"Fine with me. I'll give you whatever you need." Hillary's assurances and steady voice allowed Susan's pounding to return to a level where the veins on her forehead weren't pulsating. "But I don't think you'll learn much. The source isn't a traditional supplier of ours. We warned both Joey and Eunice the blood needed to be processed and transported properly, or it could pose a danger to the children. But, in reality, their situation was so dire, whatever dangers came with the risk... That blood was the only thing offering them a ray of hope. The boys were dead otherwise."

"Yes. But someone still profited—extorted us—by selling the blood, and I want to make sure something like this doesn't happen again."

"Understood." Hillary rose. "You can count on my full support. I will go through the records myself, speak to the staff at the surgical center where all our blood products are delivered, and find out whose signature is on the paperwork. Whatever they tell me, I'll be glad to pass on to you."

Relieved Hillary seemed so willing to cooperate, Susan stood as well. "Thank you. No matter how small the detail, any bit of information might be important. Anything you can provide will be appreciated and I'll want to talk to them myself if you don't mind."

"Not at all. But I'm confused. The committee is not going to abide by the Stratfords' request not to pursue the matter?"

"Let's just say I'm following this up on my own."

Susan registered Hillary's surprise. Ignoring it, she headed for the door, turned, and said, "I didn't see your assistant here when I came in. Is she out?"

"Called in sick today," Hillary said, reaching her and sounding frustrated. "Finding dedicated employees is one of the most difficult parts of my job."

Susan commiserated. "How disappointing." With Hillary's willingness to help, Susan now viewed her as an ally. She decided to trust her and shared her suspicions. "When I stopped in and left my card with her, she acted a tad bit jumpy when I interrupted her filing."

"Filing?" Hillary sounded confused. "I had given her some entries to work on. I didn't give her any filing to do."

"Really? Because she shooed me away from the door, telling me the room had to remain locked. I saw the filing cabinets inside and assumed she had been filing."

Hillary took a step forward and grabbed Susan's arm. "Can you show me exactly where she was?"

Pulling away from the unexpected physicality, Susan led her to the adjoining space and pointed to the door with the keypad.

Hillary asked, "Inside? With the door open?"

"Yes. I'm guessing she wasn't supposed to be in there?"

"No, not at all." Susan thought she witnessed a flame flicker in Hillary's eyes. "Thanks. I'll dig into this."

Susan made a spur-of-the-moment decision. She had intended the copy of Hector's report on Amy to be used in a different manner, but now she reasoned it might also be of interest to Hillary. Gambling it would solidify a good working relationship in determining the source of the blood, she said, "Hillary, don't ask why, but I had my reasons for looking into Amy."

Susan pulled out the copy, not at all surprised by Hillary's questioning look. "Here, this might help answer any questions you have about her. In the meantime, I'll await the information on how the blood arrived and who you paid for it."

HILLARY'S PHONE WAS at her ear the moment the elevator doors closed around Susan. "We've got to talk. No, it can't wait. Now. Right now. Where can I meet you?"

# Chapter Forty-Eight

## Student Housing

## Toronto Canada

"TELL THE GUARD YOU'RE new. You forgot something in your office, and you have to retrieve it. An umbrella, for instance." Amy was listening to Matt describing his plan for copying the file. After their day of sightseeing, they returned to the rented room. Amy still had not confronted him about flying Wilhelm to Niihau.

"And I need to have it tonight, because what?" Amy asked. "I can't wait until tomorrow?"

"Yeah. Bad example. Make it some papers, your iPad, or laptop." He searched around. "Here..." He grabbed a supermarket bag, dumping the remnants from their takeout in the trash. "Use this for the copies." Amy accepted it, squashed all the air out of the thin plastic, and shoved it in her pocket.

"Just make it quick. Get in. Do as many as possible. Put two or three items on the copier at a time. Take snaps with your phone of what you can. At any sign of a problem, just leave everything as it is and hightail it out. Don't worry about putting it back unless you have the time. Got it?"

"Yes."

"I need you to make me believe it."

She gave him a shove backward, the force behind the harder-than-necessary push due more to her frustration with him than to show she understood. "Back off, bossy boy. I've been in jams far greater than this. Much more than you can imagine."

He seemed satisfied. "That's more like it. I'll distract the guard. I'm sure I'll find some common ground with him. Just remember, I'll have my phone in my pocket, set to your number. If I sense a problem, I'll hit send, and you'll get a text from me. If you do, you're out of there in an instant."

"Got it. I'll be fine. You just worry about yourself."

Matt grunted.

THEY ARRIVED AT THE clinic to an almost empty parking lot.

At the entrance doors, Matt peered inside. A TV perched high on one wall displayed a news channel. A young girl with her head tilted back lounged in a plastic-molded chair with her feet atop another, which she had positioned in front of her.

Matt pulled on the glass door. The rattle alerted the female guard. She jolted up, came over, and unlocked it, but only opened the door a bit. She made no move to let them enter.

"Hi. I'm Amy Pryce. I work here. For Hillary Whitley. I'm sorry to bother you, but I need to retrieve some papers I'm working on. I should have taken them with me to finish up the report at home."

Matt pinched her side to indicate she was speaking too fast. Something he noticed she did when nervous. He also noted the guard eying her with suspicion.

After a quick breath, and at a more relaxed rate, she said, "I'm new here. I just started, and I'm so mad at myself." She pouted. "But I didn't feel well, and I just needed to leave."

It seemed like an eternity, but the guard finally said, "No worries."

"Sounds like you're Australian," Amy said, speaking with more confidence now that the guard had fully opened the door for them. "I love your accent."

"Didn't know I had one," the guard said. "Hang on a tick. What was your last name again?"

Matt waited beside her as the agile twenty-something girl walked behind a sleek, modern black-glass desk, picked up a tablet, and made a few entries. Matt squeezed Amy's arm in a show of support.

"P-R-Y-C-E."

"Okay. I've got you. I'll take you up," the guard said as she came around from the back of the desk.

Amy gave Matt an I-told-you-so look. "I don't want to bother you. I'll only be a minute."

"Rules, mate," she said.

Matt spoke up. "Not my business, but if you're about to leave this area, you might want to relock that front door."

The girl glanced at Matt and then changed direction toward it. Matt gave Amy *his* version of a smug *I-told-you-so* retort as he motioned for her to leave. She scurried away, bounding up the stairs.

A few minutes later, Amy bounced down the stairwell. She rushed into the lobby, cradling a package under her arm. Matt and the guard were engrossed in an intense conversation. The girl's attention focused entirely on him.

Without stopping, Amy passed them, headed for the exit. Over her shoulder, she yelled, "Wow, that felt super. I enjoy using the stairs a couple of times a day. Exercise is so great, am I right?"

Amy reached the door, turned the thumb lock, and shouted a "Thank you," to the guard and an "Are you coming?" to Matt.

Outside, they hurried away, walking briskly toward the transit stop, eager to put space between them and the clinic. Matt said, "That was fast. You know I had this. I could have kept her busy for hours. At least."

"What makes you think that?"

"She was into me. Couldn't you tell?"

Amy halted in mid-step, stymied by his attitude. She moved the pilfered bundle to her chest, wrapped her arms around it, and gaped at him. "Really?"

It forced him to stop as well. Pushing even further, he said, "Hey. We could have made a night of it. She gave me her number."

"Unbelievable," Amy said, shaking her head.

With a cocky smile, Matt turned and resumed walking, waving her on. "Come on," he yelled back to her. She reached him after a few steps. "What have you got there? You couldn't have managed to make that many copies."

"No time for slow copiers. The file was several inches thick. I grabbed the front half. This should be enough to get us started. Don't you think?"

# Chapter Forty-Nine

## Loose Moose Bar

## Toronto Canada

AFTER HER SUCCESSFUL meeting with Hillary, Susan decided lunch should be her reward. The Loose Moose, a favorite restaurant and bar, was on her route back to the train station. She entered and asked for a table—ignoring her normal place at the bar—opting instead for solitary time to contemplate her next moves.

The host led her to a seat that faced the back half of three cows. Their posteriors protruded from the wall in front of her. A strip of blackboard spanned the area beneath their hooves and tails. Under each bovine's buttocks, chalk scribblings called out individuals, employees, or customers for their bad behaviors. She was reading the accusations when her phone rang.

"Hey, what are you up to?" Frank's introductory question, the initial one he opened with before moving on to the real reason for his call, still sounded so familiar.

But today she found his call intrusive, her feelings toward him strained. "Not much. What do you want?"

"Have you heard from Mike?"

"Hang on." She adjusted her phone, minimized its screen, scanned her texts and missed calls, and returned it to her ear. "Nope. Nothing from him. Why?"

"I did. He's furious. Said you are looking into the Stratfords for some reason. Is he correct?"

"Um, not the Stratfords exactly. Why the surprise? You realize I don't intend to drop the blood issue, right?"

A waiter lingered at a reasonable distance. Susan waved him over.

"Frank, can you hold on a minute?"

As someone who had always struggled with weight, she intended today's lunch to be an indulgence she did not give in to often. She ordered a drink and one of their Epic Burgers—their description, not hers—although it was accurate. After checking to ensure it came with a side of fries, she returned to the call.

She exhaled in exasperation. "Like we always say, Frank, bad news travels fast. How did he find out?"

"No idea, but he isn't happy. I assumed he would have reached out to you by now."

"Are you calling to warn me or just add to my misery?"

"I *do* miss working with you." She pictured him shaking his head and smiling. "I'm calling for a different reason."

She registered his forceful exhale at the other end as if struggling with something. Susan kept silent, neither questioning him nor making any comment to relieve his discomfort.

"I can't let the blood issue go either, Susan. The other day, when we were trying to figure out who would be able to put all the pieces of the blood puzzle together, you mentioned blood banks, which struck a chord. I remembered something about someone at Devereux spending time at a blood bank, but I couldn't recall who. I went back through the notes I had for their personnel. I was right. Guess who?"

"I don't want to guess. Just tell me."

"Hillary Whitley. She did an internship one summer at, wait for it..." After a brief silence, "A blood bank in Switzerland, where she could have gained information about this rare blood type the children needed."

"But still..." her thoughts stalled as she considered this new information before uttering, "Thank you."

"For what?"

"My waiter just brought me my wine. How long ago did Mike ask you about me delving into the Stratfords?"

"A half hour ago. Maybe a little less. Why?"

Susan took a sip of her Cabernet. "Because I met with Hillary this morning. After our meeting, I came straight here for lunch. The walk took me about thirty-five, forty minutes. She seemed cooperative when I spoke with her, but obviously, word got back to Mike."

"Well, that is interesting," Frank said, before moving on and updating her on different projects they had been working on before her ouster. When he realized she wasn't participating, he returned to the reason for his call. "I'm surprised you haven't gotten a text or call from Mike."

Susan smirked. "My guess is he's not calling *me* because he's too busy riling up the other members to chuck me completely off the board. Thanks for the heads-up."

"I can't believe it. I'm at a loss as to what to say..."

"Say happy eating, Frank. My food is here."

Frank's information pivoted her focus away from the Stratfords and straight at Hillary.

Reaching for the burger, her eyes landed on the cow buttocks staring her in the face. She had just given Hector's dossier on Amy to Hillary. *Her* name should be added to that blackboard.

# Chapter Fifty

## Outside the Toronto Train Station

## Toronto Canada

SUSAN LEFT THE LOOSE Moose, anxious to get back to the office. With the new information from Frank about Hillary having done an internship at a blood bank in Switzerland, she wanted to delve into a few more things. She had asked Hector for his findings on Dr. Zoric and Amy, but it was possible that during his investigation into them, he had also gathered data on Hillary.

Hector couldn't do any more work for her per Mike, but she felt confident he would share whatever he already had.

Susan dug out her phone, in anticipation of placing the call as she headed toward Union Station. She took in a long breath of the crisp outside air and found it so refreshing. Especially after the overwhelming beer smell she had inhaled during her epic lunch.

Which was now causing her epic indigestion.

Her discomfort from the indulgent meal caused her to slow her pace. She inhaled another deep breath, glad for the walk. It gave her time to think.

She approached York Street—a horseshoe section of road, only used for U-turns. This useless patch of pavement resulted from a works project that split the existing street when it joined the Metro Toronto Convention Centre to Union Station.

Susan stepped in to cross. A car turned in at a high rate of speed. She snapped out of her thoughts and stumbled, but managed to make it to the safety of the street's center divider before the car flew past behind her. *Maniac. Probably in a hurry because he's lost.*

The driver navigated the turn at the road's bend. That had him headed back toward the street from which he entered. Aware of his urgency, Susan waited in the center for him to pass before continuing.

The four-door sedan began slowing. *Oh, sure. Now he wants directions after almost running me over.* Her guess was correct.

The vehicle came to an abrupt stop when it reached her.

Pedestrians in the area witnessing the strike, if any, would question themselves later. The snatch had been so brazen. The driver made a right onto Front Street, where it had come from, before Susan even started to register what had happened.

She remembered the back door had opened.

But that a man stepped out, grabbed her at the waist, and sucked her into the back seat with him... That was just starting to bloom into comprehension. The seated man held her sprawled across his lap.

Susan began to confront him when everything went black.

# Chapter Fifty-One

## Student Housing

## Toronto, Canada

*WHAT A WASTE OF TIME. Just let me talk to someone at SSI, and I'll get the information we need.* Matt was sitting on the floor using one of the walls for support. He and Amy were hunkered down inside the tiny room with the documents she had swiped. They were spread across every inch of space: the bed, the floor, and even the open, empty dresser drawers that neither Matt nor she had bothered to fill.

Yawning, he stretched his hands above his head. "Have you found anything interesting yet? Because I'm not sure what I'm looking for."

"No," Amy said. "I'm so stiff. I feel like an old lady."

"Drop and give me twenty," he said.

"What?"

"Push-ups. Do them. You'll see. You'll feel better."

She gave him a you-are-out-of-your-mind expression and opened a can of Coke instead. She returned to combing through the contents of the Stratford File. After a while, she said. "I really feel there's something in here. It's staring straight at us. We're just not seeing it. And I can't stay here much longer. I made that promise to Detective Peters, so now I'm running out of time."

"Maybe we should take a break," Matt suggested.

"We can't. We have to stay at it. We've come this far..." She looked around the room, thought for a short while, then said, "Wait. We might be doing this wrong. I first thought we should keep the file in strict order so I could put it back the same as I found it, but now I'm rethinking that. Let's organize all the same types of documents together. Perhaps we'll get a better picture."

They regathered everything that had been laid out in sequence. After re-sorting the papers into groups containing documents of a similar type, they were left with a small number of piles, each for a different category.

Surgical procedures and doctor's notes were combined in one. Invoices and memos were held in another. The labels formed a separate group, as did anything to do with, or from, the Stratford Living Legacy Foundation.

Overlooking their handiwork, Amy said, "Now, let's place each section in chronological order. Put the most recent on top. Oldest on the bottom."

With that done, Amy grabbed a stack. "I'll start with this one."

Matt picked up the papers connected to the foundation and began flipping through them. After scanning quite a few, he let out a low whistle. "You wouldn't believe the amount of money the foundation pays the clinic. I've got receipts here in the millions." Shaking his head in disbelief. "It's just mind-boggling."

Amy put down the pile of procedures she had been mulling over. "Well, I remember coming across them in my research, and I recall they are a charitable company." After giving it a moment's thought, she said, "The clinic might do a lot of charity work, and the foundation supports them for it."

"Hmm. Somehow, I don't think so," Matt said continuing to analyze them. "Each one is just a basic acknowledgment and thank you for the amount donated to the clinic. They don't give any reason for the donation or what it covers."

Convinced he could learn nothing further from the foundation's payments, Matt grabbed the memo pile. As boredom set in, his focus drifted. To Amy. *Palakiko already indicated he wasn't considering her for anything that took place on Kauai, so why is she here?*

As he watched her pore over document after document, he considered, *And why am I here? Because of Wilhelm or because my curiosity has been aroused by a crazy woman?*

He rotated his neck and rubbed his eyes. He closed them, leaned his head against the wall, and said, "I can't wait to get back in the air. Feel some freedom. This here, this room, it's too confining." On the verge of pleading, he said, "What do you say when this is done, we go and do something daring together?"

"What we're doing here isn't dangerous enough for you?"

"Nah, I mean something open and free," Matt said.

"I guess research is just too boring. Is that it?" Amy said, "What about skydiving? That's one of the things on my bucket list." Amy put down the stack in her hands.

"Matt, something's been bothering me. I need to talk to you... To ask..." He opened one questioning eye at her hesitation. The other one remained closed. "Matt,..."

"No, Wait." He blurted. He opened both eyes with a start as his face lit up with a devilish satisfaction. "Tandem parachuting. It's a version of skydiving."

"What?"

"Tandem parachuting," he said again. "It's very safe. You're connected to me with a harness the whole time. I'll be your instructor. I'll guide you through the jump. We'll be strapped together the entire time, starting from the moment we leave the plane all the way through the free fall. I'll teach you how to pilot the canopy. And, of course, how to land. You'll love it. It'll be great!"

"Sure. We can do that."

He could tell by the quiver in her voice she meant *no way*. He bolted upright. "Not a plan. A promise. I want a promise from you." He took one giant step, which brought him to where Amy sat at the edge of the bed. He drew her up. He put out his hand, his fingers curled together, with his pinky arched in the air. "Come on. A pinky promise."

Amy said, "We don't have time for this."

He insisted. "Lock your finger with mine and say the following: '*I promise to go tandem parachuting with you.*'"

Amy relented, linked her pinky with his, and recited, "I promise to go tandem parachuting with you." Then added, "If we are still alive when this is over."

Their pinkies remained locked for a few moments longer than it took Amy to make that promise. When it became awkward, Matt removed his. "You didn't have any crossed fingers, did you? Because that would be a violation. If we're going to make that leap together, there has to be an element of trust."

"Nope. None." Amy answered with a little more color to her cheeks than normal.

Matt caught sight of her flush and retreated to his spot on the floor, hiding his own. "OK. Back to work."

AMY WAS CHASTISING herself for making that promise to Matt when she should be confronting him about the log sheet. However, she hated and avoided confrontations. His signature on the sheet nagged at her. She wanted an answer from him, but she also wanted answers about Wilhelm.

Putting it off, again, at least for the time being, she decided to concentrate on finding some proof of a connection between the clinic and Wilhelm. Other than their suspicion, of course.

Hours droned on as they plowed through their heist. Amy's eyelids drooped. She let them fall and took the opportunity to snatch a few minutes to stop and contemplate what they were doing. It provoked some clarity.

Excited, Amy opened her eyes and said, "I think I may have found something." Looking up, she said, "Or maybe it's what I didn't find."

"What do you mean?"

She held up a handful of documents. "We know Baby A and Baby B needed the Rhnull blood, right? Did you come across anything in any of these records about Rhnull blood?"

Matt shook his head no.

"Like a receipt for it? Or research information on it? Or a donor who provided it? Anything at all about Wilhelm, who we know has it?"

"No. I haven't. I guess that *is* kind of weird."

Amy brought him the documents she had been holding. "These are labels for blood. Lots of them. But these are all for B Positive blood. Why are *they* in the file?"

Matt scanned through them himself. "It's possible they need to mix the null blood with a different type to stretch it." He shrugged. "What if the null blood is concentrated and the positive blood is a base? Since the Rhnull is very scarce, perhaps you add a little of the null, and it makes it all null. Like adding a little chocolate to regular milk and turning it into chocolate milk. That would make sense," he said.

"I don't know." Amy frowned. "We'd have to confirm that. Do you want to do the research or finish going through these papers?"

"You go ahead," Matt said. "You go Google. I'll keep going through the rest of this stuff. I think you might be headed in the right direction, though." Taking her spot on the bed, he returned the pile in his hand to its place and gathered up another.

Amy placed her laptop on the dresser, lifted its lid, and logged in. "OK, I'm on it." With a sly tilt of her head, she turned to him. "Should I research tandem parachuting while I'm at it?"

"What's to know?" Matt winked at her. "I'm on top. You're underneath, and we jump out of a plane."

# Chapter Fifty-Two

## Student Housing

## Toronto, Canada

A FEW HOURS LATER, slapping down the lid of her computer, Amy said, "I hate to be the bearer of bad news, but you can't combine different types of blood. It could kill the patient if they were transfused with the wrong type." Her research had taught her more than she ever cared to know about blood draws, blood types, and everything else blood-related.

Matt had continued poring over the documents. He nodded. "It was worth a shot."

They still hadn't found a connection to Wilhelm. Even after examining and re-examining the documents, ad nauseam. "We've gone through everything several times. We are missing something," Amy said. "We've come this far. I can't leave without..."

Matt rubbed his hands over his face. "I say we review what we know."

Amy picked up a group. "These look like the reports from when the boys were born. There are notes from Dr. Zoric on the condition of each. I don't see a blood type, though."

"What else?"

She chose a different grouping. "These are more of Dr. Zoric's handwritten notations. I can't read some of it. Then the ones I can make out, I'd have to look up to understand what they mean. But, I'm guessing these indicate they will need more procedures." Amy tossed them down with a quick motion, struck by her words. "Wait. Surgeries. More surgeries."

Amy spread out the reports for each procedure that had been performed on either of the twins. Then she grabbed the stack of labels and lined them up alongside the procedure reports. "Matt, where are those documents from the foundation donating money to the clinic?"

He retrieved the ones she asked for and handed them over. Stepping behind her, he watched her place them, one by one, over the procedure reports and matching blood labels. When she finished, the documents were partially aligned atop one another, resembling solitaire runs. Amy gasped. "Look at that." A cold chill made its way down her spine, causing her to shiver and cross her arms in front of herself to stave it off.

"Every time one of the twins had something medical done to them, I see a corresponding blood label for B Positive blood. And also a corresponding donation from the foundation," her voice rose with the thrill of the discovery.

"The dates aren't exact, but they are always within a day or two of each other. The blood is dated before or on the same day as the procedure, and so is the donation." Turning to gauge his reaction, she said, "Don't you find that odd?"

Matt picked up one of the runs and considered it. "So, the donations from the foundation to the clinic were to cover the procedures the kids had. Is that what you're saying?"

"This sure makes it appear that way." Amy said, "Nothing wrong with that. But what I don't understand is why the labels are for B Positive blood. If they needed a very special blood type, as Stacey told me, I would think they would have saved the Rhnull labels." The chill grew colder and spread, requiring her to rub her arms for warmth.

Amy jumped at the sound of a microwave beep. It came from the communal kitchen below. Along with the smell of sizzling bacon.

Matt checked the time. "Our roommates must be getting ready for class."

She realized they had been at it all night. Still contemplating what their findings meant, Amy said, "Unless..."

They stared at each other in a long silence that sent a different type of chill through her.

Understanding dawning, Matt finished. "They were using B Positive blood for those procedures." Shaking his head in a doubting fashion, he said, "But then, if that's true, Wilhelm doesn't fit into this at all."

"But why would Stacey have told me about the blood being so rare? She called the blood *unique* and made it sound like a big deal for the clinic. It wasn't a secret. She said it aloud in the cafeteria. It sounded to me like everybody knew about it."

"She could have been wrong. Maybe B Positive is a rare type."

"It's not. I just read that it's a very common one."

Matt moved away, rotated his head from side to side, rubbed his hands over his face, and then the back of his head. "I have to take a quick shower. I want to get over to Stratford and meet with Andy. He's the guy who interfaces with SSI for them."

Amy straightened, threw her shoulders back as her blood catapulted from icy to boiling. With one question close to a resolution, she needed to address the other. She couldn't delay any longer. "Speaking of SSI, I need to talk to you about something."

Matt rose after pulling out a casual golf shirt and jeans from his duffel. "Can it wait until tonight? Andy was out yesterday, and I want to talk to him alone before Joey gets in."

It was a failing of hers that she avoided difficult topics and confrontation. She began, "I guess it can..." Then the frustration that had been building nonstop since finding the log exploded out. "I found the log. Matt, I know it was you who took Wilhelm to Niihau."

She stiffened when he turned and took a step toward her.

"I was tricked." His words were encased in ice-cold anger. "They told me they were there to research animals in their native environment. I had no idea what they were planning with all the crates of equipment they brought." His chest rose and fell with deep breaths as she imagined him trying to tame a hidden temper.

With a pounding heart, she stood her ground. She met his eyes, boring into them. "You could have said so before."

Matt unclenched his fists and splayed open his palms. "They told me Wilhelm had a severe fear of flying, and they had to sedate him. Trust me, I had no inkling." He closed the distance between them. "Amy, I promise. We'll have plenty of time tonight." He grabbed her shoulders, frightening her for a heartbeat, before planting a quick kiss on her forehead. "I need to get going. They told me Andy starts early."

He left, leaving her numb. Amy pondered him and his story of being connived about Wilhelm.

*Do I believe him?*

*To use his phraseology: friend or foe?*

*I still don't know.*

# Chapter Fifty-Three

## Stratford Industries

## Toronto, Canada

"HELLO, MATT. WHAT CAN I do for you?" Matt relaxed. He finally reached Andy, *and* he sounded friendly.

Matt had arrived at the offices of Stratford Industries before they opened for business. After Joey mentioned that Andy always started early, Matt had hoped to speak with Andy freely. Before Joey might influence him on what he should—or shouldn't—talk about.

He found the front door locked when he arrived. Disappointed, he dialed the company's main number. A recording detailed their normal business hours, instructing callers to enter an extension or leave a general message. He didn't have an extension, and he couldn't think of another way to get to Andy.

Discouraged, he turned to leave. As he did, a shrub showing off a blanket of small white flowers next to the entrance caught his eye. At its side, a metallic plate attached to the building displayed a number for emergencies.

After a story about arriving sooner-than-expected with a delivery requiring a signature, the kind answering service operator connected him to Andy. Matt said, "I was hoping to stop in and say hello. I'm new to the firm, and I'll be heading back later today. I thought I would come by and introduce myself before I leave."

"Oh, yeah. Joey mentioned something about you coming in today." It wasn't what Matt wanted to hear. "I understand you want to talk to someone about the company's security. Why are you questioning it?"

"I'm not. I just wanted to connect with someone at SSI." By the sound of a fax or copier operating in the background, Matt guessed Andy was working inside. But he didn't offer to come to the door.

"I see. Well, the man I deal with is called Petrov. I call him Peter."

"Do you have a last name?"

"Can't pronounce it, and I don't have time to look it up. I spoke with him yesterday. He's tied up for the next few days cleaning out the home of a relative who passed away. He gave me the address. He said he'd be willing to speak with you at that location if you were interested. Do you want it?"

"Sure," Matt said to the man he considered rude. With nothing to write with, Matt memorized it. "I'm also interested in what services they provide for you and how you find working with them. Could we discuss it now before I meet with him?"

"I'd prefer you talk with him first," Andy said. "He's also curious as to what your interest is and what it has to do with your position. He suggested you meet with him first. Then, if he can't satisfy your curiosity, we can talk."

With that brush-off, Matt thanked Andy and left. He checked the transit routes, finding one that would land him close to where Petrov, or Peter, would be working. He promised Amy an update. So far, he had nothing to report, except to tell her about Andy's rudeness and his lack of progress. He thought about sending her the address, but decided against it. He'd touch base with her when he had something more to tell her.

An hour later, Matt stared at a two-story home surrounded by a wrought iron fence. Inside its gate, a narrow walk led to five stairs—and an open front door. Matt wondered if Andy had called him to alert him.

He climbed the stairs, but didn't knock. Instead, he pushed on the door. It opened wide to a room devoid of furniture. Various-sized cartons were scattered throughout. He yelled into the emptiness, "Hello. Anybody here?"

No answer came. Matt felt his heart rate increase. Something didn't feel right.

He took a few steps inside, leaving the door open. He heard no buzzing. No humming. Nothing. He went further into the home and peered into an older-style kitchen, where a strong smell of bleach hit him. A table and the countertops stood completely bare.

He moved to the base of a staircase leading to an upper floor and called out, "Petrov. This is Matt. Andy over at Stratford gave me this address. Are you here?"

A guttural voice answered. "Yes. Come up." Petrov's voice broke the uneasy silence. It made his pulse race even faster. The stillness bothered him. Like the quiet that concerns you when you're out in the woods, and even the animals aren't making any noise. "I'm packing. I'm on a tight schedule, and my hands are full."

Ready for some answers, Matt pressed the record function on his phone and dropped it into his pocket. He headed up. At the top, a small landing led to three doors, all open.

"I'm in here." The voice came from the one at the front. Matt moved toward it, guessing bedroom for the one in front and in back, as he could see the middle contained a toilet.

He thought he recognized the voice.

Reaching the door frame, he looked inside to find a man standing in the middle of taped-up cartons, hands on his hips, sporting an evil smirk.

"I thought it might be you," Petrov said. "You're the one who *stole* Wilhelm away."

Matt recognized the man as the one he had transported, along with a sedated Wilhelm, to Niihau. Although he had used a different name then. "And you're the one who told me you were researching the survival rate of animals that lived in the wild. At least that's the story you gave me for all those crates." Matt cocked his head. "You didn't mention anything about building a prison."

"True. Now I have a question for you." Matt's adrenaline kicked in as the villainous smile on Petrov's chiseled face spread wider. "Why are you so nosy?"

Matt sensed the movement at his back more than heard it. He began to turn. But he reacted a moment too late.

# Chapter Fifty-Four

## Devereux Clinic

## Toronto, Canada

HILLARY SAT AT HER desk, troubled and unable to concentrate on the work in front of her.

Yesterday, after Susan's warning about finding the new girl in the locked area, Hillary had done a quick check on the Stratford File. Verifying it was in the drawer. In the place it should be.

She left satisfied, although still perplexed as to why Amy would have been in that room. Today, however, her curiosity wouldn't allow her to remain still.

*It wouldn't hurt to check again.*

With an unfamiliar nervous feeling in her fingers, she entered the code for the door and pulled open the drawer. As she grabbed the Stratford Folder, this time extracting it rather than just verifying its presence, she could feel the difference in its heft. Lifting it out and opening it, her heart sank.

The top document, which would have been the last one she filed, was missing.

As were numerous others.

# Chapter Fifty-Five

## Student Housing

## Toronto, Canada

ALL THE PIECES OF THE Wilhelm puzzle were coming together. Amy was excited. Also fuzzy from being up all night reading through those dizzying documents. She decided she needed a short rest. She called the clinic and left a message saying she would be in today, but it wouldn't be until later.

Her nap lasted three hours. It was late morning when she awoke. She dressed, readied herself, and checked for an update from Matt. None. She sent him a message. *I'm heading in now.*

Her phone dinged with a response from Matt. *Come first to Bill's Beanery.*

She stood staring at it, confused. *Why is he asking me to meet? He knows I want to talk to Hillary about these documents.*

Amy reread his text. This time aloud. *Come first...*

*Is he asking or demanding?*

Her heart began hammering. Having spent time with him these last few days, something sounded wrong. She had snapped at him about incomplete sentence structure, but *come first* didn't sound right—even for him.

Her insides began to churn. She texted: *Call me.*

While she waited, she paced in the confined space, wringing her hands. At the window, the sight of a man loitering across the street, with a clear view of the front door, accelerated the drumbeat inside her.

*What is he doing there? It's not a bus stop. He's not with anyone else. Just standing in the middle of a block, for no logical reason. Is it me? Am I just paranoid? I need to get control of myself.*

Matt didn't call. So she rang him. It went straight to voicemail. *Now, why is your phone off?*

She collapsed onto the bed, arms stretched out to her sides, her feet on the floor. Focusing only on her breathing, she tried to bring herself to a state of Zen-like calm to quell her nervous limbs.

*What now? What's my next step?*

She stared at the ceiling, reviewing what she knew. She and Matt had witnessed Wilhelm's captivity and been instrumental in his rescue. She knew Matt brought him to Niihau, but didn't understand why. She learned about Wilhelm's rare blood type from Palakiko. At the clinic, she found out from Stacey that the babies needed the rare blood, but not how the clinic obtained it. After reviewing the swiped documents from the clinic, she and Matt had arrived at their own suspicions, but had no proof.

Amy needed answers. Or at least more information to fill in the score of missing blanks. She had come this far. It needled her, driving her crazy, like a riddle she couldn't solve. But filling in those final pieces would take more time than she had. The pressure was on her to return to DC.

She settled on what her next step would be. It began with returning the file. It was, after all, not hers. Then she would try to engage Hillary in conversation about the rare blood type that had been needed at the clinic before fessing up to taking a portion of the Stratford File.

Next, somehow in the conversation, she would reveal what she and Matt had surmised based on the multitude of B Positive labels. But none for a rare type, like Rhnull.

Hillary would hopefully fill in some of the missing pieces. Then, she would tender her resignation.

Tonight, after listening to Matt's explanation for ferrying Wilhelm to Niihau, she would schedule her return to DC, where she would set about making amends with Bonnie and her father.

Ready now to face Hillary, Amy got up, unwrapped a large purple folder she had purchased yesterday to return the documents in, and glanced out the window. The man still loitered in the same spot, sending her heart into overdrive, extinguishing the confidence she had just managed to muster up.

Crazed by the questionable man lingering outside, she decided to call for a ride to the clinic instead of risking public transportation.

With purpose now, she finished filling the folder with the pilfered papers and retrieved her purse. She searched through it, at last finding the card. The face had *Charleeez* across it in bold, colorful letters. Below it, the phrase *At Your Service* appeared, written in elegant script.

On the right-hand side, the card contained the caricature of a chauffeur: bowing in service, one hand on an open rear door, hat in the other, and a phone number at the bottom. She recalled the jovial, retired man who had talked nonstop on the ride to the hotel from the airport, offering his service at any time. Day or night.

The man across the street still lingered. By her estimate, it had been close to an hour. He could be waiting for someone, but her paranoia wouldn't dismiss him. Just like Matt's message, it didn't feel right.

She called Charlie and gave him a street location, a block behind the rear of her building. She could access that street via an exit off the kitchen downstairs and a backyard gate.

Before leaving, she removed a portion of the stolen items, culling out the ones she deemed most telling. She took snapshots of them, organized them into a file folder on her cell, and sent it to her mother. Amy asked her to scan them in and email them back, giving her an excuse about not having scanner access at the moment.

Regathering all the documents, Amy set out to confront Hillary.

# Chapter Fifty-Six

## Devereux Clinic

## Toronto, Canada

"I SEE YOU DECIDED TO show up today." Hillary's sarcasm conveyed much more than unhappiness over a missed day of work.

Amy had noticed Hillary in her office as she exited the elevator, but decided to replace the file first. Amy headed straight for the locked closet. She placed the purple folder on the desk in order to enter the code. But before she could, Hillary appeared at the entrance.

Hillary wore no trace of a smile, let alone a look of welcome. Her brow was furrowed, and her nostrils appeared wider than Amy remembered, reminding Amy of a bulldog.

Amy took a breath and said, "I'm glad you're here." She paused to steady her nerves, wanting to project a more confident attitude. "I want to talk to you. Is now a good time?" Her words didn't sound like they contained any of the force she imagined she had injected into them.

"Huh," Hillary snickered. "And what is it you would like to talk about? The information you stole."

Amy saw Hillary glance at the purple holder. She lifted her chin. "Are those the records?"

The relief of having been found out reignited Amy's confidence. "They are."

Hillary put her cell to her ear, supporting it with her shoulder. "I need you up here right now." After uttering, "Yes," she closed her phone. Returning her attention to Amy, she demanded, "Open it and show me."

Amy unsnapped the folder and pulled out a handful of documents, laying them on the desk. Still wanting answers, she said, "Don't you want to know why I took them?" Her puzzle still had missing pieces.

With her stiff, military stance blocking the exit, Hillary cast her eyes to the papers and said, "Because you're nothing but a thief?"

Amy placed a hand on top of the pile and spread the documents out across the desk, attempting to arouse Hillary's curiosity, desperate to engage her in conversation about the rare blood type. Amy picked up a sheet with a label affixed to it. She twirled it in midair. "Aren't you the least bit curious?"

"Are they all there?" Hillary's voice mimicked her posture, stern and unmoving. The elevator dinged.

Accepting defeat, Amy nodded that they were. She tossed the document on the desk with the others.

The doors opened. Two men wearing security vests spotted Hillary at the doorway and headed straight for her.

"This little snot has stolen from us. I'm contacting the police. Escort her down to receiving and don't take your eyes off her until they arrive. Make sure she doesn't leave."

"Will do."

Amy straightened her shoulders, grabbed her purse, and followed one of the guards out past a statuesque Hillary.

THE TWO MEN ESCORTED Amy to the ground floor. Neither of them spoke to her. They opened the door to a small room, slightly larger than a cubicle. Inside, a metal desk and a useless high-backed chair with wheels and nowhere to roll to, filled the room. She checked her phone for messages and had none. She called Matt and left a message for him.

With that done, she allowed herself to relax.

*It's over. The police are on their way.*

She knew she'd have to explain the entire story to them, but she already had Detective Palakiko's number memorized. With him substantiating what happened in Hawaii and Matt confirming it, her story would be verified.

*I've returned all the documents. That will surely count in my favor. I didn't sell or destroy them, just borrowed them. Shouldn't be much of a case—if any. A decent lawyer should be able to get me off with only a warning or a fine.*

*I'll have to explain it to Dad and Bonnie. But that will have to wait. Now, I just want to finish this. And go home.*

She tried the door. It was locked. She knocked, and the heavier of the two guards opened it. "I need to use a restroom." He nodded, put a hand on her upper arm as she walked out, and kept it there as they walked down a long corridor. Two glass doors with push bars sat at its end. For a brief flash, she considered bolting and dashing through them.

*But where would I go?*

The guard's hand instinctively tightened as he steered her to the right, his thoughts likely mirroring hers. He pointed ahead to a washroom. She tugged away from his grip.

She wasn't prepared for this last part. The humiliation of him having to hold on to her. It upset her almost to the point of tears. She took her time, using wet paper towels to refresh her face and hands. When she finally slid the lock open, a different man stood along with the guard.

The stranger wordlessly reached for her. The guard said, "The detective here is going to take you in." Her heart caught for a second, frightened that he might be the same man who she had seen earlier outside their room. It took a beat, but she realized he couldn't be. The one on the street had not looked up. But she could tell he was thin as a flagpole. This one was beefy.

She took a step toward him, relieved when he dropped his arm. He didn't attempt to grab her.

*At least he's civilized.*

He led her to the glass doors, depressed the exit bar on one, and let her walk out first as he followed a step behind. His silence and facial expression gave Amy the impression he was annoyed, perhaps unhappy at having to perform this menial task.

While Amy contemplated where to begin her story, he moved alongside her and pointed to the nearest car—a nondescript four-door black sedan. "Do all detectives use their own cars?"

He reached around and opened the rear door for her.

"I'm undercover," he said, stepping behind her.

Squeezed between him and the open door, Amy turned to ask another question, but didn't manage to say a word. His heart-stopping punch to her gut took her breath away as he shoved her in.

# Chapter Fifty-Seven

## Frank Gigliano's Home

## Toronto, Canada

FRANK GIGLIANO GAVE his college sweetheart a quick peck on the cheek. He closed his phone and said, "Sorry. I need to take care of this. Fix us a drink, will you? It shouldn't take too long." He considered this—the time he spent sharing a drink with his wife before dinner—the best part of his day.

Today he arrived home to an unwelcome text from Hector. After his recent conversation with the private investigator about the necessity of having him concentrate on foundation work, Frank had expected to hear from him, although it surprised him Hector marked it urgent.

In the quiet of his study, he phoned Hector. "What is so urgent?"

"Do you know where Miss Susan is?"

"No, I don't. I spoke to her yesterday, but not today. Why?"

"I've been trying her all day and haven't been able to reach her."

Frank cleared his throat. "When I asked why, what I meant is, *why* are you still in contact with her? I thought I made it pretty clear she is no longer on the committee."

"Well, Frank," Hector's nod of respect to females didn't apply to males. "You did. This is something personal I am doing for her. It doesn't interfere with what I do for your group. What time yesterday?"

" Around midday. She was having lunch."

"Where?"

The command in Hector's tone surprised Frank, making Hector sound more like an adversary than a contractor working for him. "Why the concern? I'm sure she's keeping busy." A long silence followed as Frank experienced an unusual sense of dread. "Hector, whatever happened at work doesn't negate the fact that Susan and I are still friends." He asked again. "Why are you concerned about her?"

"Her phone's been off since yesterday afternoon. You were her last call. I checked her apartment. Her cat was meowing for food, which tells me she hasn't been home in a while. So, yes, I am worried. As I said, I am looking into something for her. When we spoke last, she promised to keep her cell on. She also promised to stay in touch with me at least once a day. If you are the friend you say you are, then tell me what you can."

Hector's admonishment startled Frank. It made him stop and reflect. He wanted, and needed, this job—with two boys heading off to college in the next few years. He had found it tough being the swing vote, never expecting that his siding with Mike would lead to Susan's dismissal. It still troubled him. But, knowing of Mike's close relationship with the other board members and his firm commitment to the issue, he had chosen the safer route and backed Mike.

However, he also shared Susan's concerns about the transactions involving the clinic. His moment of reflection made him realize he needed to help in any way he could. "Well, I can tell you she was investigating The Devereux Clinic. To be more specific, the large amount of money we sent them. Susan and I had discussed the issue of blood types and who at the clinic might have information about the banks that store the blood. Yesterday, I told her the administrator, Hillary Whitley, had done an internship at a blood bank in Switzerland."

"Did Miss Susan say where she was going after lunch?"

"No, and I didn't ask. I assume home or to the office. I wasn't in yesterday, so I'm not sure if she came in or not. I can check."

"Do that. It would help. Do you think she went to the clinic to talk to Hillary?"

"I don't think so. She mentioned she met with her in the morning, so I doubt she would go back." The dread grew stronger. "I guess it might be a possibility."

"OK. Find out if she did show up at the office yesterday and if anyone knows anything about where she might be. Get in touch, no matter when, if she contacts you."

"I will, Hector. And I'll ask you to do likewise."

His evening cocktail was no longer for pleasure. It was now a necessity.

# Chapter Fifty-Eight

## Outside the Devereux Clinic

## Toronto, Canada

THE ISLAND OF PUERTO Rico is akin to many other Caribbean islands, comprised of two unofficial sections. The rich side, where the tourists and vacationers flock to soak up the rays and the white sandy beaches. And the poorer areas, where travelers seldom venture, even though both parts share the same sun.

Hector came from the less-visited side, the one without the tourists. He and his friends would often journey to the more fascinating side, where a few of them turned to pickpocketing. Although he never participated, he knew he would have excelled at it. The fear of disappointing a much-loved grandmother, who raised him from infancy, kept him from taking part.

With an island promising very little, he left as a youth and, through a series of jobs and associations, found a home in Toronto. He enjoyed his work for the foundation. A portion of the job was dry and routine, but other parts allowed him the freedom to exercise his skills as an investigator.

He often appeared at a doorstep under a false persona to either elicit information or to validate or dispute claims put forth on their applications to the foundation. Credentials are easy to replicate, and he often presented himself as a local representative of the fire, water, or gas companies.

He possessed a knack for impersonating these professionals, which, in turn, gave him access to their homes. Once inside, he found a treasure trove of data to be gleaned concerning lifestyle, financial status, and family.

Chatting up the residents with his laid-back character extracted an equal amount of information—if not more.

He enjoyed his job and loved applying his talents to foundation work, having enormous respect for the generous and benevolent work they did.

Although Susan had suggested he go back to whatever Frank wanted him to work on, Hector had not stopped. He continued delving into the doctor, the chief of surgery and a major partner in the clinic, as well as the girl who worked for Hillary.

After hearing that Frank had passed on some disturbing information about Hillary to Susan, and Susan not answering his calls, Hector's focus pivoted.

It now centered on Hillary.

Hector waited in his car in a darkened portion of the parking lot outside the clinic, wondering if Susan had returned to confront Hillary. It would be her style. He had canvassed the area when he arrived, confirming Hillary's car as one of the three parked near the entrance.

He recognized her as she left the building. Briefcase in hand, Hillary tossed it onto the passenger seat, got in, and sped away.

*Seems to be in a hurry.*

Hector followed. After two stops, a pharmacy and an ATM, he tailed her onto a road that led them away from the city. A half hour later, her car turned into an elongated driveway, with a house set far back on a rise. He saw the garage door begin to open as she passed the midway point. The home looked impressive, and the ground-level accent lights, nestled between blooming shrubs, lit the way up its serpentine, zigzagging approach.

Recognizing the address as her home, Hector parked across the street and shut his lights.

In the silence of the night, Hector pinged Susan's phone. As he sat, he pondered a myriad of ways this could go.

He imagined his frustration must be similar to what his clients experienced while awaiting news of a missing loved one. Clinging to even the dimmest of possibilities for an explanation, hoping against hope, the Jane Doe lying in the morgue matching the physical description of their loved one is still a mistake.

A light went on in one of the upstairs rooms.

*Bedroom,* he wondered. That would make sense. He opened his glove compartment and retrieved his binoculars.

As a poor child growing up, electronics were not commonplace for him or his friends. His activities took place outside, under the warm sun. He kicked balls, threw them, and caught them, but his favorite pastime was climbing trees.

He got out of the car, sprinting up the curves of the driveway, crouching, keeping to the middle, trying not to cast shadows as he passed the low-wattage bulbs. A distance away from the house, he spied a large tree that ran in a direct line across from the lit window. It should provide a decent view.

If Hillary settled into sleep, he would be able to catch a little himself—quarantined in his vehicle. If not, he would have to remain awake and vigilant. He would not rest until he found his Miss Susan.

Interfacing with her over the years as much as he had, Hector had grown fond of her. In his line of work, he interacted with some of the worst elements of society. She was different. He admired and respected her. If she needed his help, all his time and resources would be dedicated to her. Since he hadn't heard from her for over twenty-four hours, his concern grew deeper.

Finding her was now his only priority.

At the base of the tree, fond memories came to him. He began his way up with ease, starting with a short jump to the lowest branch, then around the tree's circumference to the next. Each action part of a familiar, enjoyable maze. A few more stretches and pulls, and he found himself seated in absolute comfort against the trunk of the strong oak.

He pulled the binoculars to his eyes, adjusted the distance, and watched as Hillary passed around the room. At times, moving out of his vision, only to return seconds later. He had guessed what was happening, but he needed confirmation.

Hillary opened a closet, and moments later, his suspicions were confirmed.

Hector scurried down the tree at a rate that would have made a squirrel jealous. He made it back to his car in record time.

There, he'd wait. There'd be no sleeping tonight.

# Chapter Fifty-Nine

## Empty Warehouse

## Industrial Park outside Toronto

AMY WOKE UP COLD, SHIVERING, gripped with fear, afraid she would not be leaving this place alive. Wherever this place was.

She lay on her side, lying on something hard, like a frozen slab of ice. Her eyes snapped open, but wouldn't focus. She began to cough—unable to clear away the foul taste in her mouth. A stale, dusty air attacked her throat. Her gut hurt from the strong punch she had taken.

Movement ahead caused her heart to speed up its beat. Through a haze, her eyes struggled to focus. She peered through dim light as a dark mass approached. It stopped a few feet in front of her.

At a snail's pace, the haze cleared and her view sharpened enough to distinguish an outline. Of a man. A black balaclava covered his face.

*It's him.*

Only his eyes and lips showed. But she recognized the eyes—the man posing as a detective. The one who had delivered the punch.

Amy's insides roiled, but she managed to squeak out, "Who are you? What do you want?"

He didn't answer. Instead, he turned his head to the side. Amy followed his gaze. It revealed what looked to be a body. It lay on the ground some ten feet away. One of Amy's shoes lay on the concrete between them.

Her attention returned to him as he scanned each of his two captives. He headed first to the other one, raised a leg, and kicked the still form with his shoe. His action elicited a moan, followed by something indiscernible.

It sounded like a woman.

He stood there for a while, surveying the form before moving toward Amy. Her heart stopped as he stepped behind her. He pulled on her restraint, giving it a few quick yanks. Tugging first at the one surrounding her waist and then the one securing her feet, before leaving without uttering a word.

The gritty air in the cold and cavernous building had drained Amy's mouth of all its saliva. She coughed hard, trying to expel the taste of dust off her tongue and the feel of cobwebs out of her throat.

When Amy finally worked up enough saliva to speak, she said, "Hello. Can you hear me?" Even though her head faced the form on the concrete off to her side, her words came out as a whimper.

No answer.

Occasional noises—a muffled cough, a scraping, or the sound of shuffling—could be heard in the dark abyss in front of her. Behind her, several yards back, Amy saw a solid cinder block wall. Nothing else.

At the sound of a slamming door, somewhere in the distance, Amy's attention flew to the other woman. Who didn't move.

Amy remembered hearing an utterance from her earlier, when the fake detective checked on them. Straining forward as much as her bindings would allow, hoping for any sign of life, Amy called out to the form again. "Hello. Can you hear me?"

The chill of the concrete sent another jolt through Amy. Awareness came to her in small snatches. She moved to sit up but stopped when she realized her hands were bound.

A thick rope, tied with several knots, coiled around her wrists. A chain made of heavy links encircled her ankles. The solid weight of her shackles restrained her from straightening her feet.

A cold fear, surpassing the emission from the floor, swept through her. Using her bound hands for support, she managed to sit up. Panicking, she scanned around. *Take a deep breath. Stay calm. Analyze the situation.*

Amy pressed her forearm against her right hip to determine if she had her phone in her front pocket. It wasn't there. That left her with her clothes and nothing else.

*Where am I?*

Shivering, she surveyed the right side of the open space. Empty shelves lined the wall from a foot above the concrete to the ceiling above. She estimated the place to be the height of two floors. The rest of the building appeared to be empty, except for pockets of deep darkness in the distance ahead.

*A warehouse. An unused one.*

She scrutinized the form lying off to her side, deciding it was indeed a woman. She lay flat on her back. Her head faced the roof above. Amy noticed her hands were not bound. The woman's arm closest to Amy angled out in an unusual position. The woman appeared unconscious, her legs splayed out.

*Who is she? Why is she here?*

Amy could see the woman's eye closest to her had swollen shut. The rest of her face was hidden. "Hello," Amy tried again. It came out louder this time, but still a whisper by everyday standards. "Please say something. Let me know you're alive."

Amy thought she recognized a tiny movement. An index finger lifted. Still questioning whether she imagined it or not, in a hushed voice, Amy heard, "Is he gone?"

"Oh, thank God," Amy's words crackled with joy. "Are you OK?"

"Gone?" She asked again. Her tone serious.

Swallowing hard, Amy said, "Sorry. Yes."

"Did you recognize him?"

"He had a mask on. I could only see his eyes. But I did see the man who hit me, and I believe it's the same man. How are you doing? I thought you were unconscious. Or worse."

No answer came for a few breaths. It appeared she needed time to gain strength to speak. "I feel like a sword fight is going on in my intestines, my eye is covered by something, and my head is spinning. But I'm alive." The woman let out a moan and then stayed silent.

Since waking here, Amy's body hadn't stopped trembling. At this point, she was a milkshake ready to be poured into a large glass and served with a straw. *I have to calm down. And stop this quivering.*

She knew that having control over something—no matter how small—was very important for managing anxiety and maintaining a sense of stability. She needed that now.

Although there weren't many options here.

She started with a few deep breaths. Then she began willing all her thoughts to a single place, forcing all others out, trying to establish control over something. Her memory.

*What is the last thing I remember?*

She pushed herself to recall. Things were coming back in small snippets. She fought the nervousness blocking her effort to remember.

The restroom. The clinic's guard... "The detective here is going to take you..."

The detective—who wasn't—opening the car door.

At that moment, she realized something was off.

Then the unexpected punch to the gut.

There was nothing else.

Except waking up here.

In chains.

# Chapter Sixty

## Vacant Warehouse

## Toronto, Canada

WITH THE WOMAN NO LONGER talking, Amy returned her focus to her restraints. She stared at the wide links of chain binding her ankles. Twisting around, she found a metal pillar that stretched to the roof.

She wiggled side to side on her butt. Using her bound hands, grabbing a pant leg at a time, she dragged herself back. Each movement was a struggle due to the weight of the chain. All of her effort to back up only covered a few inches.

Once her back touched the support, she bent her knees and, using the pole for leverage, began nudging herself upright.

Tightness around her waist made her stop.

She realized the chain at her waist was also secured around the base of the rusted support. The chain's slack did allow for some movement. But not much. A few inches at most.

Gritting her teeth—which at least stopped them from chattering—she braced herself for the pain to come, and leaned forward, hoping to provide some additional slack in this section of her bindings.

Then, plastering her back against the pole, she pulled in her knees and continued to edge herself up. She eventually managed to snake her way to an awkward but upright stance. She had hoped the position would give her further insight.

It didn't.

That position did, however, reduce the amount of slack at her ankles, shortening it, pinning her ankles against the pole, while at the same time loosening the slack at her waist. It allowed her already sore insides a much-needed breather.

With nothing to see, she slumped back to the floor, exhausted from the effort.

Amy heard a small moan from the woman before she said, "Tell me what you see."

"I think we are in a warehouse. The air smells stale and musty. The ceiling is probably fifteen or twenty feet high, but there are no windows. A string of four lights is above us, hanging from the ceiling, but of the four bulbs that should be lit, only one is. The rest of the place is dark. You and I are tied up. Your hands are free, but your ankle has a chain around it. I'm chained to a pole."

"Are your hands behind you?"

"No. They're tied with rope in front. I've been wiggling them, working to loosen them, but they're so tight, my hands are turning color."

"Listen to me. The fact that whoever dumped us here had on a mask is a good thing."

"What makes you say that? I wouldn't call anything about this good."

"We haven't seen their faces, so we can't identify them. So, I believe there is a chance they will let us go."

Amy didn't agree but decided not to say so. "What do you think they want? Why are we even here?"

"We must have rattled somebody's cage." The woman's hesitation between words indicated her difficulty speaking. "What have you done to get yourself in this type of trouble?"

"I don't know," Amy winced.

"What's wrong?" The woman asked, concerned.

"I'm trying to undo these ropes. I'm not getting very far." Amy looked down at the bloodied and red-stained rope. "I'm tearing off my skin."

The woman gasped and struggled to readjust her position, trying to view Amy. Amy stopped biting at her restraint and twisted around to peer at her. With more of her face now visible, Amy said with surprise, "You're the woman who came to Devereux asking about Hillary. You wanted me to leave a message for her."

"Yes, I did. I'm guessing that clinic is also the reason I'm here." The woman's voice had a firmness in it that belied the beaten-up lump of a human being she resembled. "My suspicions about it."

"You arrived just as I was swiping something from them," Amy said. "To be truthful, I went back and took much more."

"I'm Susan Fleming. I work for the Stratford Foundation." The woman who had turned her head to face Amy rolled it back toward the ceiling.

"Nice to meet you. I'm Amy. And we're going to make it out of here."

"I'm not so sure. It hurts like..." Susan took a slow, deep breath. "I am so stiff. It hurts so much to move. When that monster grabbed me and dragged me into the car, I could feel myself being scraped against something. It didn't hurt at the time. However, when he put me down on this floor, I detected a searing pain coming from my side. But with my hands like this, I can't even manage to check what's wrong."

After a silence, Susan gave a small laugh. "I have to tell you, I've traveled to some unsavory places. I've taken self-defense courses in case something like this ever happens. Jab your elbow into the chest, fling your forearm across the Adam's apple, go for their face, kick, fight, yell, scratch, they tell you." She stopped, needing a breath. "It all happened so fast. By the time I realized what was happening, I blacked out. Next thing I remember—I woke up here."

"When?" Amy asked.

"What's today?"

"Friday."

Susan thought for a second. "Yesterday—after lunch. I'd say around two o'clock."

"That makes it more than twenty-four hours. Listen, if you're right about them wearing masks and letting us go, maybe we will get out of this. If that's the case, you'll be able to get patched up."

"If the infection doesn't kill me first," Susan said in a somber tone.

"Are you a doctor? Or a nurse?" Amy asked, curious about the woman's apparent self-diagnosis.

"No. But I can feel my head getting hotter and hotter. When they first laid me here, I was freezing. Now I'd like to strip off all my clothes."

That told Amy the woman had a fever. She knew from her EMS courses, the woman needed medical care. Stat. It meant they didn't have much time.

# Chapter Sixty-One

## A Park

## Toronto, Canada

HECTOR'S INTUITION about Hillary had been right. From his vantage point up in the great oak, he spied her retrieving a suitcase from a closet and figured she intended to run. He had two questions needing answers.

*Where are you going? And what are you running from?*

He tailed her to a waterfront park.

Wide open spaces, like this one, were difficult to be invisible in. This parking area contained nothing but a few bikes positioned in a rack and an old scooter with a flat tire. Hillary parked and walked to a point overlooking Center Island. Hector put his car in neutral and guided it into the lot with his lights off, maneuvering it into the first spot in the last row.

He closed the door with a faint thud. Hunched over, he crept to a row of hedges, hiding behind them. He waited in the shadows to see who would arrive. Certain that someone would. Experience had taught him people did not operate in a vacuum.

Minutes later, a second car arrived, pulling in next to Hillary's.

It surprised him when Eunice Stratford stepped out.

*Well. Well. Well. This is interesting.*

Eunice stayed in place, twisting her neck from side to side, taking in the surroundings. Hillary started toward her. Eunice held up a hand for her to stop.

Instead of walking toward Hillary, Eunice headed in the opposite direction. To where Hector had left his vehicle. The only other one in the lot.

*Smart. I see you are taking no chances.*

She approached it at an angle and glanced into it from its side, checking both the front and back seats to ensure no one sat watching.

*There is no one inside, lady. Just leave.* Hector held his breath to see if she would take the one additional step he would have taken: checking the top of the hood to see if it was warm.

He exhaled a silent sigh of relief when she didn't.

Satisfied, Eunice made her way to Hillary.

From his vantage point, Hector couldn't hear what they were saying. But Eunice's frantic gesturing, flailing hands, and gyrating shoulders said *unhappy,* with a capital U, to Victor. Eunice reached into a pocket, extracted something small enough to fit in the palm of her hand, and passed it to Hillary.

After accepting it, Hillary turned from Eunice, walked to the edge of the point, and gazed out over the water. Eunice followed, and their conversation continued with their backs to him.

*I'm guessing you guys are done here.* Hector scurried to where the women's cars were parked and slipped beneath Eunice's for a moment before retreating further back to a large bush behind his car. He squatted in place until they both drove away.

Eunice wasn't going anywhere. He knew where to find her.

Hillary was up to something. The suitcase in her car told him so. But first, she found it necessary to conclude something with Eunice. Out here? At this late hour? Illogical actions always made Hector's adrenaline rise.

Hector followed a few cars behind her after she left the park. *Not in so much of a hurry now, are you?* When Hillary left the Gardiner Expressway and took a turn onto 427, it confirmed his guess. That is the fastest route to the Toronto-Pearson airport.

The only question left is, would she be leaving alone?

# Chapter Sixty-Two

## Vacant Warehouse

## Toronto, Canada

AMY WAS GNAWING LIKE a beaver at the rope binding her hands, aching to free them. Not only for herself, but also for Susan, who she knew desperately needed medical attention. Thanks to her father's generous gift, that awareness came from her participation in medical and survival first aid courses. Amy knew the only thing she could do for her now was keep her talking.

She called out to the woman. "Susan, may I call you Susan?"

"You may call me anything you want."

"You said you were conscious when they put you here?"

"Well, sort of. More half in, half out. Woozy, I guess you would say. But I could tell the monster who dragged me into the car with him is the same one who carried me in here. I recognized his smell. I've been drifting in and out of consciousness. At times, I could feel someone kicking me. I've been lying here hoping to summon the strength to get up and find a way out, but I'm too weak."

"Did you see his face?"

"No. I didn't."

Amy's attack at the knots in the rope hadn't made a dent. She paused for a brief rest and turned her attention to Susan. "Are you friends with Hillary?"

"Quite the opposite," she scoffed. "I was actually investigating the clinic, and just beginning to center my investigation on her. The foundation I work for should have been doing it, but they weren't. And, for reasons not worth going into now, they let the clinic extort us to the tune of millions of dollars."

Amy's curiosity was piqued. For the moment, Susan's story outweighed her fear. "Wait, what are you saying?"

"First, you answer a question for me. Were you recently in Hawaii, and did you have anything to do with a Wilhelm something, can't remember his last name, who was found there?"

"Yes. A friend of mine, Matt, and I rescued him when we were in Kauai." Hearing herself voice that accomplishment, Amy experienced a sense of satisfaction sweep through her.

It died a second later when her mind flew to Matt. *Where is he? I need to warn him.*

"You two did that on your own?"

"Yes. Then we traveled here to get some answers as to why he had been a prisoner on a private island, called Niihau."

"You exerted so much effort? Took such a great risk to pursue it?"

"We did," Amy said. Susan let out a long groan. Amy wasn't sure if it came from pain or shock at her answer. "I applied for a job at the clinic. The president of Stratford offered Matt a job. He is also an owner in the security company that paid to have Wilhelm taken to the island. Working at the clinic, I found out a unique blood type was needed for the Stratford twins."

Susan coughed. "That blood came at an exorbitant price. It cost us, the foundation, millions of dollars. We shouldn't have been paying for it in the first place—regardless of the price—even if it had been a reasonable one. The twins' father is an employee of Stratford Industries. He's exempt from receiving any financial assistance from us."

Amy maneuvered around on the concrete. It wasn't only cold. It became unbearable to remain stationary in one spot for any length of time. Leaning to a side, she asked, "But you did?"

Susan coughed again and continued. This time at a slower pace. "Somehow, they, the Stratfords, convinced the senior member of our team that they should be the exception to the rule." Her voice lacked strength, growing weaker and weaker. She paused more often, seeming to struggle with each word. "I don't know why he agreed, but he did. I got outvoted."

Amy felt helpless to do anything about Susan's ebbing strength, except to keep her from slipping off to sleep. "Susan, I agree with you. Something is off with the whole blood thing."

In a voice just above a whisper, Susan said, "Amy, I have something to tell you." Then she fell silent, needing to pause more often now. After a while, Susan breathed, "God, I'm so thirsty." Then she stopped speaking.

"Susan, Susan. Talk to me." Amy persisted.

After a long stretch of silence, Susan said, "What do you mean, off?"

Relieved to hear Susan speak, Amy said, "I swiped some records out of the file they had for the Stratfords at the clinic. When Matt and I went through it, we found what looked like labels for blood. But they were *all* for type B positive blood. Can you think of any reason there were so many entries for B positive?"

"No. That doesn't make sense." Susan said, her voice growing more faint. She seemed to be drifting away.

"We suspect the blood type for at least one of the boys was not Rhnull, but B positive. I went in to talk to Hillary about our suspicions. When I arrived, she had already figured out I'd taken the file. She notified security and had them hold me, saying she would call the police herself. One of the guards holding me turned me over to a man claiming to be a detective. Instead, he's the goon who punched me, and I guess brought me here."

Susan didn't comment. Didn't respond at all. Amy called out her name several times. Each time, louder and louder.

Her calls didn't rouse Susan, but they were overheard by someone. New sounds soon emanated from the darkness ahead.

Amy couldn't see anyone, but believing someone loitered there, she yelled into the emptiness. "This woman is sick. She needs help. She needs a doctor. If she dies, it's murder."

# Chapter Sixty-Three

## Warehouse

## Toronto, Canada

WHEN YOU ARE SUDDENLY confronted with a belief that you are about to die, fear cascades through you. Strange things force themselves to the front and center of your mind. Tommy's last day came to Amy. Her only solace with his death came from knowing he had not suffered.

She had learned his fate from an incident reconstruction report. *The bullet shattered the window, went straight through his forehead, exited out the back of his skull, and lodged itself in the headrest of the bus seat.* Based on the angle from where the gun was fired, he never saw it coming. It happened in seconds. Literally over, before it began, they had assured her. There had been no time for his brain to even register pain.

Amy guessed her fate wouldn't be that easy. After her outburst about Susan needing medical attention, Susan lay quiet, leaving nothing but a foreboding silence to surround Amy. A tortured silence that had her imagining movement in the area up ahead.

She strained to see. At first, Amy could only identify shadows that appeared to be moving. Then, as if out of nowhere, a figure started taking shape. It was large. Moving at a turtle's pace toward her. As the shadow emerged into the figure of a man, she gulped at his size.

*What had Susan said?*

Amy glanced at her, but the woman remained silent and motionless.

*She called him a monster.*

A monster capable of snatching her and dragging her into a car. A monster who brought her here. A monster.

It hit her like a shot.

The monster stopped a few feet in front of Amy. He eyed her through the slits in his mask as she watched his chest expand and recede with every breath.

From her position on the floor, with her back braced against the pole, she said, "Hello, Koa. I know it's you."

Helpless otherwise, Amy still had her voice. "But what I don't understand, Koa..." She spoke slowly, driving home each word. "Is why you are here and involved with any of this."

She paused, waiting for a reaction, but he stood mute, continuing only to stare. "You come from a beautiful island with a wonderful history. Professor Longo taught me all about your culture. He told me about you and your family."

The monster facing her didn't move, except to breathe.

"The professor explained about the traditions you hold dear. About the hula. He said it's not just for entertainment. It's a way of storytelling, passing down beliefs and customs. The one I watched told the story of a girl who pined on the shore for a loved one, a sailor, to return to her." Amy continued to gamble that she might be able to reach him. Reason with him. The longer he showed no reaction, the faster and more erratic her heartbeat became. It skipped beats as fear crawled up her body.

*It is him. Isn't it? It has to be.*

Amy drew her knees in and, using the pole for support, struggled to push herself up off the concrete and into some form of standing. The masked man took a small step back.

In an uncomfortable, but somewhat upright position, Amy continued, taking advantage of the fact that her voice projected better in this position than from the floor. She had to make an impact on Koa. To somehow reach him. To make him realize what he is doing here is wrong. She drove more emotion into each word. "Every night she would go out into the moonlight."

Amy fought the resistance from the chain as she willed herself to continue. "Then she would reach to the heavens, pleading for his safe return.

My heart broke at the thought of someone pining their life away for a missing loved one. A mother, perhaps. Never knowing."

She paused for a few breaths, hoping to remind him of his situation. "Yearning for a child. I can't imagine what that must feel like. Her days. Her nights. Always wondering." Amy started speaking slower, pausing more often for effect, gambling she could get through to him. "Where is he? What's he doing? Hoping and praying. Day after day. What an excruciating life that must be. I can't imagine how much she is suffering."

Her words didn't appear to have an impact on Koa. She tried a different tactic. "Your cousin, Kalani, told me everyone misses you—not just your mother. Professor Longo, too. He loves you. He took a huge chance, risking his career, by going to Niihau to search for you. He still has faith in you. He said you are a good person. Is he wrong?"

From the midnight-black distance beyond, a noise made her stop. In moments, a second masked figure approached, grunting his presence. In a gruff voice, he asked, "Problem?"

"No," Koa said. His response loud and strong. "I just came to tell her the man she came here with is dead. And he won't be coming to save her."

# Chapter Sixty-Four

## Hotel Bar

## Toronto Canada

BLUE LIGHTS DANCED along the base of the mirror, causing the bottles in front of it to sparkle, tantalizing onlookers to come in and partake.

Joey Stratford was experiencing another rush of excitement. He feared it might be the drink. *Am I becoming an alcoholic?*

Joey sat on the end stool, which he chose for privacy. He said, "Hit me again." He pondered the tattooed young man with the multicolored hair and heavy hand, guessing he was new to the job since he poured a generous amount of vodka into each tonic.

*He doesn't care. It's not his business. Not his problem. It's the hotel's.*

A bearded, heavyset man entered the intimate lobby bar. His belly, hanging low over his belt, shouted years of indulgence. With a full row of seats available, he chose the one next to Joey.

*Just like in an empty parking lot. I park my Jag as far away as I can, and when I return, some joker is in the next space.*

The overweight man asked, "What do you have on tap?"

The bartender rattled off a few choices. The man chose the first. Then wiped a glob of spittle from the side of his mouth.

It made Joey wonder if he should call it a night. His canceled flight left him with nothing else to do until morning. Deciding he wasn't ready yet, he said, "I'll have one more."

"Women," the stranger said. "I think it's God's version of a joke. Put them here to see how much we could take." The newcomer turned to Joey. "You married?"

Joey nodded.

"Get along?"

*I should have gone upstairs.* Joey didn't want to talk.

To anyone, let alone this slobbering drunk. But, because of his young wife's vision, he now dared to dream of a life he could not have envisioned until much later in life, only at retirement. She deserved credit for that. "She's wonderful," Joey said. "More than I could ever have hoped for."

"Then why are you here," he belched at Joey, spewing out a sour odor of sauerkraut and beer, "with your old friend, the bottle?"

Joey waved his hand back and forth in front of his face to clear the smell as their drinks were placed in front of them.

Joey guzzled his. He turned toward the man, ready to leave, when a raging alcohol-induced fire swept through him, extending outward from his core to his fingertips and the edges of his toes. Leaving in its wake a cocky, confident calm. "I have to go. But before I do, I want to tell you something." His words came out in a choppy, start-and-stop fashion. "I have the best wife in the whole world."

"Sure you do. Whatever you say," the man said and returned to his beer.

Uninhibited, Joey said, "I'm president and CEO of a company, but I hate my job." The words spilled easily from his lips.

"Want a medal?"

"You know why I love my wife so much? She came up with a plan. A plan that will make us both rich, and I won't have to put up with all the..." Joey found himself a little confused. He couldn't remember the next word he meant to say.

"Since you're so happy and rich, I think you should buy the next round."

"Sure. Why not?" *I should celebrate what's about to happen.*

The glass-wiping barkeep overheard. The next time Joey reached for his cut-glass tumbler, it was full. He didn't remember it being that way.

"What I don't get is why you hate your job. You're the boss, aren't you?"

"You would think so. My grandfather started the company. Then my father ran it. They loved it and lived for it. I'm not them. I can't seem to get anything right. I used to be a salesman when my father ran the company. At least then I spent part of my days outdoors. Now, I'm in the office most of the time."

With a slur, he said, "Why is that?"

"My father died, and I became president and CEO." With a sudden urge to share, Joey raised a finger to the bartender, who understood.

"I have a board that wants me to increase revenue and cut costs. I decide to raise prices, and the sales staff balks. Customers want more, not less, they argue. They advise me to advertise. I do. That cuts into our dwindling funds. Now it's their turn to bring in the dough. They tell me competitors with newer products are hampering our sales. I can't win. Whatever I do is never enough."

Joey took another long drink. "I have no idea how to, and no interest in, fixing these things. I feel like I'm a truck without a driver, a ship without a captain, a jumbo jet without a pilot. I am at a standstill, nonproductive, useless." He put down his glass with a heavy thud and burped.

His new friend, resembling a bobblehead, was staring at his beer, nodding in total agreement.

"I am ready to escape. All I want to do is be left alone to paint. Gorgeous landscapes. And beautiful waterfalls."

"So what's the big plan?" The man managed to ask.

"I can't tell you. I can only say it may involve some..." Joey struggled for a few seconds trying to spit out, "deception."

When he thought about being free from all the pressure, he couldn't contain his excitement or hold himself in check. "Of course, there will be some people who will be affected by it. It will hurt. I'm sorry." He shrugged. "But it's unavoidable."

Joey looked to see if *Nameless,* sitting next to him, still agreed. But his head no longer bobbed. He sat immobile, in a beer-induced stupor, his hands cupped around the glass, his head bowed, resting on his chest.

To the unconscious man, Joey said, "It doesn't matter. I didn't want this. I didn't ask for this. Therefore, I am not responsible for what is about to take place."

# Chapter Sixty-Five

## Vacant Warehouse

## Outskirts of Toronto

AMY SLUMPED TO THE concrete. A weight, hundreds of times heavier than the metal chain binding her, plunged her down. The two masked men turned to leave.

*Matt is dead!*

Somewhere deep in her soul, reason had always told her she wouldn't have been able to save Squeaky, the gang member knifed back in DC. It had happened so fast. There was nothing she could have done.

*But Matt... I should have stopped him.*

She closed her eyes. Pictured him winking. Susan had shared pieces of the puzzle, which helped complete the full picture. Amy now knew they were on the right track. But she would never have the opportunity to tell him. He would never know.

The floodgates opened wide. Tears streamed down her face. She thought back to the morning they first met, his playfulness. *I'm wearing my sneaky shoes. On or off?*

Her eyes burned, but the tears wouldn't stop. Her body shook. *Do you want to live dangerously?*

Amy sobbed alone. Susan had long ago stopped speaking. She lay motionless, the only sounds from her were occasional murmurings.

In the emptiness, sorrow turned to anger with Amy chastising herself.

*What was I thinking? How, without any expertise, any support, or any training, did I imagine I could just waltz into a situation and do what? Single-handedly fix it?*

*Why is this place spinning?* Fear surrounded her. A tightness grabbed hold of her core. *I can't breathe.* She gasped for air. *I can't breathe.*

It wasn't just physical stress. Her heart was being shredded apart by regret.

It had always been a source of frustration that she had been powerless after the death of her brother. Too young at the time to do anything about it, she vowed to make some change, to have some impact during her lifetime to ensure he hadn't died in vain. To that end, she had geared her education and her life's direction with that in mind.

She thought about dying. And how helpless she was to do anything to fix things now. Of how no one would ever know what she and Matt had uncovered. Of how her parents would suffer at the death of their second child. Of how they would torture themselves, wondering why she was here and what she was trying to accomplish.

As the gasping became more pronounced, the tears stopped. She realized it wouldn't be long. Her life would soon be over.

Without ever having made any constructive change.

Anywhere.

At all.

# Chapter Sixty-Six

## Vacant Warehouse

## Outskirts of Toronto

KOA REFLECTED ON AMY'S reminder of his homeland after delivering his news about Matt. Guilt grated on him after hearing her words. He and Petrov had retreated to the little room at the front of the warehouse, which served as an office.

Petrov said, "I leave. One hour." He let the door slam on his way out. His message clear—you stay here and make sure no one else comes in. And, of course, no one leaves.

Koa waited until the car pulled away before returning to a broken high-backed chair to consider the man. That he spoke with a thick accent and that his name was Petrov was the total extent of his knowledge about him. Even after working with the guy around the clock, he still couldn't say where he originated from.

He had asked when they first met, but Petrov cautioned, "Too many questions make you trouble." He understood the warning, and as a result, they didn't speak much. Usually, the conversation only concerned what Petrov needed him to do.

When Petrov returned, he said, "Hold door," and headed straight for the washroom. It meant he wasn't alone.

The pedestrian door at this makeshift office often stuck. In addition, after being opened, it would spring back at a brisk pace. Koa went to it and held it open. The woman entered, turning a shoulder away as she passed. Koa wondered whether her action arose from fear or arrogance, curious if his size frightened her. She resembled a tiny bird in comparison to him.

She stood in the center of the room, not touching a thing, waiting for Petrov. When he re-entered the office, she asked, "Is everything good?"

Koa answered instead. "She is worse. Not talking anymore." He believed he had somehow injured the woman when he grabbed her off the street, pulling her into the back of the car. He had stepped out with ease and taken hold of her. But ducking in first, required him to drag her in as well. He felt her catch on something. When the woman's body snagged, he yanked her in with all his strength, knowing the allotted time was up.

Earlier, Petrov had warned he would only have four seconds to get her in. Petrov had taken the additional step of testing the native Kauaian, making him recite one, two, three, four, out loud to ensure he knew how quick it would be. "After four," he said, "I go."

At home on Kauai, they had medical facilities to treat her wound. She needed care. He had been told the women were causing trouble, interfering with something big the company had planned. Since Petrov said these women were to be held only for a short time, he assumed she would have wanted the information.

The woman ignored him and addressed Petrov, "What about the second one?"

When he hesitated, she said, "Never mind. I'll see for myself." She marched toward the back.

Petrov shot Koa a warning look, put on the balaclava, then turned and hustled after the woman who headed to where the two captives were being held.

# Chapter Sixty-Seven

## Vacant Warehouse

## Outskirts of Toronto

HOURS LATER, AMY FOUND herself alive. Barely. Her bout of gasping, shivering, and crying had exhausted her. The entire cathartic episode after hearing of Matt's death left her numb and cold. On the edge of defeat.

Her body had taken a pounding. Her spirit was severely wounded. Both were beaten and battered—but not broken. She still managed to breathe.

That breathing was beginning to slow along with her pulse. Both were returning to rates somewhere in the vicinity of normal. She drew in a shaky breath and imagined an invisible cloak of determination wrap itself around her.

She decided she didn't want to die.

Not now. Not like this. Not after coming this far. She had spent her last five years in search of her life's direction—unsure exactly of what it would be.

Somehow—against all logic—the darkness and dreariness of this warehouse shone a light to her, revealing a path. She took a fraction of a second to congratulate herself for having pursued the strange man with the blue eyes on Niihau. It had been the right thing to do.

A slight smile found its way to her face, exposing those dimples she loved and had managed to benefit from in so many situations. Despite the fact that they were useless to her here, they weren't her only strength.

Feeling somehow resurrected, she shouted, *"Dangerously,"* as loud as her raw throat would permit into the darkness. Then she began vigorously scraping the rope binding her hands against the cement with a powerful resolve.

# Chapter Sixty-Eight

## Vacant Warehouse

## Outskirts of Toronto

SUSAN STIRRED WHEN she heard Amy yelling, 'Dangerously.' *What's happening? Why is she shouting?*

She lifted her head a slight bit and opened her good eye, straining to see. The light was too dim. She rested her head back down. Unable to see anything else but the darkness ahead and the ceiling above, Susan could only listen. She recognized the sound of purposeful footsteps. Like someone approaching in high heels. They sounded like they were coming from the emptiness in front of her and Amy. Along with the footsteps came the sound of an accompanying slow, sharp clap.

At the sound of someone coming, Amy halted her so far futile attempts at the rope. A small figure stepped to the edge of the light. As she did, the clapping ceased.

Surprised to see a familiar face, Amy cried out, "Eunice?"

Eunice took a step closer to the two prisoners. She glanced toward Amy, but her focus settled on Susan.

Susan found a renewed strength at the utterance of Eunice's name. Her one eye opened, shocked that Eunice had wound up here as well. She moved her head to look in the direction of the clapping. Behind the tiny presence stood one of the masked men. Not the one who had grabbed her—the other one. This time, brandishing a gun.

238

It took a few beats, but then, like a train slamming into a stalled vehicle on the track ahead, it hit her. The man wasn't pointing the weapon *at* her. Eunice had walked in of her own accord. Her hands free to clap.

Realizing Eunice was not a captive, Susan pleaded, "Eunice, get us out of here. Please, I need a doctor."

"You need so much more than that." Eunice's response came with spittle, which didn't quite reach Susan. It landed a foot or so short of her. "You're pathetic. You almost spoiled our plan."

An eerie silence wafted through the air. Susan lay numb and dumb with shock. She attempted to use her right arm, the good one, to force herself into a more upright position. When she finally managed to brace herself with a palm against the concrete, she said, "What plan? What are you talking about?"

With open condescension, Eunice said, "Did you *honestly* believe all of the money you finally agreed to provide was for the clinic? That *they* would get to keep it?"

Susan said, "For the children, yes, I did."

Eunice moved closer to Susan as she spoke. Susan gaped at the vileness emanating from Eunice. Hate laced her voice, anger wrinkled her skin, and the corners of her lips were dragged down in disgust. "You were the one against it. I had to go out of my way to convince Mike. Lucky for me, he's a stupid old man, and I'm an attractive young thing."

Having spat out her vitriol, Susan watched in awe as Eunice inhaled a deep breath, exhaled, and restored her expression to its normal faux facade. The one Susan remembered from her initial request for help when they all met in the Presidential Suite.

"I should have gotten rid of you earlier," Eunice said. "This would all have been so much easier."

Susan's face went through a transformation of its own, displaying her astonishment at Eunice's words. Her mouth hung open while her one open eye protruded dangerously from its socket. Her eyebrows and forehead stretched high, to an almost impossible length. Eunice's words may have shocked Susan, but they didn't deter her. In contrast, they seemed to spur her on. She asked, "Then what did happen to all the money? Where did it go?"

Completely composed, as if recounting a well-known tidbit, Eunice said, "Hillary took some of it. We had to give her a small portion. She was, of course, instrumental to the plan. As a registered nurse and head of the clinic, that put her in perfect position to authorize the payments for it, switch the blood, and then administer it."

At Eunice's *switch the blood* phrase, Amy spoke up, sputtering, "That's why I saw all those B-Positive blood labels and nothing for Rhnull blood. The twins *never needed* the special blood, did they?"

Uncovering another piece of the scheme, Amy turned to Susan, and said, "They wanted money from the foundation. So they came up with a *ploy* that the babies needed it."

Eunice clapped again. This time faster than before. Eunice came to stand in front of Amy, who edged away, pressing further back against the pole. Studying her, she scoffed. "For a kid, you're not half bad."

Amy glared up at her. "I guess you get to keep most of the money, minus Hillary's cut. What I don't understand, though, is why. Your husband already makes a humongous salary. Why not just divorce him, take half of what he's got? It happens all the time. You could have started over, and no one would have gotten hurt. It would have been so easy."

Eunice smirked. "Who says I leave him? *We* is the correct pronoun here. We." She emphasized the two-lettered word. "We go away after all of the misfortune we have endured." She crossed her hands over her heart and feigned a sigh. "Who could blame us after such a devastating tragedy?" A greater level of confidence and connivance crept into her voice, Eunice said, "My husband then resigns his position after the IPO is released. Then we live happily ever after because he will be free of all his burdens."

When the depravity of Eunice's scheme sank in for Susan, she said, "Eunice, are you telling me they didn't need the Rhnull blood? You made it all up?"

Eunice whirled around. "You had all the money, Susan." Her words were bullets, aimed straight at the injured woman. "Money that belongs to Joey, and by extension, me. You guys gave away millions like I give away tips. And Joey, my poor Joey, has been forced to wake up every day hating his job but doing it because his father decided, long before his birth, this would be his destiny. They robbed him. Of his free will. They drove it into him from his youth: this would be his life. Work. Work. Work. Then make sure you *fund the foundation* so it can help others. *Others?* What about him?" She shrieked. "Do you know what they did to him when he was just a child?"

She didn't wait for an answer. "As a kid, starting as young as six, his father forced him to attend meetings with lawyers, accountants, and other professionals where they would talk about things he didn't understand, using words he couldn't pronounce. He dreaded it. Hated it. It made him feel so inept. It destroyed his self-esteem. Took away his self-confidence. Even his effort to escape to a men's room brought him no relief. There, he heard others at the urinals joke about the stupidity of having him attend, mocking his ability to contribute anything. His father stole his life."

Eunice took a long, sobering breath.

"And you, Susan, you stole his money."

# Chapter Sixty-Nine

## Vacant Warehouse

## Outskirts of Toronto

AT LAST! THE PICTURE on the puzzle was becoming clear for Amy.

Eunice's phone chimed. She must have recognized the ringtone. Without hesitating, she turned away, extracted it, answered, and kept it at her ear.

The call lasted only a few seconds. Replacing her cell, Eunice returned her attention to them.

Amy still wanted to know more. She pressed Eunice. "So, let me guess. When Baby A and Baby B were born, you realized almost from their birth that their prognosis wasn't great, and you cooked up this scheme."

Eunice shrugged. "Joey and I were ready to leave anyway. He was already working on the IPO." Plumped-up lips opened wide to expose perfect teeth. The woman appeared eager to explain. "The plan had always been he would step down after it went public. He would turn the management of the company over to others and leave it all behind."

Eunice's eyes widened to the size of golf balls, and the fingers on both hands spread open wide as she said, "Then it all came together." Amy watched as a deviate revealed her innermost, twisted thoughts. "Why not profit from our misfortune?" Her words sent shards of glass pulsing through Amy. "I remembered what Hillary told me about a rare blood type. She was dissatisfied working at the clinic, claiming to have all the responsibility while Dr. Zoric reaped all the profits."

Eunice patted her tummy and lower front. "Although he does do great work. I can personally attest to that. It's amazing how much damage carrying those kids for five months did. I needed a little fixing. I can't imagine what I would have looked like if they had survived all nine."

Eunice yawned as if bored. "Hillary was easy to convince, and such a natural at all the deception. When I delivered early, she told the staff we were *very special clients* and she would be responsible for everything related to the twins' care. As the boss, no one questioned her. She recorded the blood type as Rhnull. Then she made a big hullabaloo over it."

Amy listened in disgust, thinking the ice coming from Eunice's mouth would cause frostbite if the woman came any closer.

Eunice began pacing in front of Amy as if giving a lecture. "The first batch of blood came in legitimately. The blood had to come in as Rhnull since everyone knew about it, including Dr. Zoric. We never knew whether it might be tested or analyzed somehow. We had to have the real thing, just in case." She paused and faced Amy. "By the way, it never was. Tested, I mean. Having a quantity of B positive on hand, their actual type, was easy enough. When the first Rhnull blood arrived, Hillary switched the labels and hung the bag. Nobody even suspected. Easy peasy."

Eunice moved next to Susan. She squatted, leaned over her, and inches from her face, in a gush of fury, said, "Then my part came in. *I* had to convince *you* we needed to pay millions to secure the priceless blood to save our kids."

After delivering that vitriol, Eunice rose, saying, "Knowing in reality, we wouldn't be able to acquire more of it from the regular sources, we hired someone to *borrow* Wilhelm for a few weeks. He would have been let go. He was never in danger. We just needed a few weeks of his time. No big deal—until Bozo over here..." Eunice gave a disapproving nod toward the masked man standing off to her side. "Panicked when he found out an unauthorized helicopter had flown low over the island. And decided to handle things his own way. Unfortunately, you had changed apartments for some reason, leaving that old couple there instead."

Astonished and annoyed at how smug and cavalier Eunice sounded about her plan, Amy couldn't help poking a hole in her balloon. "You do realize those payments can be traced, and they will find out the funds were returned to you, don't you?"

Susan sounded aghast. "What? What do you mean the money was sent back?" Amy's revelations must have ignited something in Susan.

Amy explained. "Well, I'm not sure of all the details, but I do know the bank codes indicate that similar amounts of money flowed back to the same banking institution they came out of. I imagine they went into your account, Eunice. Am I correct?"

"No. Not our normal one." Eunice contemplated Amy. "But you are a smart girl. It's a shame your talents won't be put to further use."

Amy's study of Hinduism, courtesy of her father's gift, had taught her that a person makes an earthly choice to become divine or demonic. She knew which one Eunice had chosen.

Eunice sighed as if exhausted. "The IPO goes off on Monday. Once it's done, we'll be set for life. Joey and I will be gone. Somewhere where no one will be able to touch us."

She began walking away. Petrov followed her. Before being engulfed by the shadows, she turned back to the stunned women. "I'm sure the boys will take good care of you until then. They'll bring you something to eat soon."

Susan lay flat on the concrete again, moaning, "Oh God."

As Eunice's footfalls faded away, Amy said, "I wouldn't count on the boys bringing us anything. At least not anything good."

# Chapter Seventy

## Streets of the City

## Toronto, Canada

HECTOR NERVOUSLY TAPPED his fingers on the steering wheel as he drove, speculating on what he would learn when he reached the airport, confident that's where they were headed.

Frustrated with being unable to do anything more for the moment, he depressed a speed dial number. One he had been trying intermittently over the last many hours. With a heavy heart, he heard the phone trill three times. He reached a finger to silence it, knowing the fourth ring would result in a recorded statement to leave a message.

Before he could, the phone was answered. By a man. "Hello. Who is this?"

A sudden rage filled Hector. His heart sank. His Miss Susan was in jeopardy. He knew it. But experience had taught him to suppress his anger. He needed a sharp mind now. Any necessary retribution would come later. He would see to it.

Hector's foot lifted off the gas. Out of instinct, he maneuvered from the middle lane over to the slowest one, looking for the next exit. "I might ask you the same question," he said to the stranger speaking to him on Miss Susan's phone.

"Just someone who needs to get in touch with a friend. Can you unlock this phone for me? Do you have the code?"

"No, I don't. But, you say you need to reach a friend?" Hector wondered whether it was a taunt meant to provoke him. "I can help you with that," he said in his most conversational tone. "But, first, you have to do something for me. Tell me where you got the phone you are speaking to me on." Hector took the first exit he came to, pulled into a lot, put the car in park, and left the engine idling. He closed his eyes and held his breath, hoping not to hear the answer he feared most. *A dumpster.*

"What does it matter how I got it? Let's just say I found it, okay?"

"The person who owns that phone is a friend of mine. She is very important to me. I just want to know how you came to be in possession of it. I'll help you. But you have to help me."

"I don't have time for this," the man said. "Look, pal, it's a long story. There's no time to explain it now. But I have nothing else on me. No cash or cards. Can you call my friend for me? I need to know where she is. Are you in or not?"

"Yes. Yes. I'll help you," Hector said in a level voice. "What is her number?"

He gave Hector the number. "If you don't get an answer from her, try The Devereux Clinic. I don't have that number. You'll have to look it up."

Hector said, "I know the place." Then he asked with a sincere-sounding interest, "Is she a patient there?"

"No. She works there. I need you to place those calls as fast as you can and get back to me. She may be in some trouble."

Hector held his voice steady as he headed toward a route that would lead him back to town. "Why the urgency? What type of trouble is she in, your friend? I'm a private investigator? Maybe I can help."

"The trouble Amy may be in is an even longer story than how I got this phone. Please..."

Hector cut him off. "Did you say Amy? What's her last name?"

"Pryce. Why?"

Hector tried to suppress his surprise. "You say she's at the Devereux Clinic?"

"Working there, yes."

*This man is involved somehow.* Hector's intuition had never failed him before. He relied on it now. "That's very interesting. Because I was just following Hillary Whitley, who looks like she's on her way to the airport, getting ready to leave town."

The man yelled, "That's who Amy works for!"

"And what's *your* name?"

"Matt Conners."

"Well, Matt, we *need* to talk."

# Chapter Seventy-One

## Vacant Warehouse

## Outskirts of Toronto

EVERY PART OF SUSAN'S beaten and battered body hurt in some manner. Each movement excruciating. For the moment, she lay dumbfounded, the pain of her injuries ignored as comprehension of what Eunice had revealed sank in.

*It was all a ploy. An evil, sickening ploy for money that Eunice and Joey felt entitled to.*

*I was right, Mike. But what's more important, you were wrong. Are wrong. Whatever part you played in assisting them contributed to their theft. You are just as culpable as they are. You don't deserve to be in a position to dictate where the foundation's funds go any longer.*

*I'm not sure how, but I promise, I'm going to see to that.*

# Chapter Seventy-Two

## Vacant Warehouse

## Outskirts of Toronto

"SUSAN." AMY KEPT HER voice low. "Susan. We have to get ourselves out of here." After being exposed to the face of evil and hearing Eunice's chilling explanation, Amy's fear and anxiety morphed into a drive to survive. It spurred her into action. She forced herself to sit as upright as possible. Engulfed by her chains, she looked anew at the humongous mass of metal shackling her.

"I agree," Susan said in a weak voice. "Any ideas on how?"

With a renewed determination and clarity, Amy abandoned the attack on the rope at her wrists, which thus far had gotten her nowhere. All the gnawing at it, trying to soften it with saliva before scraping it against the rough concrete, had been a wasted effort except to dye it scarlet.

Eunice's presence had been a sharp dose of reality, sparking a renewed commitment in Amy. She examined the shackles surrounding her. A door banged closed in the distance. Amy said. "Shh. Did you hear that?"

"I did," Susan said. Then came silence. A silence more troubling than any noise. Susan seemed to be testing her extremities with small movements. She said, "I'm just about frozen stiff. What about you? Can you move?"

"I can maneuver a bit, enough to somewhat stand. Other than that, I'm secured with a chain to a post behind me. You have one around you, too."

"What am I chained to?"

"Don't know. Yours trails off into the darkness ahead. I can't see the other end. I'm guessing it's attached to something. Can you try your right foot? That's where it is fastened. At your ankle."

Susan slid her foot out an inch or so and then back in. "A little."

"That's a start. See what else you can manage."

Amy twisted herself within the rusted chain confining her at the waist to study her bindings. The links were thick and weighty. Each link measured about two inches in length. Wide enough for her to fit an index finger inside for leverage. A padlock at the base of the pole secured the restraint.

"I'm fastened with a giant chain, like something to be used in connection with commercial construction. It's heavy, but if I can just find a way to loosen it, then..."

*Calm down. Think. There has to be a way.*

Amy took slow, deep breaths to slow her racing heart. She began pulling on and tugging at the links from various areas and angles, analyzing how she had been bound. It took a while, but through trial and error, Amy followed its path, straightening it in her mind.

She reasoned whoever had bound her started by placing the middle of it at her waist in front as she lay prone on the floor. Then twisting it around her back before wrapping it behind the pole and then bringing it out again to wrap around her ankles. Both ends then went back to the beam and were secured with a padlock.

In its current form, the restraint provided just enough slack to allow her to move away from the pole at one end, either with her legs or upper body, bringing the opposite side closer to the pole.

She had managed an awkward stance when she confronted Koa. As she did, her torso stretched a short distance away from the support as her feet were pinned to it.

When she returned to the floor, her legs were able to extend out a little, though her knees couldn't straighten. In that position, her back was forced nearer to the pole. In both positions, she could feel the knot at her back.

With the weight of the metal, any movement required an effort. "If I could just maneuver in tight enough up against this albatross at my back and tuck my feet in, I might have just enough room to push the chain up and off."

"I wish I could help," Susan said, regret apparent in her voice.

With a fervor desperate to succeed, Amy positioned her back as near to the beam as she could manage. Kneeling, she pushed her ankles toward the pole. Bending forward, she used her upper body to pull the section constricting her waist as far away as possible to provide the largest degree of slack. "Alright, here goes. Wish me luck."

In that position, she plunged her elbows under the rusty metal, wiggling them around to force her elbows further and further down, beneath the chain, thus lifting it higher up her core. Pausing to take a couple of deep breaths for strength, she whispered, "Making progress."

With both elbows pinned in position between the chain and her body, she used her forearms to inch it further up her chest.

Her arms ached. The small movements were exhausting. But she had to keep going. She couldn't stop.

"Susan, how are you doing?"

After several attempts, Amy managed to squeeze her bound wrists under the chain, which gave her the ability to force the links higher toward her neck. Amy took a few more breaths for strength. Then, with a final effort, she brought her shoulders into her ears and turned her face to the side. Using her bound hands, she shoved the heavy restraint up, over her head.

And off, freeing her upper body.

"Susan, I did it. Can you hear me? Say something?"

Amy's feet were still entangled in metal. But now, despite its weight, she found ample slack. With her bloodied fingers—the ones she could no longer feel—she tore at the links surrounding her ankles, managing to push them off and release herself.

"Susan, I'm out of my chains. My hands are still tied, but I can move." Amy crawled toward her. "I'm coming over to you. Let's get yours off you."

"Susan, Susan." The woman had gone quiet again. Amy pressed her cheek against the woman's forehead.

Susan was on fire.

And Amy was on her own.

# Chapter Seventy-Three

## Vacant Warehouse

## Outskirts of Toronto

ON THE FLOOR ALONGSIDE Susan, with one bare foot, Amy realized the task of finding an exit now fell to her. Susan was out for the count.

Amy tried to stand. It was difficult, but somehow she managed. On shaky legs, she retrieved her missing shoe, thankful its rubber bottoms would mask her footsteps.

Starting a count at one, she took her first tentative step in the direction Eunice and the armed guard had come from. Step by careful step, she put more distance between herself and Susan. Each one drew her deeper into the abyss. Soon, the overhead light behind her dimmed to the extent that she felt blind. Swinging her bound hands in front of her from side to side, she utilized them as a white cane.

She counted as she walked, but fear may have caused her to miss a few. *How many steps so far? A hundred and fifty?*

In front of her here, the area held large metal drums that blocked her forward path. She changed direction, gravitating toward another source of brightness off to her side.

*A hundred and fifty, then go left.*

This new sliver of light helped her identify and avoid additional large items in her path. This area of the building contained several large metal pieces of equipment.

She resumed counting, beginning again at one. Besides huge drums and other large machinery, there were also piles of wood. Long planks of it. In addition, stacks of empty wooden crates mounted atop each other stretched halfway to the ceiling. They appeared to extend back quite a distance.

Each step brought her further from Susan and closer to the new source of light. Across from an open space in front of her, another stack of carelessly placed crates reached halfway to the roof. To her right, a light shone down the length of the wide area between her and the sloping crates.

*It must be an aisle to move this heavy equipment around.*

She needed to change direction again. *How many steps was that? I lost count. A hundred fifty, left for a while, then right.* That's all she had. To this point, she had seen no doors or windows.

Amy paused, waiting for her galloping heart to slow as she summoned the courage to take her next steps in the new direction.

*There has to be an exit somewhere. It has to be where that light is coming from.*

She drew in a deep breath, stepped into the space, turned to her right, and realized she was correct. A wide break in the concrete wall opened into what might be an office. The loading dock door ahead was elevated, in its open position. She fled toward it, holding her breath.

Before reaching the track on the side of the opening, her leg brushed against a white carpenter's bucket packed with strips of wood, a rusted pipe, and a metal bubble level protruding from its middle. She almost knocked it over, exposing herself. Thankful it didn't fall, she exhaled a slow, quiet breath. She flattened herself against the concrete to stay hidden.

During those quick steps, she had glimpsed a brief section of the room behind her. The wall looked to be made of plywood, and the single window had bars on it. An empty corkboard contained pins, but no papers hung there. It confirmed her thinking that she had reached an office or a workspace. *Which must have an exit.*

Daring to peek, she began to extend her head around the wall. Faint sounds coming from inside caused her to jerk back before taking a solid look.

*Who's in there? One of them? Both?*

That peek did reveal another window—with bars.

But not a door.

After another long exhale, she reasoned it must be on the far side. Which meant, to see that angle, her head and at least a portion of her upper body needed to penetrate the space. It would put her in jeopardy. It risked revealing her presence to anyone there.

It didn't matter. It had to be done.

KOA STOOD BEHIND A cracked section of cloudy glass at the barred window of the office's door, thinking about his island home. The sight of an approaching vehicle broke his concentration.

He had been expecting Petrov.

But not what Petrov was bringing with him.

HIDDEN IN DARKNESS outside the office, Amy readied herself for a better look at the area.

The slamming of a car door stopped her.

She waited. Then came the sound of a door opening, followed by the unwelcome, accented voice of her fake detective. It paralyzed her. "Problem," she heard him ask. She reasoned he must be speaking to Koa.

Who had probably been alone before.

Now they were both there.

Her eyes closed in defeat. *Not now. Please, not now. I made it this far.*

Uncertain of what to do next, she concentrated on the footfalls and the noise she could hear from inside. By the sound of it, items were being shuffled around, like someone was searching for something.

There were no distinct sounds to indicate where each of them was or which way they might be facing. She couldn't remain there. She couldn't tell how long they would stay in that office, either. At any moment, one of them could come out and see her.

She needed to find that exit before going back for Susan.

*Now or never.*

She stepped to the side of the door. Bracing her bound hands on the doorway for support, she carefully slid her head around it, far enough into the room to survey the area. This time, in seconds, her gaze scanned the small, prefabricated office in its entirety. The look had been brief, but she memorized the entire layout.

It had been worth the risk.

She found the exit.

Along with the two cans of petrol on the floor next to it.

# Chapter Seventy-Four

## Warehouse Office

## Outskirts of Toronto

IN THE SMALL OFFICE at the front of the warehouse, Koa asked, "What are you looking for?" As usual, Petrov didn't answer.

Petrov continued riffling through the drawers of the dented metal desk that stood against a back wall. As he bent to open the lower ones, his shirt rose, exposing the gun tucked in at the small of his back.

Worse, the two five-gallon cans of gasoline Petrov had brought with him remained at the side of the door.

Koa knew what they contained. A sickening feeling began taking hold of him. This wasn't what he signed up for.

From the start, he had questioned whether he'd made a mistake taking the job, beginning with the man on Niihau, whom he had come to know as Will. But having faith in his fellow man, he believed what he had been told. He had convinced himself Will would indeed be let go after a short time, despite the makeshift prison he was confined in.

Koa never received a satisfactory explanation as to why Will needed to be there in the first place. That fact hadn't ceased to nag at him. Since Kalani, his caring but interfering cousin, drugged him to drag him home, Koa would never know if Will would have been released or not. But his suspicions had been aroused.

Still, he held on to his beliefs.

He had been promised money. Lots of it. He had been warned it might be dangerous—but he wasn't afraid. Especially since they told him he would be trained to protect himself.

This opportunity seemed too good to pass up for Koa. From a very young age, he knew he wanted to see the world. The island of Kauai was just too small for his big dreams. Their father had taught him and his brother to fish, hoping they would follow in his path. His brother, Abelino, loved it. Koa enjoyed it—he just didn't *live* for it.

His mother must have sensed his nature, and as a result, he always felt closer to her. Now, he was a disappointment to his mother as well. He couldn't bring himself to face her after Kalani forcefully brought him back to Kauai. For that matter, he couldn't face his cousin, either. His dream of bringing back gifts for his mother from exotic places and watching her face light up with joy would never come true.

Koa's discomfort and unhappiness had reached a turning point after being instructed to *take the nosy man out and make him disappear.* Only then did Koa realize Will would never have been released. If he had been given the kill instruction before dragging the poor woman into the car—an action he now regretted—he would have refused to comply. But her abduction had occurred first.

Earlier, when Petrov arrived with the boss lady, Eunice, he told them the woman needed help. Both of them had ignored him, stomping off instead toward the two prisoners. Koa had listened from a distance. He didn't quite hear everything they said, but he knew the boss lady wasn't happy with either of the women. It made him fear for their safety. Since that order to kill, he had been wrestling with how to remove himself—and now, them as well—from this horrific situation.

He had never agreed to this.

He wished he could take it all back: the job, leaving Kauai, all of it—and just go back to finishing his studies at the university.

But how? What could he do about it? The feeling of despair swallowing him made him realize his moment had come. Something worse was about to happen.

Petrov stood as if he had either found what he wanted or had satisfied himself it wasn't there.

With his heart rate accelerating and dreading the answer, Koa asked, "What are those for?"

"Bring one," Petrov said, before lifting one of the cans himself. "Come."

Koa followed Petrov into the warehouse, but without the other can. He watched as Petrov began splashing around the liquid from the open spigot at the top of the one he had brought.

Koa's fingers balled into a fist. He stood a few feet behind Petrov. In one quick action, Koa moved forward and grabbed a fistful of Petrov's shirt. He yanked him backward, letting out an ear-shattering wail of anger and frustration.

Petrov lost his grip on the canister. It dropped from his hands. He stumbled away but managed to stay upright.

Koa charged at him like a bull.

Petrov was prepared for him. He started punching and jabbing the Hawaiian. Attacking his face and upper body. Koa's attempts to wrestle him to the floor were thwarted by Petrov's closed-fist punches.

In normal situations, with his bulk as a deterrent, Koa needed only to be present to intimidate or unnerve an opponent. He had never fought like Petrov was now doing—landing continuous blows to sensitive areas.

Koa found himself taking defensive positions as he was forced closer and closer to the ground.

WATCHING FROM THE SHADOWS of the doorway, Amy stared in shock and horror as she witnessed a dazed and struggling Koa manage to regain his balance, stand, and straighten. He took a wide swing at Petrov. But the effort failed. His foot slipped, forcing him to the concrete.

Petrov bent over him and began delivering a walloping to his face—striking him without mercy, nonstop.

Without any time for rational thought, Amy grabbed the bubble level sticking out of the bucket near her, somehow managing to hold onto it with her numb fingers. She flew forward, coming to a stop behind a bent-over Petrov.

Koa lay motionless beneath him. She raised the long metal bar up to her side and over her head. Wielding it like a golf club, she used it to strike Petrov, slamming him on the back of his head with all the force her exhausted body could muster.

She heard the sickening sound of his skull cracking.

Petrov's raised right hand went limp. Then his upper body began to slump.

The level fell from her hands. Her heartbeat bellowed so loudly in her ears, she feared her eardrums would burst.

For a fraction of a second, the world stood at a standstill. It resumed in ultra-slow motion. Ever so slowly, Petrov's body fell off to the side from his position atop Koa.

Koa's dazed face, with one open eye, stared up at her.

Her pulsating heartbeat pinned her in place as sweat streamed down her back. Her mind reeled at the thought of what she had just done. Then a sudden jolt of adrenaline spiked through her.

She turned and ran.

Back toward Susan, calling out as she did, "Susan. Susan, we have to go. Now!"

# Chapter Seventy-Five

## Vacant Warehouse

## Outskirts of Toronto

SUSAN WAS FEVERISH. Fighting to stay positive, Susan forced herself to call up thoughts of better times. Focusing on the good she had accomplished with the foundation's money. Basketball courts and other facilities they had built, scholarships they had funded, homeless shelters and organizations they had sponsored. She concentrated on the happiness, the gratitude, and the appreciation of the recipients, which were etched forever in her mind.

With inspiration from those gleeful faces, she refused to submit to the piercing pain shooting through her. She lifted her upper body to a position where she could see the chain at her ankle.

*Only one ankle.*

The chain carried weight, as she had already determined from moving her foot. With her head in that position, she could see the links were large, as Amy had described. She tried to touch it.

Her good hand wouldn't reach. Not even close. She lay her head back down.

Lying very still and concentrating, her resolve strengthened. She kicked off the shoe on her left foot. Then, using the toes on her freed foot, she tried to dislodge the chain, searching for a way to get under it. As Amy had.

Digging her left toe into her right ankle, she managed to finagle at least a portion of her big toe a tiny way under one link.

*Can't stop now. Too much more to do.*

After repeated tries, she felt a smidgen of movement. It spurred her on.

Her commitment grew stronger with each additional iota of space until her toes found a bit of leverage underneath the chain. With a final grip, she spread the chain further away, although her ankle was still not free. She let out an exhausted breath.

Then, she heard Amy yelling her name.

# Chapter Seventy-Six

## Vacant Warehouse

## Outskirts of Toronto

AMY FOUND HER WAY BACK to Susan. She put her shoe back on, managed to remove the loosened chain at her ankle, and crawled up to her side. "I found the way out. We have to go. Are you ready?"

"I will never be more ready," Susan struggled to say.

Amy reached for Susan's left arm, but Susan cried out at her touch. Amy moved to Susan's other side, hoping her right arm would be strong enough to use. Her left was useless. "Alright. Let's give this a try. I'll help."

Susan whispered, "I have a cat back home that gets very prissy if not fed."

"Can't wait to meet her."

At Susan's right side, Amy dragged her bound wrists under Susan's right arm, bringing them to Susan's armpit. "OK, let's get you up."

"Him," Susan corrected. "My cat is a male."

Amy smiled at the bit of normalcy with Susan's correction. "Can't wait to meet *him* then."

With a solid hold, she began lifting, managing to raise Susan to a sitting position. Amy felt the heat emanating from the woman. "Here we go," she said as she rose alongside Susan, attempting to lift the woman.

Susan helped with the effort, but struggled. Amy managed to maneuver Susan up into a hunched, but not quite vertical position. Susan tried to take a step. She crumbled. "My feet. I can't feel them. I can't stand."

Without warning, a strong whoosh traveled past them, as if a powerful blower had been turned on. Turning her head, Amy saw the orange hue coming from the direction of the office. She knew in an instant what it meant.

*Petrov must have regained consciousness. And lit the gasoline.*

She couldn't yet see flames, but she knew they were there. She thought about the planks of wood and stacks of crates she came across before finding the office, and how they would fuel the fire. Fire also needed oxygen, and this place certainly had plenty.

With no time to waste, Amy reset her hands under Susan's arm. "I know where the exit is. It's in this direction. I've got you, Susan. We can do this."

They tried again. "It's no use," Susan cried. "This won't work." Turning onto her belly, Susan announced, "I'll crawl." Her version of crawling meant placing her good forearm on the ground ahead of her and dragging the rest of her body to it. Then repeating the movement.

The use of only one arm made it difficult. Amy squatted every other step to help move her with a little tug. "You're doing great. Susan. Keep moving," It was a slow process for the feverish woman who was already burning up.

A loud pop indicated the fire was doing damage somewhere up ahead. Amy's understanding of how fire burns and how it spreads gave her both hope—and scared her to death—at the same time.

The scary part was knowing the heat and smoke from the fire were being drawn up toward the ceiling into the space known as the overpressure area. There, the heat and smoke would spread out, radiating heat back down to the objects below, warming them up.

Heated enough, they would release pyrolysis gases, which would add to the mixture above, making it even more dangerous. The overpressure itself might begin burning. Or, the heated items below could reach their auto-ignition point. The temperature at which they would spontaneously combust.

The hopeful part was, because the warehouse was so large and the ceiling very high, coupled with the fact that Petrov had only splashed gasoline on empty concrete, the fire might burn itself out. That could give them enough time to get out. Assuming, of course, that Petrov hadn't added more gasoline to anything else.

Within what seemed like moments, Amy could see the first tendrils of smoke swirling above them. She hadn't expected it to happen so fast.

She didn't mention it to Susan. She didn't have time to dwell on it either. They had to keep going. Behind them, smoke swirled around the single bulb, diminishing its light. That area now even darker than before.

A look ahead indicated how low the smoke had already come. The air turned acrid. Amy struggled to speak. Downplaying the crisis, needing to keep Susan's spirits up, Amy managed to choke out, "You're doing great. Let's keep going." Amy wondered if Susan realized they were headed toward a real fire.

By now, crackling and pops in the distance told her more than just empty concrete was burning. *Petrov must have managed to spread the other can of gasoline.*

They continued inching their way through dense smoke. It drifted lower and lower, faster and faster, as Susan crawled slower and slower. Amy felt the difference each time she rose after bending to assist.

They reached the area containing the tanks and larger items. "Susan, this is our first turn. It's not too far from here."

After what seemed like an eternity, they reached the aisle area, their last turn. Pulling Susan into it, Amy peered through squinting eyes to see flames ahead. They flickered on either side of the aisle, but the center—the part they needed to pass through to reach the exit—appeared to have already burnt itself out.

Amy lifted her head to the ceiling. The heat and smoke from the flames on either side of the aisle were still being drawn up into the ceiling area. Amy bent again and gripped Susan, knowing they needed to move faster. Almost crawling alongside her, she pulled on Susan.

Her tongue tasted bitter, as if a layer of dust covered it. She couldn't stop coughing. It was almost impossible to speak or swallow because of the effort required and the irritating fumes. Their throats hurt. The heat and dryness stung their eyes, forcing them closed, allowing them at best to squint.

They forged ahead. Practically blind. Each step hotter.

Then, from a glance, Amy thought she saw it—a lick of fire in the smoke above.

Her heart stopped mid-beat. It was the worst possible thing—the crucial sign firefighters feared. *Flashover:* The *instant* in which a fire burning within a structure transforms into a structure that is completely *on fire.*

It meant everything in the warehouse could burst into flames in an instant. *Everything.*

All at once.

Everything would be on fire.

Including them!

# Chapter Seventy-Seven

## Vacant Warehouse

## Toronto, Canada

WITH A RAW AND ACHING throat, Amy croaked, "Susan, it's now or never. We have to hurry."

With the possibility of an impending flashover, time became even more critical. Amy dropped to her knees alongside Susan, literally dragging her by her good arm, needing to convey the urgency.

Somehow, Susan found an inner reserve of strength, giving Amy a nod before propelling herself a bit further. After a few more feet, Amy could feel the heat from the concrete below her knees, realizing they had reached the burnt-out aisle area where Petrov had splashed the gasoline. It meant they were near the office. And the exit.

*Can't stop. I can do this. I have to hold on.*

The next few pulls on Susan brought them to the threshold of the office. They had just passed the area where Petrov had beaten Koa, and she had slammed Petrov. Her glance, which was all her blistering eyes could manage, made her believe only one body lay on the floor. It made sense because someone had started the fire. If the body on the floor was Koa, it meant Petrov might still be here to finish the job. *We have to get out before he finds us.*

She stripped those thoughts away, focusing all her energy on the task at hand. The continuing crackling and pops reminding her of the danger they were in. Somewhere in the mix, Amy heard the sound of glass shattering. The fire must be burning hotter.

Her strength was ebbing. She couldn't stop coughing. It required a breath before each pull on Susan, who was now unable to function much. Each forward movement could be measured in inches. Amy yanked on Susan—out of necessity—hoping the feverish lady could contribute more to the effort.

There was no response as a sudden, strong whoosh of air blew above them. Amy reset her bound wrists under Susan's good shoulder and attempted another pull.

*We are so close. I just need a moment to catch my breath.*

Then Amy felt a pressure from behind. A force yanking at her. Susan's arm lifted away as Amy was pulled from Susan.

*He found us. Please, no. Not now. We are so close.*

# Chapter Seventy-Eight

## Outside a Vacant Warehouse

## Toronto, Canada

AMY BECAME SUDDENLY aware again. *I must have blacked out for a moment.*

Constant coughing prevented her from relieving her dry mouth. Her eyes were pinched closed. She couldn't open them even if she wanted to. The thick, acrid smoke had already done its damage. But she sensed a brightness behind her closed lids.

*The flames! They're getting closer. Susan...*

In her blindness, she reached for the woman and found herself unable to move. Something held her locked in position. Her arms were pinned at her sides.

*Something must have fallen across me. I have to get this off. Susan needs my help. She won't make it out of here alone.*

Struggling against the restraint. Amy tried to raise her hands to the item at her chest. She began pushing at it, coughing and gasping for breath as she did so.

Then came a new sensation. A pressure on her shoulders, along with a force hovering above her. She shook her head, trying to deny him.

But he won.

He managed to cover her nose and mouth with one quick action.

Then a gush of air rushed into her. Fresh and cooling. Her body sucked it in before it might be taken away, fearing she would never get enough. The oxygen mask would leave white stripes on her soot-blackened face due to her thrashing, but it was doing its job, reviving her. Her eyes burned too badly to force open.

Bewildered, a good minute passed before she realized the cracking and popping sounds were gone. These sounds were different. Someone was talking.

*Are they speaking to me?*

"Don't push on the straps. The rope is off your wrists." *That voice. It sounds so familiar.*

The cadence in his words was soothing. Tender.

*But it can't be.*

"I've got you. You're on a stretcher."

*Could it?* She fought to open her eyes, but her lids wouldn't lift.

"Stop pushing on the straps, will you? Can't you just listen for once?" He squeezed her shoulder.

*It is him! It's Matt. He's alive!*

# Chapter Seventy-Nine

## Susan's Hospital Room

## Toronto, Canada

TORONTO GENERAL HOSPITAL is a major teaching hospital and organ transplant center. Amy and Susan were each treated there for their respective injuries. They admitted Susan. She was on her third day of a heavy regimen of antibiotics.

She was suffering from a severe infection, the byproduct of her injuries from being dragged into the car by Koa. Her sprained ankle, along with untreated lacerations and the deep puncture wound on her right thigh, was cleaned and dressed. Her dislocated left shoulder went through a closed reduction—or, as she described it, *was popped back into place.*

Amy was also checked over and released after being treated for smoke inhalation and a variety of other non-life-threatening injuries. They released her with bandaged hands and advised her to follow up with her personal physician.

In Susan's hospital room, Amy was ensconced on a windowsill. A self-assured Matt, who had also been treated and released for cuts and scrapes to his hands, stood nearby. His injuries were the result of his breaking through the glass window on the office door to reach in and unlock it.

He was once more expounding on how he was still among the living. He had already explained his escape to Amy and Susan. But, with the shock of him still being alive, some of the details were obscured, requiring him to recount it again.

"After I was slammed on the back of the head in the house Andy sent me to, Petrov and Koa shoved me into the back of a car. For some reason, maybe because of my height, they didn't use the trunk."

Matt moved to the far side of Susan's bed where her last bag of heavy-duty antibiotics was dripping at a snail's pace down a clear tube and into her arm. "I came around in the car, but I wasn't on my game enough to go on the offensive. I decided I would need to overpower the driver. There was a phone on the floor, and I thought I could use it as a weight. Maybe whack him with it. Instead, I managed to remove my shirt without him noticing. Then I formed it into a length of cloth to mimic a rope and went with a twisted sleeve as a garrote."

Amy said, "I'm guessing they were bringing you to the warehouse we were in."

"I don't think so." He gave her a you-are-dead-wrong look. "Koa told me the Russian gave him instructions to make sure no one ever sees or hears from me again. He showed me proof. Koa opened the trunk. In it, I saw a folded tarp with a brand-new shovel. He was supposed to kill me and bury my body."

Susan spoke up. "I don't remember you telling us that part before. That must have been terrifying. Did he just let you go?"

"No. Of course not. I've taken a few punches in my day, and I realized the hit I took could have been curtains for me, especially when you think of the heft Koa could have put into the blow. For sure, it was a good wallop, but it could have been far worse. I was out for a while, but I came to and found myself squeezed on the floor in the back of a car. As we drove, my head cleared. I saw the phone on the floor, half-hidden under the front passenger seat, and grabbed it. I could tell we were driving through city streets at first. Then, his speed increased, and I guessed we were on a highway. When his speed slowed again, I reasoned we must be taking an exit. I made my move. I sat up as quick as I could and strangled him from behind."

"You both could have been killed," Amy shrieked. "Convenient how you also left this bit of info out before. You only said there was an accident. That Koa hit a tree."

"Can I please finish my story?" His admonishment came with a slight pout, which she suspected was forced to disguise the smile he was hiding.

"Why not? Doesn't look like I could stop you even if I tried."

Matt picked up where he left off. "I realized the guy's heart wasn't in it when he whacked me. I surprised him from behind while he was driving. But with my makeshift garrote around his neck, he didn't react as you'd expect. No flinching, swerving, or swearing. Just a hand trying to protect his neck. It was as if he didn't care. He did, however, take his eyes off the road to look in the rearview mirror and, by accident, drive off the road. I knew he wasn't a killer. Petrov, on the other hand, had laid out in detail what he expected Koa to do. He had entered the GPS coordinates for where he was to get rid of me. After the accident, I managed to get out of the car first. Koa's door was lodged against the trunk of a large oak."

Matt took in a long breath. "I took a chance. I helped him get out. We talked, and he admitted he didn't want to kill me. I tried to convince him to leave with me, but he wouldn't. He did give me a message to give to his mother when I get back, though. After that, I suggested he get rid of the tarp and dirty up the shiny new shovel to make it look like he had done what he was supposed to. He let me ride back with him and dropped me off at a gas station before we got back in town. All I had on me was the phone. It was locked, so I couldn't use it, but I did answer it when it rang, and I ended up speaking with a Hector Lopez."

Susan spoke up. "Matt, that reminds me. I wanted to talk to you in reference to doing something in Koa's memory. Even though he was involved—up to his neck in all of this—he did play a crucial part in our survival by releasing you."

Matt acknowledged her words, nodding, looking too choked up to comment.

Susan turned to Amy. "Before they chase you two out of here, I wanted to ask you something. What I am interested in is where you got your information on the bank codes and the money transfers you were talking about. Was it all accurate?"

"You want to know my secret source." Amy smiled with a newfound pride. "It's my mom. She's worked with numbers and puzzles all her life. She's a forensic accountant. She was the one who found out that the money coming back to the sending bank was not going back to the same account. Not to the clinic's, but to one for Stratford Industries, which Joey had control of. It struck her as odd. After a great deal of analysis, she reasoned it was coming in to inflate the sales of Joey's new line of snowboards. After depositing the money, someone at the company made it look as if it was revenue. Income from sales, which it wasn't. With those pumped-up sales, the presumption would be the new line was already a winner, and therefore, the IPO would appear as a much better investment, worth a great deal more than it was. She suspects it was where Eunice and Joey intended to make the real money. And it would all look legitimate on paper because Joey owns millions of shares. Every additional penny in earnings would add dollars to each share he owned. My mother said it wouldn't have been caught for quite a while. By then, it would have been too late."

Susan smiled, shaking her head. "I see where your tenacity comes from." A loudspeaker, announcing that visiting hours were over, interrupted her. "I'm out of here tomorrow. Don't forget about the luncheon."

# Chapter Eighty

## Susan's Condo

## Toronto, Canada

SHORTY TIPTOED ALONG the back of the love seat where Amy and Matt were seated in the spacious open area of Susan's condo. They were feasting on a fabulous array of sandwiches and desserts. Susan had insisted on having it catered, although she implied it would be a simple luncheon.

A bottle of champagne sat on ice, unopened, in the center. The three of them indulged in water or soothing teas, their throats still sore, a lingering irritation from the effects of the fire. In addition, Susan still required antibiotics, and no alcohol was allowed for her.

During her stay in the hospital, Susan had filled Amy and Matt in about her involvement with the foundation and her suspicions about the clinic, which caused her to be taken prisoner and wind up in the warehouse.

Frank became a daily visitor—renewing their friendship in the process. He brought Susan up to date on all that had transpired after her dismissal. In addition, he detailed his actions in going to bat for her after the alarming call from Hector notifying him that she was missing. All outlays—of any kind—were stopped. He provided the board a detailed overview of the Stratford case for their review, and, overriding Mike's request, he had stayed in continual contact with them until their relief at hearing she was found. Alive.

This morning, her first stop after being released had been to attend a board meeting at the foundation before sponsoring this celebratory luncheon. "I'm delighted to say the emergency meeting I asked for was successful," Susan said. "I didn't have to threaten them with exposure or a lawsuit. Before I even started, they informed me of Mike's voluntary retirement and their unanimous motion to have me replace him. I'm the new chair of the Evaluation Committee. Frank and Denise will be the other two members. And the board has on its agenda the task of bringing on a seventh member to replace Mike."

Susan picked up a plate of pastries from the table and offered them around. "Amy, suffice it to say, if any skin grafting or surgeries are required for your wrists, they will be covered by the foundation."

"Thanks," Amy said as she put down the fork she had been awkwardly holding between a thumb and index finger. "The doctor said we'll have a better picture when these bandages come off, but he said it looks like I might get lucky."

"The same goes for you, Matt," Susan said as the doorbell buzzed. "Anything you need," she called over her shoulder as she limped to answer it.

Moments later, Susan returned, accompanied by a dark-haired, olive-skinned man. "Amy, Matt, this is Hector Lopez. I believe you two gentlemen are aware of each other."

Matt leapt out of his seat. A split second later, he was pumping Hector's hand in thanks. "It is so very much a pleasure to meet you."

Amy approached him, holding up her bandaged paws, and gave him a hug of welcome instead.

Susan said, "By the time Hector arrived at the fire, we had all been taken away to the emergency room. He stayed and spoke with both the police and firefighters, and has been working with them over the past few days, tying up loose ends. I'm glad he found time to be here today."

Hector settled in a chair and looked to Matt. "Now, it is *my sincere* pleasure for us to talk face to face. I hope you appreciate my reluctance at first to give you any information. Since you were calling me from Miss Susan's phone and, with her missing, I could only deduce you had something to do with it."

Matt retook his seat and shook his head. "Tell you the truth, I took it to use as a weapon. Other than that, I have no idea why I snatched it. I just did."

"Was it just lying there?" Hector asked.

"Yes. Under the front passenger seat."

Shorty found his way into Amy's lap, cuddling and purring. When Matt glanced around the room, he found he had everyone's attention. "After Koa dropped me off with nothing, I knew I had to get to Amy to warn her. I couldn't use the phone. I couldn't unlock it, but when it rang, I answered it."

Hector interjected. "And since you were speaking to me on Miss Susan's phone instead of her, I needed to find out why, who you were, and how you obtained it."

Hector looked to Susan, explaining, "We played cat and mouse for a little while. Neither one of us wanted to divulge anything to the other. We didn't know who the other was or what part he played in all the goings-on. At some point..." Hector nodded to Amy. "Your name came up. I remember thinking, What does Amy Pryce have to do with this? I knew who you were because Miss Susan had asked me to investigate you."

Susan mouthed *sorry* to Amy before returning her attention to Hector.

Hector continued. "At some point, the man speaking to me on the other end of the phone said, 'I need to get in touch with her.' That got my attention. I told him I needed to find the woman whose cell he was using. He told me of the setup at the house and that he got that address from Andy at Stratford Industries. I wasn't sure of the complete connection, but we filled each other in with more and more details."

Matt cut in. "Hector put the pieces together, though. He had been following Hillary after she met Eunice in an out-of-the-way spot. While there, Hector put a tracker on Eunice's car. We both knew of her involvement with the clinic because of the twins. The same clinic Hector told me Susan had decided to look into."

Hector nodded to Matt, "I didn't see how all the dots connected, but I think by that point we both were satisfied that somehow this all tied together. It didn't take us long to realize we were both on the same side."

Matt shook his head, "But if you hadn't put the tracker on Eunice's car, we never would have known about the warehouse."

Susan cut in. "Well, I can't say thank you enough."

"Ditto for me," Amy said.

Matt continued. "Once he knew we were on the same team, Hector shared your password with me, and I unlocked your phone. Since he was closer, he headed back to Devereux to check on Amy, and he asked me to check out the location where Eunice had been. He couldn't figure out why someone like her would make a stop in such an industrial area. I used your phone to book a ride and gave the driver directions based on the tracking information Hector transmitted to me. It led to the warehouse where you were both held. I saw the smoke as we were approaching. I called it in and knew it spelled trouble.

"The office door was locked when I arrived. I could see flames deeper inside. I could see someone lying on the floor at the entrance to the warehouse. It took a while to break that glass. As soon as I broke through, that nasty smoke came billowing out. I could hear the sirens in the background. I found you first, Amy. The fire engine pulled up as I was dragging you out. By the time I went back in for you, Susan, the firemen were inside helping. They took over from there. They found and pulled Koa out. They cut a path through the flames and worked on putting out the fire. Those guys are heroes."

Matt said, "I'm sorry Koa died on his way to the hospital. But at least I have that message for his mother."

Susan said, "Amy, I can't tell you how much I regret passing Hector's information about you to Hillary. At the warehouse, I tried to tell you what I had done when I realized who you were, but I couldn't find the right words. I felt so dumb and guilty for doing it. Can you forgive me?"

"Of Course," Amy said. "You didn't know. I might have done the same thing if our roles were reversed."

Matt turned to Hector. "Do we have an update on Eunice and Joey?"

Hector, who had helped himself to a sandwich, said, "Those two! They were arrested late last night as they were about to board a private jet. With the tracker still active on her car, I gave the authorities my login and password and they tracked them there. They arrested them as they were about to leave the country. They have both lawyered up. Joey is already arguing he didn't think his wife would go that far. Claiming, he only knew about the extortion with the foundation." Just before taking another bite, he said, "Apparently, he viewed it as somehow justified."

Susan said in dismay, "I still can't get over the lengths Eunice and Joey went to, all because they felt entitled to the foundation's money. I have to admit, it was a brilliant scheme. Although I could never have imagined it, let alone implemented it."

Hector said, "Interpol, which already has a wealth of information, has been updated about all of this and has broadened their investigation. The Stratfords' assets have been frozen, and all of the policing agencies throughout Europe have been alerted about Petrov. By the way, his surname is Bogrov. The authorities already have a long list of data on him. It seems he's been a freelancer for hire since leaving Mother Russia. He won't get far. Same for Hillary. She fled to Switzerland. They know where she is."

Hector appeared to just notice the bottle of champagne. "Why isn't this open?" He raised an eyebrow to Susan.

"Oh, heck with the doctors," she said. "Hector, would you do the honors?"

As she rose to retrieve the flute glasses, Amy and Matt joined Hector at the table. When their glasses were filled, Susan gave the toast. "To all those who care enough to become involved and not allow evil to flourish."

They lifted their glasses and drank, all in varying amounts.

Amy said, "No matter how evil and conniving Eunice is, it is still a shame she lost two children. She's already paid a huge price."

Hector put down his empty glass and gave her an unusual look. "I wouldn't be so sure about that. Interfacing with Interpol and sharing notes over the last few days, I discovered activity on Eunice's computer not long before the twins were born. It revealed she had been researching ways to induce a miscarriage."

Amy said, "Sad as that is, it makes sense. Eunice said Joey always felt he had to do what his father wanted, as if his father bore him for his desires. It appears Eunice is of the same ilk. The children were there for her needs. She used them to get what she craved."

Susan shook her lowered head. "My friend Eileen said she had nicknamed her Evil. But she has no idea how correct she is."

Matt interjected, "Well, with our testimony, along with all the evidence against them, I'm sure they'll pay for their crimes, and I hope they get what's coming to them."

Hector rose to leave, saying he still had more paperwork to attend to. "So, do you two return to the States tomorrow?"

Matt answered. "I'm headed back to Hawaii right after Amy and I make a short stop to complete a pinky promise."

"Don't ask," Amy said in response to Hector's quizzical look.

Susan looked at her watch and said, "Don't you two have a call to make?" She pointed to French doors off to the side. "You can use the study."

# Chapter Eighty-One

## Study in Susan's Condo

## Toronto, Canada

"HELLO AGAIN, DETECTIVE Palakiko," Amy said when he answered his phone. "Matt is here with me. Did you get an opportunity to fill in Professor Longo on what went on up here?"

"I have. I've invited him here, and he is joining us on this call. We are on speaker."

"Hello, Longo. I'm not sure if you've met Matt Conners. Matt and I have some news to share with you about Koa."

The professor said, "I can't say that I've met him, but I've certainly heard a good deal about him from Detective Palakiko."

Matt spoke up. "I'm glad you're both there because I wanted to speak to each of you. Detective, I'll text you my flight information. Professor, if he didn't already tell you, I'll be accompanying Koa's body back. Amy tells me you are close to his mother. Since you are, please let her know I'll also be bringing back a personal message from her son. Please tell her I'd be willing to help with whatever arrangements need to be made."

"And professor," Amy said, "I want you to also let her know that Koa will be returning with honor."

"I don't understand. I thought..." Amy could hear the hesitation in the professor's words. The detective must have told him of Koa's involvement. "I know, professor. It's a long, involved story. Matt can fill you in on the missing pieces when he returns. But for now, just let her know Koa is coming home and she should be proud of him."

"I will," he said. "I'll be most interested in hearing the entire story myself."

"Longo, there's one more thing," Amy said. "The other woman who was captured and rescued along with me, she works for a charitable foundation. Because of Koa's actions, which were indirectly instrumental in our rescue, the foundation has established a generous fund in his name. They want his mother to be involved in how that money will be used. Perhaps for scholarships in his memory, since he never finished. I thought you should be the one to deliver that news as well."

"It would bring me great happiness to do so," the professor said.

"I guess that about covers it." Amy looked to Matt to see if he had anything else. He shook his head that he didn't.

"Amy," the detective said, "will I be seeing any more of you on my island?"

She smiled to herself. "You know, detective, it may not be for a while, but I think you just might."

WITH THEIR PHONE CALL to Hawaii completed, Amy turned to Matt and said, "Oh, about our pinky promise..."

"You're not trying to wiggle out of it, are you?" Matt asked.

"No," Amy assured him. "I'm not. But I would like to enjoy the event with more functional hands. I'd like to hold on for myself, just in case you're not as good as you think you are in maneuvering things." Turning serious, she said. "Plus, I can't take any more time off right now, not until I complete my promise to Bonnie."

Amy had resolved a lot of things during these last few days. In a phone call to her best friend, she had apologized and explained the delay in starting the job Bonnie had lobbied so hard for her to get. Amy promised to correct that as soon as she returned. In the end, Bonnie's concern for her friend overrode her annoyance. She had even admitted to Amy that she was proud of her for getting involved. And, on a separate note, anxious to hear about it when Amy returns.

Matt said, "I think you mentioned the temporary gig with Bonnie is for three months, while your mother's visit with you and your dad will be only for three weeks, right?"

"Yes to both. Are you keeping tabs on me?"

During the time Amy would be working with Bonnie, she would also be renewing the relationship with her mother. It was the second call she placed on the day of the fire. Her first call had been to her father.

The conversation with her mother turned out to be uplifting and freeing—for both of them. Her mother's absence would also be addressed soon. After hearing of Amy's harrowing story, and as a result of their long-overdue talk, her mother requested three weeks of immediate family leave. She would be returning to DC within the week.

"I just don't want you skipping out on a promise," Matt said. "No giving me some lame story that you can't make it because they need you to start your *job* up here." He made air quotes around job.

Amy's unexpected reward for her involvement in not giving up on Susan at the warehouse and for pursuing Wilhelm's abduction in the first place came yesterday. At Susan's emergency board meeting, Susan had sung her praises and convinced the board they needed to bring in new blood. She received approval to bring Amy on as her assistant. It would begin when Amy's commitment to Bonnie finished. She would be working for the foundation in Toronto. The offer came with a generous salary and a one-year contract. After which, both parties would re-evaluate.

During her time in Toronto, Amy had come to realize she was driven—just like her mother. More than she ever would have believed, or cared to admit. She already knew her life's work would be guided by honoring and upholding her promise to Tommy. It would, in some manner, focus on fixing injustices or improving situations—at least, to some extent. This position would help her fulfill that promise.

Her only hesitation before jumping at the offer came from concern for her father. She hesitated at first, fearing he might feel she was deserting him too—-because of the distance. During her phone call with him, he put all her concerns to rest, saying, *That's terrific news. Toronto has always been on my bucket list.* It sealed the deal for her.

She accepted the position and, in typical fashion, dove right in. She had already given Hector a person to research. A *Mrs. Winters,* whose name she had found in the homeless girl's tent.

"You know you're not getting out of this. I have your number," Matt said. "Do you still have mine on speed dial?"

"I do. And I just might consider keeping it there," her dimples smiled at him. "I may need to check up on you every once in a while."

Matt let out a long sigh. "OK. Today we'll settle for a long and relaxing dinner at the CN Tower as it spins us around. Then, three months from now—when you are done with Bonnie and before you start up here—we'll complete our promise. We'll get back together just so we can risk our lives—again. By jumping out of a plane."

He gave her a familiar wink. "After what we've been through... How hard could that be?"

# ACKNOWLEDGMENTS

I hope you enjoyed reading my novel. It was a long journey for me to finish this one. I started just prior to the 2019 COVID pandemic, and although that gave me a lot of free time, as it did for many others, I just didn't seem to be able to put down on paper the words that seemed right.

In order to help this manuscript come to fruition, I had to call on some very special people to help guide me through some areas of this fictional piece of work to bring it to life. However, since this is a fictional piece of work, any inaccuracies you may come across in it are solely mine.

My thanks go out first to Detective David Whitmer, of the Ocean City, MD, Police Department, who pointed out some of my misconceptions and set me straight on police procedures.

Also helping me on my journey was Dr. Seyed Safavynia, of New York-Presbyterian Hospital/Weill Cornell Medicine, who helped me define the injuries that I inflicted on poor Susan.

And, last but not least, my gratitude to Fr. Thomas Underwood, a retired professional firefighter of thirty-three years, who schooled me on the effects of fire and the possibilities of surviving a burning building.

I would also be remiss if I didn't once again extend my thanks—and condolences—to friends and family who read earlier, choppier versions of this manuscript. Their comments and opinions helped point out things I was just too close to and had completely missed.

And, finally, my thanks, as always, to my husband, Nick, for supporting, encouraging, and (many times) nagging me to not ditch the project when I felt like doing just that.

And, more than finally—if that's grammatically correct—thanks to you, the readers, for reading A Perfect Ploy. I would be very grateful if you would leave an honest review. You can use Amazon.com/review/create-review?asin=1733354247 if you purchased it from Amazon, or wherever you purchased it. Or you can leave it at my website, BarbaraNicholson.com. Your review matters because real feedback from real readers makes all the difference to indie authors. It helps encourage other readers to give the book a chance. If you do decide to leave one, you have my thanks in advance.

I write to entertain and read to be entertained. I truly hope you did enjoy it—that it entertained you enough to transport you to another world—at least briefly.

Warm regards,
Barbara